THEODORE TERHUNE STORIES

A Case of Books

A THEODORE TERHUNE MYSTERY

BRUCE GRAEME

With an introduction by J. F. Norris

 Moonstone Press

This edition published in 2021 by Moonstone Press
www.moonstonepress.co.uk

Introduction © 2021 J. F. Norris
Originally published in 1946 by Hutchinson & Co Ltd
A Case of Books © the Estate of Graham Montague Jeffries,
writing as Bruce Graeme

ISBN 978-1-899000-36-4
eISBN 978-1-899000-37-1

A CIP catalogue record for this book is available from the British Library

Text designed and typeset by Tetragon, London
Cover illustration by Jason Anscomb
Printed and bound by CPI Group (UK) Ltd, Croydon, CRO 4YY

Contents

INTRODUCTION

It Takes a Village... to Solve a Murder

Twelve Chimneys... Three Ways Farm... Timberlands... Willow Bend...

On the basis of the title of this introduction you might think that these are quaintly named villages in Bruce Graeme's series of detective novels. But as we learn in *A Case of Books*, they are in fact some of the stately homes—one of the key ingredients in the fictional British villages of detective novels—that dot the countryside of Bray-in-the-Marsh, home to Theodore I. Terhune, full-time bookseller, part-time writer and accidental detective. Of course, the other key ingredient is plenty of crime to keep the gossip-mongers deliriously happy at teatime and the amateur detective distracted from his full-time job. In *A Case of Books*, the sixth title in the Terhune series, the owners of these houses, indeed all of the denizens of Bray-in-the-Marsh and its environs, step out from the perimeter of the story and appear in much larger roles than their usual cameos in earlier books.

Take for instance Anne Quilter. As business increases, and with Miss Amelia, his elderly spinster assistant, growing increasingly dotty and haphazard in her suggestions, Terhune hires a new teenage assistant to help him with the bookshop, one who never make mistakes like those of Miss Amelia, who, for instance, mistaking John Paddy Carstairs, a comic novelist, for a writer of non-fiction, sells two books to a customer seeking books on housekeeping and cooking based solely on the titles: *Vinegar and Brown Paper* and the somewhat naughty *Curried Pineapple*.

Anne, by contrast, suffers no fools, knows the stock much better than her elderly colleague and is trusted as an assistant manager of sorts when Terhune is off assisting the police.

But Anne cannot abide the way Terhune indulges his customers. "You are positively *nice!*" she chides, pointing out how he spends too much time in conversation with gossips and chit-chatters who have no intention of buying books. She also accuses her boss of caring only about the books and not the actual business, a criticism that gives him pause and will come back to haunt him later in the story.

The customers we have met in previous books take on greater significance in this adventure, and will appear in the climactic book auction, which brings out not only Terhune's customers but some oddly sinister book agents from foreign countries.

Those customers include the following:

— SIR GEORGE BRERETON, who is always boring everyone with tales of his fly-fishing expeditions and in search of books on angling.

— ALICIA MACMUNN, the prattling and absent-minded mother of Julia, Terhune's on-and-off-again partner in detection. Alicia's book on heraldry with its missing pages served as the springboard for Terhune's globetrotting adventures in *Seven Clues in Search of a Crime*. We haven't seen much of Alicia since then and her presence here is a welcome delight.

— Catty DIANA PEARSON, who can always be relied upon for dishy gossip, if not for dipping into her purse and buying books.

— Doctor ARTHUR HARRIS, who is always in search of detective novels and a has a penchant for John Dickson Carr.

— THOMAS HUNT, a farmer, who comes in "to know whether Raymond Bush had published any more Penguins". Bush was a horticultural expert who wrote books on how to care for fruit-bearing trees, though Graeme does not bother to mention this.

— And JEREMY CARDYCE, who appears in passing looking for books on common law. Cardyce, a veteran barrister, previously appears in a much earlier novel by Graeme, *Cardyce for the Defence* (1936), involving an odd divorce case, in which he turns detective to solve the mystery of "amnesiac adultery". He was also instrumental in helping Terhune and Detective-Sergeant Murphy in the final pages of *Ten Trails to Tyburn*.

Books are perhaps the central character in this outing. Arthur Harrison, a noted collector of Tudor incunabula, is found stabbed with an unusual weapon in his library. The bookcases have been ransacked—something was quite obviously being sought among his vast collection of books and manuscripts. Faced with a missing book as the possible motive for murder, Murphy coaxes more help from Terhune, who must consult with his numerous customers and his fellow booksellers, and enlist the aid of both Anne and Julia in browsing the many catalogues he receives.

Julia and Terhune, who previously undertook intense bibliographic research in *House with Crooked Walls*, team up again to catalogue books from the Harrison library that are to be sold at auction. Terhune is always surprised by the industry and curiosity which Julia displays when she sets her mind on a book project. This time Julia goes at her assigned tasks with a feverish bibliomania to rival Terhune's own bibliophilia. She loves the work so much that she vows to buy a book as a souvenir of her time in the library of Twelve Chimneys. In one of the many action sequences, Julia and Terhune are interrupted in their work by burglars and a fight ensues. When Terhune has chased them away he finds an object left behind that quite possibly could be the mysterious weapon used to kill Harrison.

A Case of Books is a bibliophile's celebration of all things related to the world of books. It is practically the paradigm of all "bibliomysteries" from the Golden Age of detective fiction, providing the reader with an insight into how a deceased collector's estate is handled, how the books must be catalogued, and how a book auction is run from start to finish.

In the auction scene, the true highlight of *A Case of Books*, a competition of sorts develops between the village folk and the city dwellers, two factions whom Graeme depicts in marked contrast to one another. Belittling and sneering gush from the urban book snobs when the village people spend a few shillings on cheap books the professionals would not touch even for a handful of pennies. The centrepiece of the auction is the bidding war on Lot 160, which consists of a few books that Terhune estimates will go for only a few pounds. The final realized sale price is astonishing not only to Terhune but to everyone in the room. Immediately the books in Lot 160 are of great interest to Murphy. The sale and the books set off a whirlwind of police work, eventually revealing the motive for Arthur Harrison's murder.

As in other novels in the series, a local murder reveals a hoard of secrets from the past. The detective work involves the decoding of strange marks in an arcane book, the uncovering of forgotten legends, Nazi looting and some intriguing insights into Argentinian culture that in true Graeme fashion are instrumental in helping to solve the various mysteries. Terhune is also aided by comments and snatches of conversation that occur early in the book and will probably be dismissed by most readers as entertaining background. But the labyrinthine story of *A Case of Books*, set almost entirely in Theodore Terhune's not so quiet village of Bray-in-the-Marsh, proves that it takes the many wagging tongues and curious-minded citizens of a British village to solve a murder.

J. F. Norris
Chicago, IL
September 2021

A Case of Books

Chapter One

Only rarely were both Terhune and Anne Quilter absent from the shop, but it did happen occasionally, and the last Tuesday in May chanced to be one such day.

It was less unusual for Terhune to be away; it was his custom, on the last Tuesday of every month, to visit London to select and buy the latest publications, and to negotiate other sundry transactions with buyers and sellers of second-hand, rare, and antiquarian books. So, usually, Anne's was the sole responsibility for carrying on that day's business in the shop at Bray-in-the-Marsh. But the inexorable law of averages, which prevents any series of events from being one hundred per cent trouble-free, this exasperating, intangible, natural law made its power felt on the last Monday in May, that is, the day before Terhune was due to pay his monthly visit to Charing Cross Road, and sundry roads west. Anne, cycling back to her work after the midday meal, was knocked down by a skidding car.

Fortunately, she was not seriously injured. But Doctor Harris had ordered her to remain in bed for the remainder of the week, so Terhune had quickly to arrange for Miss Amelia to act as Anne's substitute.

The indirect consequences of Anne's unfortunate accident were first brought to Terhune's notice just one week later, by which time Anne had returned to work, none the worse, apparently, for her mishap. Shortly after four-thirty p.m., a small Austin pulled up in Market Square, just outside Terhune's shop. Through the glass-panelled door he saw a woman emerge from it, and cross the pavement with the very obvious intention of entering the shop.

She was a stranger; he inspected her with all the curiosity of the countryman in whose village complete strangers are rare. She was tall, slim enough for her thirty-odd years, a false blonde, pleasant-looking, but dressed in clothes which bore the hallmark of the inexpensive *chic* of suburbia.

The door opened; she entered with a purposeful stride, and moved across to Anne's desk, which stood before the lending-library shelves on the left.

Anne smiled a welcome. "Good afternoon, madam."

The woman snapped: "Good afternoon. Who owns this shop?"

"Mr. Terhune, madam."

"Is he available?"

"He is at his table over there, madam, towards the back."

The newcomer swung round, saw Terhune, and made towards him. Suspecting trouble he rose quickly.

"You wish to speak to me?"

"If you are Mr. Terhune, I do."

He smiled disarmingly, and indicated the chair which stood beside the desk.

"Won't you sit down?"

She sat down, unbendingly. "My name is Mrs. Rowlandson. Less than two weeks ago my husband and I moved into this neighbourhood. From London," she added with a note of condescension. "We have purchased *Willow Bend*."

Terhune nodded. He knew *Willow Bend*, a small, but rather charming house, standing on the Toll Road, about half a mile south of Wickford. Its late owner, a man named Jellicoe, had died earlier in the year, since when the house had been empty.

"We have only been married a few weeks," Mrs. Rowlandson continued. "Until last year I lived abroad with my parents, in a country where domestic labour was cheap, so you will realize that I have not been accustomed to doing housework."

Terhune could make neither head nor tail of the reason for this long explanation; but he murmured politely: "Of course."

She continued: "Last Monday afternoon, as I was passing through Bray, I caught sight of your shop. I thought it might be a good idea for me to buy a book on household hints, so I called in." Mrs. Rowlandson paused—whether for dramatic effect, or whether to give her the opportunity of regarding him accusingly, he didn't know. He smiled wryly; he suspected that Miss Amelia had been up to her tricks again—the poor old dear was so incredibly willing, so desperately anxious to please everybody.

"There was a woman here. Not a young woman—" A slight movement of her blonde head indicated Anne. "An elderly female. With teeth—"

"Miss Amelia," Terhune murmured.

"I am not in the least interested in her name," Mrs. Rowlandson snapped. She stared angrily at him. "I suppose you know your business, Mr. Terhune."

"I have been a bookseller for several years," he informed her modestly.

"Then your past experience does you no credit."

He did not dare glance at Anne; he had a vague idea that she was making rude faces at Mrs. Rowlandson's back—Anne was still very young!

"You met Miss Amelia?" he prompted.

"I did, indeed. To my cost, I might say. Believing that this was an efficiently run establishment I asked for a book on household hints. Do you know what that—that stupid woman sold me?"

He tried to think of titles in stock. "*Elizabeth Hallett's Hostess Book*, or *Enquire Within*?" he suggested, not very hopefully. Then, as an afterthought: "Not the eight volumes of *Every Woman's Encyclopedia*? A little old-fashioned, for these days—"

"NOT *Every Woman's Encyclopædia*," she interrupted firmly. "The book I purchased, stupidly without first examining it, was entitled *Vinegar and Brown Paper*."

The sound of a muffed explosion came from the direction of Anne's desk. Terhune choked. Painfully! *Vinegar and Brown Paper* was a light-hearted novel by John Paddy Carstairs, as far removed from sweet domesticity as the moon from green cheese.

"I am very sorry," he began. "It was extremely stupid of Miss Amelia. She should have been more careful—"

"You have not heard all," Mrs. Rowlandson interrupted again. "That foolish woman sold me another book by the same author which she claimed was a cookery book."

A cookery book by John Paddy Carstairs! Anne made a dash for the door, and disappeared. Terhune stared aghast at his visitor while he tried desperately to remember the author's titles, and identify Miss Amelia's second *faux pas*. Presently a horrible thought occurred to him.

"Not—not *Curried Pineapple?*" he gasped.

She nodded, and his self-control collapsed. Soon he could see Mrs. Rowlandson only through a mist of tears. *Curried Pineapple* a book of recipes! Ye gods!

Presently he recovered; but he had to take off his horn-rimmed glasses, and wipe the lenses dry, while he gazed anxiously at his visitor.

"You must forgive my rudeness," he pleaded. "Please!"

Then he saw that her eyes, which he had thought were so frostily blue, were twinkling.

"I'm not really cross, Mr. Terhune," she told him. "Even though I have only lived in the neighbourhood for a few weeks I've heard all about Miss Amelia. Poor dear! I think she's so sweet. Isn't she rather good at fine needlework?"

"I believe so."

"In that case I hope she will be able to spare me an occasional afternoon. But there, I didn't really come here to complain or talk of Miss Amelia, but to ask—" She paused, to smile confidingly at him. "Have you any other books by that author I can borrow?" He made a move.

"*And* some genuine household and cookery books?" she added, "One or two Elizabeth Craigs, perhaps?"

A little more than fifteen minutes later, Mrs. Rowlandson left, with an armful of books. As the door closed behind her the telephone bell rang. Terhune picked up the receiver,

"Hullo."

"Mr. Terhune?"

Terhune thought he recognized the matter-of-fact, vaguely Irish voice of Detective-Sergeant Murphy,

"Speaking, sergeant."

"Are you busy at the moment, Mr. Terhune?"

The question produced a delighted grin on Terhune's round, healthy face. A grin not of amusement, though it might well have been, seeing that he had done no more strenuous work during the past hour than sell the latest Philip Hughes to Isabel Shelley, and a mixed selection of books to Mrs. Rowlandson. No, the grin was one of slightly heartless—but very human—excitement: Murphy wasn't in the habit of ringing up during Terhune's working hours unless something unusual had happened.

"No," he replied eagerly. "Why?"

Murphy did not answer the question. "Would you care to come over to *Twelve Chimneys*?" he asked instead.

Twelve Chimneys! A house well-known to Terhune, for it was the home of Arthur Harrison, an ardent—and wealthy—book-collector. During the years he had lived at Bray-in-the-Marsh Terhune had sold many rare books to Harrison. Fairly recently Harrison had paid him £40 for a copy, in excellent condition, of Bode and De Groot's *Complete Work of Rembrandt*, and a similar amount for a rubbed copy of Saxton's *Atlas of England and Wales*, published in 1579.

The shadow of misgiving succeeded excited interest. "Nothing's happened to Harrison, sergeant?"

"I'm afraid something has, Mr. Terhune," Murphy replied evenly. "He's been killed."

The news shocked Terhune. Not on account of his having lost one of his best clients. Nor on account of the man himself, whose nature had not been one to command affection. Terhune's regret was prompted by the reflection that the man's plan to collect the finest private library in the world of Tudor publications had come to a premature end.

"A car accident?" he asked.

"Worse than that. Mr. Harrison was murdered—less than an hour ago."

"Good Lord!" So that was why Murphy was 'phoning. A case of homicide. But who on earth had murdered Harrison—as inoffensive a man (when he was not bargaining for books!) as anyone could wish to meet. And why?

"Can you come along to the house?" Murphy went on. "I believe you might be of help to us in our preliminary inquiries."

"I'll come at once, sergeant," Terhune agreed promptly.

"Thanks, Mr. Terhune." To the hearer there appeared to be a note of relief in Murphy's voice. "Then I'll expect you in about ten minutes."

Having arranged with Anne that she should see to closing up the shop at five o'clock, Terhune collected his bicycle from the small shed at the rear of the premises and set off for *Twelve Chimneys*, He proceeded along St. James's Road, which bounded Market Square on the east, but at the south-east corner of the square, turned left into the Ashford Road which, running in an easterly direction, passed through Wickford and Willingham before losing its entity and becoming merged with the Folkestone Road.

Before he had travelled far he had left the outskirts of Bray behind and only the countryside, rich, burgeoning and fresh with spring colour, bordered the winding, hedge-bordered road. Normally he would have been conscious of the details of the scene—the several tones of green in the woods on his left: the presence of two black lambs among the sheep grazing in Farmer Chitty's fields; raddle hedging and ditching at Ponds Farm; the drawn blinds at Canal Cottage (so Grandmother

Tobin had passed away at last, poor old soul!); Fred Pyke discussing the ploughing-up of some permanent pasture at Wilson's Hill Farm (not before it was time, for it was hummock-strewn and impoverished)—a dozen other such matters perhaps, for the countryman's keen eye misses little of his neighbour's activities, good or bad.

But Terhune noted none of these things. He was still thinking of Harrison's death, and his reflections were gloomy. Of what use ideals, ambitions, hobbies? Sooner of later they were all brought to an abrupt end by the Eternal Reaper. And then—what? Rarely, a continuation, by others in loving memory—for instance, Madame Curie. More often, a callous dispersal, followed by oblivion.

Take Neil MacDonald, for instance, who had died less than a twelve-month ago. Neil MacDonald had devoted a lifetime to philately; specializing in used issues of the British West Indies. Within six months the executors had sold the entire collection, in a hundred lots, at public auction. Now poor Neil MacDonald's priceless collection was scattered over the seven seas. What had taken fifty odd years to amass had been dispersed in as many minutes.

Was all this part and parcel of the cycle of life? he reflected dismally. Take the line of lovely old oaks which bounded Lady Kylstone's property, *Timberlands*, on the west. More than a hundred years old, every one of them. How long would it take man to fell a specimen? A matter of hours. And lightning, to blast it? A fraction of time. What of man himself? taking twenty-one years to reach physical maturity. A careless step, a slippery road, a faltering aircraft engine, a hurricane, any one of a thousand mishaps—and twenty-one years of growth could be destroyed in a moment equally unrecordable by time.

Even the means of remaining alive was subject to the same law of slow, plodding ascent followed by a precipitous descent. The turnips, for instance, which even as he passed, were being sown in the seven-acre field on his left. What took months to grow, would take seconds to eat. Those lambs in the next field—was not the same equally true of them? And even when their naked carcases arrived at their eventual destination, the dining-table, would it not take a matter of minutes only to eat what had taken hours to prepare and cook?

Mother Nature looked with jaundiced eye, it seemed, upon everything progressive—and as Terhune passed *The Hop-Picker*, which stood on the outskirts of tiny Wickford, his thoughts completed *their* cycle, and returned to Harrison's library.

What would happen to the thousand-odd choice volumes Harrison had assembled during his lifetime? Was there a relative with an equal enthusiasm for sixteenth and seventeenth century publications who would take over the library complete, love it, care for it, and make it grow? Or would some generous patron buy the library and present it to the people—the finest monument of all to human endeavour?

A short distance past *The Hop-Picker* Terhune turned off the Ashford Road into Toll Road, which passed through Farthing Toll, and later divided, to proceed east to Dymchurch, and west to Rye. Here, the journey was easy-going, for the road gradually descended towards the Canal, at a gradient which made pedalling unnecessary. He was soon opposite the Parish Church of Wickford, from which point the smooth grey water of the Canal was visible through the trees, also some of the twelve chimneys which gave Harrison's home its name. A few hundred yards farther on a short, gravelled drive connected Toll Road with the house.

Miss Baggs opened the door to him. Miss Baggs had been Harrison's housekeeper for a long time—"fer mor'n twenty year, maid an' old maid," claimed Frank Houlden, the lessee of *The Hop-Picker* who, besides having to maintain a local reputation for wit, possessed a phenomenal and intimate knowledge of everyone living within two miles of the inn. Miss Baggs was round and dumpy, and normally put one in mind of a large-sized, walking and talking doll, with her vivid, apple-red cheeks, her round china-blue eyes, and crisp muslin apron and fichu above a black, silk frock. But the tragic face which stared pathetically at Terhune was ashen; the china-blue eyes revealed evidence of emotional strain.

"Mr. Murphy is expecting you, Mr. Terhune," she whispered, opening the door wider for him to enter. As he stepped into the spacious hall, so did Murphy, from a door at the rear.

"Ah! I thought it might be you, Mr. Terhune. Will you come right in?"

Terhune walked towards the room which he knew to be the library. Murphy greeted him with a handshake; then, having seen that Miss Baggs had vanished through another door on the far side of the hall, asked:

"Are your nerves steady?"

"He's inside?"

"Yes. And not looking too pretty."

Terhune nodded. Years of inhuman, bloody war had long since hardened him to the gruesome sight of corpses. Murphy stepped aside, so Terhune entered the library.

Although the sun was still bright, every electric globe in the room was on. In this disconcerting glare every detail of the tragedy was stark. First, the deceased. In the middle of the room was a large, oak table, a handsome period piece which was used as a desk. Here, it had been Harrison's usual habit to sit for many hours, during the early evening as well as in the daytime, sometimes reading his recent purchases, sometimes studying sale catalogues, sometimes listing and relisting his own collection, and attending to the hundred and one other details connected with his absorbing hobby.

Harrison had been seated at the moment of death, for his head and shoulders had fallen forward across the desk, partially concealing some papers which had been spread out before him and upsetting a book-rest with book, both of which were now balanced precariously on the edge of the desk.

This first quick glance also revealed a small, but ominous stain on the dead man's jacket, just below the left shoulder blade—but no weapon.

That was all, so Terhune turned his attention to the room itself, an extraordinary sight.

Except for a small space by two radiators which heated the room, the walls, from floor to ceiling, were entirely concealed by bookshelves and books. The majority of these shelves were glass-enclosed, on these Harrison had kept the most precious, or the most cherished, of his books. On the other hand the southern wall—in which were set French windows opening out on to a lawn—housed only open shelves. These Harrison had kept for the residue of his library, books of small value, but great knowledge; reference books, dictionaries, encyclopædias, lexicons, maps, guides, catalogues, and modern histories, geographies, biographies, and the like.

All these shelves, both glass-enclosed and open, Harrison had always kept scrupulously in order, with every book in its place, dusted and upright. Now, what a change! All but two of the glass-enclosed shelves had been cleared of their contents, which were lying on the floor, higgledy-piggledy.

Terhune's first reaction was one of anguish at the wanton treatment of rare and precious books, many of which were fragile with age, and liable to suffer irreparable harm from split spines, bent covers, torn pages. He turned, with the intention of voicing his indignation, but recollected that the death of a human being was a greater tragedy than possible damage to a few old books.

"Poor devil!" he exclaimed feelingly. "What killed him, sergeant? A bullet?"

Murphy shook his head. "Cold steel."

Terhune grimaced. Murder was always beastly, but death inflicted with a knife, particularly in the back, was, in his opinion, one of the beastliest, the meanest, methods of homicide. Only the administration of slow poison seemed a more evil way of killing a human being. Nevertheless, the mention of cold steel aroused his curiosity.

"What kind of weapon, sergeant?"

"You're asking something I can't answer. I haven't found it yet. P.C. Dix is searching the house and garden, but it's my idea, at the moment, that the swine who stuck Mr. Harrison in the back took the weapon away with him."

"What was it? A knife?"

"Probably, but Dr. Edwards hasn't been here yet, so I can't properly say. He's on his way home now, from an operation at Tenterden. Offhand, I should say something long and narrow was used. The slit in the cloth is something less than an inch."

Terhune stared at the sprawling body. "It looks as if he died pretty soon after the blow."

The detective nodded. "Almost at once, I should say, judging from the absence of bleeding, I'm willing to bet he didn't recover consciousness. The slightest move would have upset the book balancing on the edge."

"How long do you reckon he has been dead?"

Murphy looked at his watch. "Just about the hour. Miss Baggs 'phoned the police at four twenty-nine. According to what she has told me since I've been here the body was still warm when she discovered it."

"How did she know?" Terhune asked swiftly.

A dry smile parted Murphy's thin, colourless lips. "You're becoming quite the regular detective, sir."

Terhune grinned. He had come to know the other man well enough to realize that the detective's remark was in no way a reproof. "You shouldn't encourage me, sergeant."

"Pure selfishness, Mr. Terhune. You've been too useful in the past." He became business-like again. "Returning to Miss Baggs, she says she was sure he was dead the moment she saw his attitude—she was a trained nurse before she became Harrison's housekeeper—but to make sure she felt his pulse."

"She didn't disturb the body?"

"She says she didn't."

"I think, from what I know of her, that you can believe her. Any clues yet?"

"Not a sausage," Murphy answered glumly.

"You know why he was murdered?"

"I have one theory—but I daren't think about it too seriously for the moment."

"Why not?"

"It's too ruddy fantastic for a mere copper to swallow." He paused, and glanced slyly at Terhune. "That's why I've sent for you, Mr. Terhune. I've an idea this murder is going to be right up your street."

"My street!" Terhune was not able to follow the sergeant's reasoning. "What do you mean?"

"Books!" the detective exclaimed briefly as he indicated the mass of books on the floor.

Chapter Two

"Look, Mr. Terhune," Murphy continued. "Those books are not lying all over the floor without some damn' good reason, and the sooner we find out what it was, the better. Do you mind if I ask you a few questions?"

"Of course not."

"I suppose you've had dealings with Harrison, you and him being both so crazy about books?"

Terhune nodded. "I've lost a good customer in Mr. Harrison. I've sold him dozens of books in my time, in addition to which, for the past two years or so, I've acted as his agent in buying certain titles on his behalf,"

"Then I take it that you know something about this library of his?"

"A good deal."

"What kind of books did he collect?"

"Three kinds. In the first place he specialized in books published during the Tudor period. He would buy, for this particular collection, any book published up to the end of the seventeenth century. His collection of *incunabula* was reputed to be one of the finest private collections in the world."

Murphy's expression was comical. "Do you mean books on poultry-rearing?"

Terhune's eyes twinkled. "*Incunabula* is a Latin word meaning, figuratively, the origin or beginning of things."

"So when you speak of books as being incun—incun—what you said, Mr. Terhune—I suppose you mean books published in the early days of printing."

"More or less. Actually, books printed previous to the year fifteen hundred."

"As long ago as that. Were there many?"

"Experts have reckoned that as many as twenty million copies of books were printed in Europe during the fifteenth century."

"Bedad! Twenty million!" Then Murphy's amazement changed to suspicion. "You'll not be having me on toast, now, Mr. Terhune? I always thought Caxton didn't start printing until nearly the beginning of the sixteenth century?"

Terhune laughed. "I'm not exaggerating, sergeant. England was a newcomer to printing—mostly because it had to be subsidized in those days—in comparison with some of the European countries. Block printing on vellum began in the twelfth century; and on paper, sometime after the thirteen-fifties, I believe. But if you are referring to books printed by a press, these were being published in Paris, Cologne and Venice some time before Caxton came back to this country, in 1476, after printing, or helping to print, one or two books in Bruges."

"But glory be to God! if there were twenty million of thim books still about surely most of 'em wouldn't be worth more than a few shillings each?"

"You're right, they wouldn't, sergeant, book collecting, like the collection of most rare articles, being sometimes a form of snobbishness. But I didn't say that all the twenty million were still extant. It was estimated, in 1905, that there were only about thirty thousand *incunabula*, complete and incomplete, left in the world at that date—the Lord only knows how many still exist after two world wars."

"And Mr. Harrison had some of these incun—thingumajigs?" Murphy asked in an awed voice.

"He did, the lucky devil!"

No sooner was the exclamation out than Terhune regretted it. Was Arthur Harrison a lucky devil, to be sprawling forward on his own desk, the victim of a murderous attack?

Terhune hurried on: "But Harrison didn't only collect *incunabula*, sergeant. He was equally keen on fine bindings, also illustrated books—I don't mean any old illustrations, of course, but hand-blocked, or hand-painted pictures, and even some of the more modern books which had illustrations of special interest."

"Like that book on Dutch costumes you showed me some time back—the one with pictures that had to be printed more than twenty-five times to get the colours true to life?" Murphy broke in eagerly.

"Yes, As a matter of fact I sold the very copy you looked at to Harrison—it may be lying somewhere beneath that pile over there, near the window."

"Ruddy shame!" Murphy exclaimed, quite sincerely.

"In addition, he wasn't above buying ordinary, modern books for his own recreation—most of those he kept on the open shelves."

Murphy stared down at the books on the floor, "Getting back to the thingumajigs, some of them would be worth a fairish amount, wouldn't they?"

"Fairish!" Terhune agreed. "But although Harrison was moderately wealthy, and spent practically all his income, so he told me, he wasn't a millionaire. Some of his choicest prizes he had tracked down for himself, before the last war, and purchased at quite moderate prices."

"All the same, I put this to you, Mr. Terhune. From your own knowledge of Mr. Harrison's collection, did he own a book worth the price of a man's life?"

"Not one that I have seen."

The answer appeared to gratify Murphy. He nodded his head in agreement.

"Just what I thought."

Terhune was puzzled. He was not able to follow Murphy's reasoning. "You think that Harrison was killed on account of a book?"

"That's just what I *don't* think."

"Why?"

"Because, however much a book might be worth, no man with an atom of common sense would risk his neck to steal it."

"Why not? Many a man has risked his neck—and lost it—in stealing something he could turn into money."

"Not if that something was rare enough to be traceable—which it would be, wouldn't it?"

Terhune nodded,

"See here, sir, can you see any book lying about now which would be worth a few thousand pounds, say? Or if you can't, tell me any old title, for the sake of argument."

"*English Historical Portrait Miniatures*, for instance. I saw the four volumes which comprise this title sold for twelve hundred and fifty guineas."

The sergeant groaned. "Saint Patrick! All that money for four blinking books of portraits. I should want them jewelled or something for that price."

His hearer chuckled. "They were jewelled, sergeant. The centre bar of the clasp mounted turquoise, amethyst, cornelian and ruby."

"Jewelled books, bedad!" The sergeant made no attempt to hide his disgust. "And how many people are there in the world who would give that price for a set of ruddy books?"

"Probably only a handful or so, if you are referring to private buyers."

"Right, and you could probably tell me their names, couldn't you?"

"Possibly."

"Are there any people, other than private buyers, who might buy books of that sort?"

"All the big booksellers, for instance. Maggs, Sotheran, Myers, Edwards, Grafton. Or, of course, the books could be put up for auction through Sotheby, or Puttick and Simpson, or the Parke-Bernet Galleries in New York."

"That's what I thought. Then if we circulated a description of the stolen books to all the private buyers, the leading booksellers, and the principal book-auctioneers, what chance would the thief have of selling the books without leaving a trail behind him wide enough for a blind man to follow?"

"Not much, I should say."

"Exactly. That's why no professional crook would touch one of Harrison's books with a barge pole."

"Perhaps this isn't a professional job."

Murphy pushed the tip of his forefinger into Terhune's shoulder.

"This is a pro. job or my name isn't Tim Murphy. Take a look at that body. Where would you say Harrison was when the knife was stuck in his back?"

"Sitting at his desk."

"And facing it?"

Terhune studied the position of the body. Everything pointed to the fact that, at the moment of being stabbed, Harrison had been sitting at his desk in a perfectly normal attitude.

"Probably," he agreed.

"Good! Now the desk is placed sideways in the north-east corner of the room, isn't it? Which means that both the French window, in the south wall, and the only door, in the west wall, are visible to anyone sitting behind the desk."

Terhune nodded.

"Now look at the spare chair facing the front part of the desk—"

"Its usual position, by the way."

"Just what I thought. It's for the use of visitors, I take it?"

"Yes."

"Suppose you are Harrison," Murphy continued crisply. "And suppose a stranger comes into the room. Do you sit quietly behind your desk and let the other man walk round to your back without at least keeping sight of what he is up to; or turning round at the same time in that swivel-chair if only out of politeness and nothing else?"

"The other man might not have been a stranger, sergeant."

A smile passed across Murphy's face. "I have already classified that possibility as clue number one. And yet the idea of this stabbing business being done by somebody known to Harrison doesn't smell right to me. Anyway, for the sake of argument let's assume that a stranger has come into the room. Perhaps he has come on some business or other. What do you do?"

Terhune reflected. "Perhaps I get to my feet, shake hands with him, then tell him to sit down. Or maybe I don't rise and shake hands. But in any case I tell him to sit down."

"Of course you do. And the man sits down, doesn't he?"

"I suppose so," Terhune admitted doubtfully.

"Well, if he doesn't, then I repeat, you don't just sit still and let him mess about behind you without seeing what he is doing. No, the stranger is sitting down, and you are talking to each other when, bingo! you're stabbed and dead without ever knowing what happened to you."

"You mean that two men must have come in?"

"At least two, Mr. Terhune. But probably only two; more would have been a crowd, and might have made even the most innocent of men suspicious of what was happening. No, as I see it at the moment, two men come into the room—or perhaps I should say, two people, in case one was a woman. Harrison invites his visitors to sit down. There is only one chair. One of the men, or the woman, sits, and begins to talk to Harrison. The second person turns to the bookshelves, pretends to be interested in the books, and wanders along the shelves till he reaches a spot where he can stab Harrison in the back. Does that theory make sense to you?"

"It doesn't make nonsense."

"Which every other theory which I thought of so far does," Murphy said glumly. "But if it's anywhere near the truth then the crime was premeditated; if it was premeditated it was very carefully planned; and if it was planned then it must have been a pro job, for amateur murderers don't usually set about the job in pairs." Terhune frowned his perplexity. He was not prepared to criticize Murphy's deductions, but the idea of two professional criminals entering the library with the intention of murdering Harrison—well, in the sergeant's own words: "it didn't smell right." What could be the motive for such a cold-blooded murder? was a reflection which worried him. Harrison had lived his adult life in *Twelve Chimneys*. In consequence, the details of his life were almost as an open book to the inhabitants of Bray-in-the-Marsh. It was known, for instance, that Harrison, a bachelor, rarely left his home. There was a good reason why he had no need to, of course. His was a lovely home from every point of view; it stood in several acres of land which not only supplied the needs of the inner man, from the large kitchen gardens, the walled orchards, and the greenhouses, but also catered for the spiritual man, for a landscape gardener had planned it, and turned it into a miniature fairyland for the solitary-minded, which Harrison was. Here a sunken garden, overlooked only by a creeper-enclosed pergola; there a shrub-enclosed, natural gold-fish pond filled with carp, orfe, rudd and tench; here, a bower beneath the low-hanging branches of a centuries-old fir; there, a long, rambling walk, walled in by flowering shrubs, ornamental grasses; trimmed conifers, and planted with bulbs, flowers, and ferns in variety. Wherever you walked in Harrison's garden you encountered attractive corners or cul-de-sacs, each containing something to give it character or charm—an ornamental stone bench, a mossy statue, a bird-bath, a fountain—

This garden of *Twelve Chimneys* was a world of its own, in which Harrison was more than content to pass all the hours he spared from his beloved books. So he seldom went beyond the boundary line of his own property; when he did it was usually to attend a book-auction, or to visit booksellers in London and elsewhere.

Of his relatives, little was known; it was believed that he had a nephew in one of the North American countries, and an aged cousin in the Orkneys, but Miss Baggs, who was the source of as much as was known of him, said that she had never heard of any other relatives. His circle of friends was equally restricted. Sometimes he asked Winstanley to dine with him, sometimes Dr. Edwards—upon which occasions the two men talked of little other than roses—and sometimes Edward Pryce—several of Pryce's famous sunsets had been painted in the grounds of *Twelve Chimneys*: in addition, Pryce shared Harrison's interest in illustrations. But few other people visited the house with any regularity, and Harrison visited none if he could avoid doing so.

He was not very much liked by the local inhabitants. Alicia MacMunn maintained that she positively disliked him, indeed. So did Olive Brereton. But Harrison was a notorious misogynist, so it could be that pique was responsible, that pique which many women automatically feel for any man who remains unaffected by the need for woman's companionship.

Such was the background of Harrison's life and character—a background which seemed to harbour no sinister shadows. The idea of Harrison's being the premeditated victim of "professional" criminals seemed too far-fetched a theory to be credible. Why should anyone want to murder the inoffensive little man?

This objection Terhune passed on to the detective, who laughed sourly.

"I wondered how long it would take you to come back to the question of motive. Before I begin guessing perhaps you can answer one or two questions,"

"I'll try."

"Have you any idea what Harrison was worth?"

"Miss Amelia told me once that Harrison had inherited something a little less than seventy thousand pounds from his father."

"Before or after estate duty was paid?"

"Good Lord! Miss Amelia wouldn't know anything about that."

"She probably got the information from some newspaper, in which case that amount was probably reckoned before the payment of death duties. What was the amount of duty in those days?—" Murphy did not wait for Terhune's reply, which, in any case, would have been unhelpful. "Suppose he inherited about sixty thousand net. Sixty thousand at, say, an average of four per cent, less present income tax—" A slight pause. "He was probably worth anything from sixteen hundred to two thousand a year net. Do you believe he spent that amount of income each year?"

Terhune did a sum in mental arithmetic. "Miss Baggs, say, one hundred and fifty; the girl, Mary, another fifty; two gardeners at the same each, that's five hundred; rates and taxes, say another hundred. That's six hundred. Say another four hundred if you like for all other living expenses, and two hundred for general maintenance, indoors and out—one thousand, two hundred."

"Which would leave a balance of anything up to eight hundred—"

"Don't forget the books," Terhune interrupted quickly.

"He wouldn't spend eight hundred a year on books?" Murphy's maimer was slightly scandalized.

"No?" Terhune pointed down at a book which lay, open, on the ground close to the door. The open pages revealed a watercolour drawing of a large-sized bird. "If that book is what I think it is—" He picked it up, and examined it. "It is. You see this volume of *Birds of Washington* by Dawson and Bowles, published in Seattle? It's one of eighty-five sets, signed by the author. To buy the book to-day wouldn't leave much change out of ninety pounds."

Murphy whistled. "Ninety Jimmy-o'-Goblins for this?"

"Yes."

"What is it—one of the thingumajigs?"

"On the contrary, it was published in nineteen hundred and nine. And there's another—"

"All right! All right!" the sergeant exclaimed hastily. "You've made your point. I can see it wouldn't be hard to spend eight hundred pounds in a year."

"Why did you ask about his income?"

"I was wondering whether he made a hobby of collecting other things besides books."

"Such as?"

"Jewels, for instance."

Terhune was puzzled. "Why jewels?"

"Because they are things which crooks could dispose of without much difficulty. You see, Mr. Terhune, we've got to find some good reason to explain why all the books are on the floor. To me it looks as if someone has gone along the shelves, systematically emptying them merely by putting a hand behind the books and pulling them forward until they overbalanced and fell on the floor."

Terhune looked with sad eyes at the untidy masses of books, and could not contradict the detective. "But why should anyone want to do that, sergeant?"

"In the hope of finding something behind—a packet of jewels for instance."

Jewels! Terhune shook his head doubtfully. He could not think of anyone less likely than Harrison to collect jewels.

The sergeant's sharp eyes were quick to recognize his companion's reaction to his theory.

"You don't agree?"

"Frankly, I don't."

"I don't blame you." Murphy thrust his hands deep into his pockets, and rocked to and fro on heels and toes. "I don't know that I have very much faith myself in the jewel theory. But something was hidden behind the books on one of the shelves, and if it wasn't jewels or money, well, you tell me what it was."

Terhune shrugged. His mind felt blank on the subject.

The sergeant became unexpectedly testy. "Bedad! I hope I run across someone who can give me some hint as to what the murdering swine got away with, or a fat chance we'll have of recovering it."

"If you don't know what it is the men were after, how do you know they got away with anything?"

Murphy's irritation disappeared as quickly as it had shewn itself. A slow smile made a rare appearance.

"That's one to me, Mr. Terhune," he exclaimed ingenuously. "You see those shelves just by the window—the glass-enclosed ones, I mean. The books there are still intact. Why? Because the thieves found what they were looking for just before they reached there. Otherwise, they would have emptied the books out of those as well. Don't you agree?"

But Terhune did not have the chance of either agreement or argument for just then Doctor Edwards entered the library.

Chapter Three

While Doctor Edwards, the police surgeon for the district, was examining Harrison's body, Murphy beckoned Terhune outside. "I want to ask Miss Baggs some more questions. Would you like to be present?"

The answer was never in doubt—Murphy knew that before he asked the question, as his dry voice only too well revealed—so the two men went in search of the housekeeper. They found her in a cosy little room towards the rear of the house. There was a small wood fire in the grate; its red glow illumined the gay chintzes and bright cushions, the sewing-machine in one corner, a basket of needlework beside a large armchair, all the little bits and pieces of feminine occupancy which gave character to the room, and lastly, Miss Baggs herself, She sat in the armchair, and stared dry-eyed into the fire, but neither its warmth, nor its glow gave any colour to her cheeks, from which the usual apple-red colour had disappeared. Her hands, limply idle in her lap, trembled,

"May we come in?" Murphy asked through the half-open door. Then, quickly, as she moved: "Don't move, Miss Baggs. I just want to ask you a few questions."

"Come in, sir," she said tremulously, adding, as she saw Terhune: "I'm afraid there's only one other chair." She began to rise. "I'll get another."

"No, you won't, Miss Baggs. I will." Terhune forestalled her by leaving the sergeant to deal with her. He saw the kitchen near by, and a chair by the table, so he borrowed the chair and took it back to the housekeeper's room, where he found the detective sitting close to the armchair, patting one of her plump hands.

"Don't you worry, Miss Baggs. You'll sleep to-night. Doctor Edwards will see to that. He will probably give you something to take. I've already asked him to come and see you afterwards."

"Thank you, Mr. Murphy, I've never taken a sleeping draught yet, but I know I shouldn't sleep to-night without one." But the strained expression still remained, "Draught or no draught, I'm not staying in this house to-night. Nor is Mary. She's going off to her mother's, at Appledore, and I'm going with her."

"It must have been a terrible shock to you," Murphy said sympathetically. "But I think that the men who killed Mr. Harrison got what they came for. You won't be troubled by them again. Besides, I can arrange for a constable to remain on guard for the next few nights—"

She shook her head obstinately. "Mary wouldn't sleep here to-night if there was a dozen policemen about the place, and I won't stay without her. I'm not so young as I was—"

"There, there, Miss Baggs! Nor shall you stay if you don't want to."

She relaxed. "I oughtn't to be so stupid, me being once a nurse and all, but when I went into the library, and saw him lying across the desk—" She shuddered, but her voice became a shade stronger as she continued: "Who killed poor Mr. Harrison, Mr. Murphy? And why? There wasn't a kinder man in the world than him. Wouldn't hurt a dog nor cat, he wouldn't, still less a human being. He might not have been much of a one for other people's company, but that was only because he loved his books so much. And his garden."

"We don't know much yet, Miss Baggs. That's why I want to ask you a few more questions."

She said nothing, so Murphy took her silence for consent. "Suppose we start at the beginning, Miss Baggs," he began gently. "You have already told me that both you and Mary were out this afternoon. Were the two of you often away from the house at the same time?"

She nodded her little round head quickly, as if detecting a vague suspicion in his voice. "Oh! yes. Every Monday and Friday afternoon, from about two o'clock to five-thirty. We used to go into Ashford together, to do the shopping. Mary's afternoon off was a Wednesday—"

"Quite, Miss Baggs. I don't think we need worry about Mary's other time off. How long have you and Mary been in the habit of going into Ashford every Monday and Friday?"

"Ever since Mary has been in service here. That would be four years come next January. Before that Agnes used to come with me—Agnes Brown was the maid here until she married young Ted Cooper, Sir George Brereton's chauffeur."

"So it would be common knowledge in the village that Mr. Harrison would be in the house alone on the two days in question?"

"Yes."

"I see. Now, did you know that Mr. Harrison was expecting a visitor or visitors this afternoon?"

"He wasn't expecting any visitors. If he had been I shouldn't have gone to town." There was a note of asperity in her voice. "I should have sent Mary by herself."

"How do you know that Mr. Harrison wasn't expecting visitors?"

"Because he would have told me so."

"But suppose he had not wanted you to know that somebody was calling upon him?"

Her round eyes became reproachful; apparently it was beyond her power of imagination to think of Harrison's having a secret which he had kept from her.

"Why shouldn't he want me to know?"

The sergeant decided not to pursue a line of interrogation which might evoke resentment. He answered diplomatically: "I am sure he wouldn't have wanted to deceive you, Miss Baggs. So you think the visitor to *Twelve Chimneys* this afternoon was an unexpected one?"

"I am sure he was," she maintained obstinately.

"Then we will leave it at that. Now, with regard to the telephone.

I noticed that there was a receiver on the desk in the library. Is it a direct connection with exchange, or an extension?"

"It's the only 'phone in the house, Mr. Murphy," she replied, looking somewhat puzzled.

"Where is the bell? In the library?"

"No. In the hall, above the library door."

"Where it can be heard all over the house?"

"Yes."

"Was it rung to-day—I mean, at any time while you were in?"

"Once. This morning, about ten-thirty."

"Do you know who rang?" he asked eagerly.

"The Rector. Mr. Harrison told me so later. He asked whether he might come along to-morrow afternoon to fetch some books Mr. Harrison had promised for the Church Bazaar." Her china-blue eyes misted. "And now it's too late. Mr. Harrison is—is—" She choked over the dread word, and left it unsaid.

Her answer, satisfactory from one point of view, was, from another, disappointing. So far everything pointed to Harrison's visitors as being both uninvited and unexpected, a fact which would militate against quick identification. But patience and dogged perseverance were Murphy's *forte*—as indeed they have to be, and are, of all successful detectives. He passed smoothly on to the next sequence of questions.

"So we've now established that when you and Mary left this house about two this afternoon, you had no reason for anticipating, or suspecting, that visitors would call on Mr. Harrison during your absence. Now, Miss Baggs, you said just now that you usually arrived home about five-thirty—by the four-thirty-five from Ashford, I suppose?"

She nodded.

"Then how did it happen that you arrived home an hour earlier than usual?"

The two men could see by her strained expression that it distressed her to bring her memory forward to more recent happenings. Fortunately she was a common-sensical little body, so, with a quick gulp, she spoke in a somewhat toneless voice, while concentrating her gaze upon something on the floor—the pattern of the carpet, Terhune believed.

"We had finished our shopping early, Mary and me, so we went along to Forrests' Stores, meaning to have a cup of tea, which we often used to do if there was time before catching the bus home. Well, just as we were going in Mrs. Pettigrew came out—"

"The Rector's wife?" Terhune interrupted.

"Yes, Mr. Terhune."

"The Rector of Wickford?" Murphy asked, in his turn.

"Yes, Mr. Murphy. That's the Rectory, just along the road before you reach *Twelve Chimneys*."

Murphy's eyes twinkled. That much was already known to him. But he said nothing, and nodded encouragingly.

"Mrs. Pettigrew stopped to ask how Mary's mother is, Mrs. Oliver being poorly, the poor soul. While we were talking Mrs. Pettigrew asked whether we were on our way back to the village. I told her that we was, so she said she was too, so would we like to come back with her in her car. That was better than hanging about waiting for the bus, so I said we would."

"So you arrived back home about an hour earlier than usual?"

"The clock in the church said twenty-five past four, as we went by, but it's nearly always three or four minutes fast, so I suppose it was nearer twenty past."

"Where did Mrs. Pettigrew drop you; outside the Rectory, or here?"

"Outside the kitchen door here."

"Then what happened?"

"We came into the house. Mary went up to her bedroom. I came in here, took off my hat and coat, gave the fire a poke to liven it up, and then—" She began to falter.

"And then, Miss Baggs," Murphy prompted gently.

"I—I went into the library, to tell Mr. Harrison we was home, and ask him whether he would like a cup of tea."

"Try to be brave, and tell us about everything you remember seeing. Every little detail you can possibly think of."

Tears trickled down her rounded, wan-looking cheeks from the corner of each downcast eye. "I didn't see nothing else but—but just Mr. Harrison," she replied, falteringly. "Mr. Harrison lying face forward on the table, just like he was dead."

"What did you do?"

"I wasn't really frightened at first, Mr. Murphy. I thought he had just fainted. So I began to hurry towards him. Then I saw his—his back."

"Well?"

"I knew the stain was blood—I've seen too many bloodstains in my time not to know one when I see one. I guessed something terrible had happened, so I tried to feel his pulse. When I couldn't feel it I knew there was nothing nobody could do to help Mr. Harrison, so I picked up the telephone and asked for police."

"Is that all?"

She nodded.

"There was nothing else you noticed, however insignificant?" Murphy persisted.

She shook her head agitatedly. "Directly you had finished speaking to me on the telephone, Mr. Murphy, I hurried out of the library, and haven't been back there since."

"I see. Now, Miss Baggs, did you enter the library before leaving the house this afternoon?"

"Yes, to tell Mr. Harrison that Mary and me was just leaving."

"Did you, by any chance, notice whether the French windows were open or closed?"

She gave the question thought, but finally shook her head. "I don't remember looking at them, but you wouldn't find it easy to make me believe they was open."

"Why not?"

"There was a cool nip in the air this afternoon, and if there was one thing that Mr. Harrison couldn't abide more than another it was a draught. I've never known those windows be open much before the middle of June, or after the first week or so in September."

One or two more questions followed, but they added nothing to the little the sergeant knew or suspected. Presently Murphy brought the interview to an end, by rising to his feet and telling Miss Baggs to rest quietly where she was for the time being. Directly she realized that the sergeant had finished with her an obstinate expression settled upon her face. In a decided manner she said that, if she were not wanted any more for the time being, she wasn't going to rest quietly in her own, or any other room; she was going to put a few things together right away, so that she could leave the house at the same time, or even before the police did, even if it meant her standing in the road thirty minutes or more to catch the last bus as far as Ashford, where she hoped to get a distant relative of sorts to take Mary and her in his car to Appledore. All this in one long, breathless sentence.

From the housekeeper's sitting-room the two men returned to the library where they found Doctor Edwards just finishing his examination.

"Ah! just in time, Murphy. I was coming to look for you." He waved his hand at the body. "There's not much doubt about cause of death. It's as neat a bit of murder as any I've ever been connected with. Whoever stuck his knife into poor Harrison's back knows his anatomy. I shall be surprised if the p.m. doesn't reveal a ruddy bull's-eye."

"The heart?"

"Of course I mean the heart. If the weapon didn't pass clean through it I'll eat my hat."

"Then death was instantaneous, I suppose?"

"As near as makes no odds."

"What kind of a weapon was used, doctor?"

"Something long and pointed—"

"A stiletto?"

"Give it what fancy name you like, sergeant, but the flesh in the back has an inch-long wound, while that near the left breast is less than an eighth of an inch."

"Would you say that the blow was delivered by someone who is expert with a knife?"

Doctor Edwards was a cautious man. "It could have been a lucky stroke."

"But if it wasn't one hundred per cent luck? Would you agree that the murderer had skill?"

"And knowledge. Anatomical knowledge, I mean."

"Well, then, skill and knowledge?"

Edwards gave a dry grin. He was in a corner, and knew it. "A person who didn't know something of the whereabouts of the heart, shoulder-blade, and so on, probably wouldn't have achieved such a clean stroke in the proper place," he compromised.

The answer was all Murphy wanted. "Then I'm sticking to my theory that this was a pro. job," he asserted.

The police surgeon's eyebrows twitched. "Why should an habitual criminal want to kill an old stick-in-the-mud like Harrison? I thought he hadn't any interests outside books and his garden." Murphy shrugged. "As far as I know at the moment, he hadn't. But it's early days yet. And take a peek at all the books on the floor. It looks as if the crooks swept them off the shelves while searching for something hidden behind them."

Edwards stared at the heaped-up books on the floor. "Which they found over there by the window, I suppose?" he said presently. "That's my present theory."

"Strange!" the doctor murmured. "Ruddy strange!"

I I

Strange indeed! This, by general agreement of the inhabitants of Wickford, Bray, and the other villages near by. And the strangeness was in no way mitigated, during the next few days, by the absence of any evidence that the police authorities were making progress towards an arrest.

As always, as soon as the news travelled around that Terhune was once again connected, however remotely, with a crime, people flocked into his shop to buy books. As always he was bombarded with questions. As always he remained—outwardly at any rate—his cheerful, courteous and likeable self, parrying most questions with a skill which long practice was beginning to make perfect, while, at the same time, cunningly slipping in a few questions of his own, designed to elicit any information about Harrison which might prove useful to Murphy.

Among the people who visited the shop during the days immediately following Harrison's death was Edward Pryce. Pryce was a frequent, though not regular, visitor, being only a moderate reader, and then only of books by or about artists, past and present.

Pryce entered the shop, just before five o'clock on the Thursday, and was lucky enough to find only Terhune present. Being a forthright character he made no attempt to dissemble.

"I say, Terhune, is it true that you were at Harrison's home just after his death?"

Terhune nodded. "Sergeant Murphy sent for me."

"A damned shocking business! Poor old Harrison. Not everybody liked the old fellow, but I got on well enough with him. Perhaps because we both shared a passion for book illustrations. Look here, Terhune, I am going to ask straight out what may be an impertinent question. Don't answer it if you would rather not, or if it's betraying any sort of a confidence. But do the police know why Harrison was killed?"

An easily answered question, "So far as I know, they don't. The only theory they have—if I can say this in confidence—"

"Of course."

"Their only theory is that Mr. Harrison was murdered for something of great value."

The artist stared at Terhune with incredulous eyes. "Do you mean one of his books? I shouldn't have thought that any book was worth a man's life."

Almost Murphy's own words, Terhune reflected. "No," he replied aloud. "Not a book."

"What else of value was Harrison likely to have had?"

"You were more intimate with him than I, Mr. Pryce."

The other man shrugged. "Was any man really intimate with Harrison? I doubt it. He wasn't the type to share intimacies; his soul was too wrapped up in those books of his to leave room for normal emotions. But what kind of something else of great value have the police in mind? An old master? A curio? A—a—damn it! I can't think of anything which would have interested him."

"A collection of precious stones, for instance?"

The artist gesticulated his scornful rejection of this theory. "Nonsense, Terhune, Harrison was no more interested in precious stones or in jewellery than I am in Siamese cats. What gave them that strange idea?"

"Three-quarters of all the books in the library had been tumbled off the shelves on to the floor. Murphy's idea is, that the murderers were looking for, and found, something hidden behind the books. The first obvious answer to the question, what is both valuable enough to warrant the risk of hanging, and small enough to hide behind books, is—a package of precious stones or jewellery."

"I see!" Pryce exclaimed reflectively. "The police idea isn't quite so foolish as I believed at first. All the same—" He shook his head. "The idea of Harrison's possessing a packet of valuable stones or jewels doesn't agree with the man's character. So far as I know he didn't care a rap for jewellery—in fact, he said once that he wouldn't exchange his Desmoulins Bible for all the diamonds in the world."

"Except that he could have sold all the diamonds in the world and have bought himself some more books," Terhune commented drily.

"I'll agree with that statement," Pryce retorted swiftly. "Therefore, if he had had any diamonds he wouldn't have hidden them behind his books; he would have sold them as quickly as possible, and reinvested the proceeds in, as you say, more books."

"Then what could he have had at the back of his bookshelves to tempt men to murder him?"

"God knows!"

A long silence followed Pryce's fervent exclamation. At last Pryce spoke again.

"I can't begin to think what he might have hidden away behind his books. I know it sounds stupid, and, probably, immaterial, but I can't even imagine *how* he came into possession of anything valuable. You see, he was such a queer, solitary-minded kind of chap. To prise him away from his books and his garden was as difficult as making me believe that foxes like being hunted. Almost the only times he left the neighbourhood of Wickford were those when he was chasing a book. He would go anywhere for a book—but you know more about that side of his character than I do.

"Visitors to *Twelve Chimneys* were as rare as his visits to other people. In fact, Edwards and myself were the only people to visit him with regularity. So you see what I mean when I say that it isn't easy for me to imagine how or when this packet of stones, or jewels, or whatever it was, came into his possession. I've added the word *when* because he told me, only last week, that he hadn't moved off his property since the second week in March."

"Not even to an auction sale, or to the London booksellers?"

"That is what he told me. If he bought any books during that time he must have done so by correspondence. Haven't you sold him any?"

"Since the second week in March?"

"Yes."

"Only two, neither of them expensive. The first was a copy of de Tizac's *Animals in Chinese Art*—"

"I know the book," Pryce interrupted eagerly. "I've spent hours looking through it."

"He paid me three guineas for that, and five pounds ten for a copy of Hall's *Union of the Famelies of Lancastre and Yorke* with margins cut into."

Pryce looked surprised, "You usually sold him more than two books in ten weeks, didn't you? At any rate he always seemed to be telling me of some new book or other which you had sold him."

"I have sold him more than that number of books in ten weeks, but I've also sold him less," Terhune explained. "It all depended whether the kind of book he wanted came into my possession or not." Then Terhune was unexpectedly reminded of something.

Pryce's eyes, trained to observe, were not slow to note the expression which crossed Terhune's face. "What's the matter, Terhune? Have you just thought of something?"

"Yes. Three weeks ago I offered him a copy of the sixteen thirty-five edition of *Montaigne's Essays*. He refused it."

"Because he already had a copy?"

"No. He hadn't. I knew that before I offered it to him."

"Then why didn't he have it?"

"I don't know. He wouldn't give me a reason."

For a second Pryce looked surprised. Then he dismissed the subject with a shrug. "Perhaps he was economizing after his one and only holiday in the last umpteen years."

"His trip to Stockholm last December?"

"Yes. Maybe he went gay for once in his life. Good luck to him if he did," Pryce glanced at his watch. "I'd better be going now, Terhune. I'm due home for tea and crumpets. You might let me know if you do get to hear anything further about Harrison's death. I think it's a blasted shame that such a harmless old chap should be murdered by ruddy thieves. May they hang as high as the church steeple."

With which sentiment Terhune felt in complete agreement as he watched his visitor stride briskly across empty Market Square.

Chapter Four

Twenty-seven hours later Terhune had another visitor, Murphy, this time. The sergeant relaxed into the deep, roomy armchair in the study with an exclamation of satisfaction, and automatically pulled out his pipe and tobacco-pouch. It always gave the bluff Cockney-Irishman pleasure to enter Terhune's masculinely untidy study with its shelf upon shelf of books—Terhune's own collection—its desk, piled high with papers, books, catalogues, and everything else under the sun, its warm, cheerfully-crackling log fire, its characteristic slightly-musty smell of old books and fragrant tobacco smoke, its tobacco-ash-strewn rugs, and above all, its atmosphere of serenity. Here was a very small, and very intimate world in which, Murphy felt convinced, no troubles of any kind were permitted to intrude, which no woman was ever allowed to spoil by tidying up, and lastly one in which he could drink, smoke until the room was in a fug, and yarn with Terhune; a tiny world, in fact, in which, for a few hours, he could be himself without self-consciousness and embarrassment.

And, so, although he was a happily married man—a loving husband and father—Murphy often seized upon the flimsiest excuse to visit the room above the bookshop, while Terhune, for his part, was equally glad to see Murphy. He liked the sergeant because Murphy, although having no especial brilliance or learning, did possess a practical common sense second to none. One could always rely upon his giving a considered, unprejudiced and logical opinion upon any subject within his comprehension. No man was more qualified, but less inclined, to speak for and as the Man in the Street.

With the help of Murphy's pipe the room was soon fuggy enough to make them both feel happy. But while the sergeant toasted his feet, and sank lower and lower into the chair, Terhune poured out a whisky and soda for his visitor, and a beer for himself, so neither of them spoke for awhile, until at last Murphy lifted his glass.

"Cheers, Mr. Terhune!" he toasted simply.

"Cheers!" Terhune returned.

Both drank, or rather Terhune drank while Murphy sipped. Then Terhune asked:

"Any news, sergeant?"

"About what?" the detective asked blandly. Sometimes his humour was inclined to be ponderous.

Terhune grinned, but played the game. "The men who killed Harrison?"

"Oh! Them!" Murphy dropped pretence; his mouth hardened as he took his pipe out of his mouth. "Not a ruddy thing." He was evidently disturbed, for his tongue was commendably not loose as a general rule. "I think everybody in the village must have been asleep that afternoon. Not a soul that we've questioned so far had sight or sound of the crooks, either coming or going."

"I suppose they came by car?"

"They didn't travel by bus, at any rate. We questioned the two drivers, Binks and Wood—you remember them in the Charles Cockburn case? Both of them not only swear that no strangers travelled in their buses at any time during the day, in either direction, but both were able to give us the names of most of the local people who did.

"We've checked up also with the ticket collectors and porters at Ashford station. They were not able to help us much, for there were a fair number of people travelling last Monday. But, for what it is worth, nobody there is able to remember seeing two or three strange men travelling together; either the travellers were unaccompanied, or with a family, or with female companions, or were known to the porters as local residents, or regular travellers. Of course, they could have cycled to Wickford from anywhere, but—" The sergeant shrugged. "It's only in Chesterton's Father Brown type of stories that murderers go about on bicycles, which is psychologically unlikely in these days."

"Don't forget Raffles," Terhune reminded the other man.

"Old Raffles! Yes, that's right; he and Bunny used bicycles, didn't they? But Raffles wasn't a *murderer*. It's that particular crime which sticks in my gullet. Cold-blooded murder—or hot-blooded murder, too, if you like—and bicycles don't mix. A murderer's natural impulse, on his way back from a crime, is to hide himself from everybody, to take advantage of dark places and shades, to keep clear of populous districts. But a bicycle perches a man up in the air for everyone to look at—it all but throws a limelight upon him—at least his guilty conscience creates that impression as he rides along in the middle of a road—or am I talking nonsense, Mr. Terhune?"

"I think you are probably ninety-nine per cent right, sergeant, although it is unusual to hear you speak of psychology. I thought you were far too matter-of-fact."

"So I used to be. It's your influence which has changed me," Murphy admitted gloomily. "And having a complex like that doesn't help a poor copper with his normal job of work, I can tell you. I very nearly argued myself out of arresting a doubtful character two weeks ago because I got a crazy idea that a man who walked along a street smoking a pipe couldn't possibly be a housebreaker. A pipe is a domestic article, I told myself; something to smoke before a fire, or when one is reading a newspaper, or having a friendly argument with a pal at the local. No crook I've met has ever smoked anything but cigarettes—except one who made money by visiting widows and other bereaved people and pretending that he owed money to the dead person, and that his conscience wouldn't be at rest until he had paid up his debt in full."

"With a dud cheque, I suppose, made out for a pound or two more than the debt, which the widow was only too grateful to cash for him?"

"Yes. Well, that particular bastard used to smoke cigars in the belief that a cigar created more confidence than a cigarette."

"And did it?"

"It damn' well did."

"Then that proves that a psychology complex can be useful. But what about your pipe-smoker?"

"The old Adam in me was stronger than the psychology bug. I took a chance and asked him what was in the attaché case he was carrying. He took his pipe out of his mouth, laughed, and said: 'Stolen goods.'"

Terhune chuckled. "What had he really got inside the case? The manuscript of a new novel, or somebody's washing?"

The sergeant's face brightened with a slow-spreading, beatific smile. "All Mrs. Grayson-Jones's silver. And to think he very nearly got away with it just because he was smoking a pipe!" His expression sobered. "But I'm still convinced that Harrison's killers didn't travel to and from Wickford by bicycle."

"I suppose they don't live in the village?"

"We aren't forgetting that possibility, naturally, but I'm willing to bet ten to one against." The detective turned gloomy again. "Between ourselves, Mr. Terhune, the case hasn't progressed one jot since I last saw you, and the Chief Constable is hopping mad about it. He hasn't had to call the C.I.D. in on a case for more than two years, and is anxious to keep up the good work. No, from all we've been able to find out so far the men might have materialized from nowhere and gone back there—though it's Buckingham Palace to a sixpence that they came from London."

"Did you find any fingerprints?"

"Several, probably all from the same pair of hands, but Records don't recognize them."

"Did nobody in the village see a strange car about at any time during the afternoon?"

"Nobody," Murphy stated emphatically. "But if the murderers had had enough savvy to take their car up the drive and leave it immediately outside the front door it would have been hidden from the road by that thick belt of evergreens bordering the road. The only places from which it might have been seen while parked there were the Rectory windows on the south side, and the north-east windows of the house where that man Jellicoe used to live—"

"Willow Bend."

"That's the place. I made inquiries at both houses, but nothing came of them. The Rector was out digging most of the afternoon; his wife was in Ashford, as you know, and the maid didn't move out of the kitchen. The man at *Willow Bend*, Rowlandson, was in town; the wife says she was in Bray—"

Terhune laughed. "I can confirm that statement, sergeant. She was in my shop, telling me how not to run my business."

"Well, there you are. So nobody saw a car. That helps a lot." Murphy sounded quite bitter about the villagers' errors of omission.

Terhune refilled the glasses. "Then you haven't a clue of any sort?"

"No," the sergeant barked. He stared at the fire. "But one fact has come to light," he continued, musingly. "I don't call it a clue to the crime—as yet—but it's damned mysterious, and it's meself that would like to know more about it."

He turned his head in Terhune's direction. "Mr. Howard, the solicitor, 'phoned me up this morning, and asked me to go round and see him. I did so, and he told me that he was Harrison's executor. In that capacity he began a preliminary investigation into the deceased's affairs. He didn't expect this to be a very difficult task, he told me, for at the time the will was drawn up Harrison had deposited with Howard a list of the securities which then represented his capital. Incidentally, Harrison's capital was round about the one hundred and twenty thousand mark, which is a tidy sum to possess even in these days, bedad!"

If a vague expression of envy reflected itself in the sergeant's eyes, it was not long there; Murphy stirred uncomfortably, and continued:

"Yesterday morning Howard sent one of his clerks round to the Westminster Bank to check up the list of securities, which Harrison had lodged with the bank for security reasons during the war—and by the way, although it has no bearing on the case, Harrison, for all his interest in books, was a knowing old bird where his finances were concerned. This morning the manager told me that Harrison often bought and sold shares, and always to his own advantage.

"Anyway, Howard's clerk went round to the bank, as I told you, to check up on Harrison's holdings. Of course the two lists didn't agree, which wasn't surprising in view of what I've just told you about selling and rebuying whenever it paid him to do so. But—and here's the point, Mr. Terhune—the disparity between the total value of the securities according to Howard's list, and the securities in the Westminster Bank vaults, was seventy-five thousand pounds."

"What!"

Murphy was rather gratified with the result of his surprising news.

"I thought that would make you sit up. Yes, Mr. Terhune. Instead of holding securities for one hundred and twenty thousand pounds, the Bank had only—in round figures—sixty thousand pounds' worth. And if you can't make sixty thousand agree with one hundred and twenty thousand, I'll make that difference clear in a moment.

"You can guess what kind of a shock Howard had when his clerk returned with the information about the size of Harrison's fortune. He went hareing off to the Bank then and there. It didn't take him long to discover these two facts. Firstly, that on the thirtieth day of June last year Harrison had been worth one hundred and thirty-five thousand pounds—note that the capital sum had increased by fifteen thousand since the will had been made. The second fact was this. Seven months ago, about the beginning of December, Harrison realized more than half his capital—the missing seventy-five thousand pounds, in fact. Three days after the money had been put to the credit of his account he went to the bank and drew out the whole bang-shoot—*in cash*!"

"Good Lord!" In his amazement Terhune flicked his cigarette, not yet half-smoked, into the fire. "Seventy-five thousand pounds in cash! Fancy walking about with that much money in one's pocket."

"He couldn't have stuffed that much into his pocket," the sergeant said solemnly. "He took the entire amount in one-pound notes."

Terhune whistled. "Something begins to smell."

"To high heaven!"

"Any ideas on what he did with the money?"

"None. But if that money didn't have some connection with his murder, and the theft of what was hidden behind those books, then I'll eat my hat."

With which deduction Terhune did not, at first, feel inclined to argue; it was far too reasonable. Perhaps Murphy had been right after all in believing that the property stolen from Harrison's library had consisted of precious stones. The dead man, it seemed, had always been quick to take advantage of any opportunity to increase his capital; it could have happened that he had seen a chance of buying a parcel of stones which, at some later date, he would be able to sell at an increased price. Yet a few second's reflection brought doubts.

"Look, sergeant, if you had risked more than half your fortune to buy something of value, would you take no more care of it than merely to hide it behind a lot of books?"

"Glory be to God, that I wouldn't! Not at all, at all! I'd stow it away in the deepest, thickest vault I could find. And then I probably shouldn't sleep at nights for thinking of what a charge of explosive might do. But don't you be forgetting this, Mr. Terhune; as I see things, Harrison's been going agin the law."

"Because he drew all the money out in one-pound notes?"

"Of course. If he had wanted the money for a legitimate purchase he could have paid by cheque. But even if there had been some good reason for not paying by the usual method he could still have paid with Bank of England notes. No, somebody didn't want the trail of that money to be followed, though whether Harrison was the cautious one, or whether it was the seller, we don't know. Perhaps they both had good reasons for wanting to be cautious."

Unexpectedly, Terhune remembered his conversation with Edward Pryce that afternoon, "I wonder if he bought whatever it was he bought in Stockholm."

"Stockholm! What's this about Stockholm?" Murphy asked sharply,

"Edward Pryce was in the shop yesterday, discussing Harrison's death, also his visit to Stockholm last year, his first holiday for Heaven knows how long."

The sergeant sat upright. "When was this?"

"In December, according to Pryce."

"December!" Murphy slapped his knee with his hand. "He withdrew the seventy-five thousand in the first weeks of that month. Bedad! This case no longer smells. It stinks."

There was no doubting the nature of Murphy's inference. Harrison's so-called "holiday" had been an excuse—if the inference had any foundation in fact, of course—to visit Stockholm for the purpose of buying something which, presumably, he had no legal right to buy. But the problem of identifying that something seemed, with every new factor brought to light, to be more insoluble than ever. What had Harrison purchased in Stockholm? And why? And why, having come into possession of it, why had he been so incomprehensibly, so crassly careless in his choice of a place of concealment? Fancy daring to hide something worth £75,000—or even more—behind a few books!

But this reflection led to another. Had he really been careless in choosing such a hiding-place? Could he have acted intentionally, on the theory that the safest hiding-place is often the most conspicuous? Had he possibly convinced himself that no sane person would think of looking behind a book for an article of such great value?

This thought prompted a question. "By the way, sergeant, did the thieves enter any part of the house other than the library?"

"If they did they left no traces behind. Why?"

"I was wondering whether Harrison was stupid or cunning in using one of the bookshelves as a hiding-place. Your answer indicates the first possibility as being the more likely."

Murphy nodded. "My thoughts have been travelling along much the same lines. What made the thieves ignore all the usual hiding-places—a locked drawer or cupboard in his bedroom, or a safe, or what would you? How were they able to find what they wanted almost without taking the trouble of looking for it? The only answer seems to be that Harrison had talked too much at some time or other. And if he had been careless once then it would be no surprise to find that he was careless the second time, with his tongue."

For some minutes after that neither man felt inclined to talk. They smoked hard, stared at the flames caressing the fresh ash log which Terhune had just added to the fire, and pondered upon the mystery of Harrison's death.

At last Murphy took his pipe from his lips, leaned forward in his chair and knocked out the charred tobacco over the fire; a multitude of pin-point flames sparked into momentary existence.

"I don't like it!" he exclaimed emphatically. "Nothing makes sense."

"It certainly doesn't seem reasonable for an astute man like Harrison to be quite such an utter fool," Terhune agreed.

"Seventy-five thousand pounds!" Murphy muttered, as if he found it hard to believe that any man could have so much money. "Only a lunatic would invest seventy-five thousand pounds in something, only to hide it behind some books, without even a lock to protect it from curious hands. And I don't believe even a lunatic would broadcast its whereabouts. Speaking of lunatics, would you say, from having met him many times, that there was any chance of his having been a bit soft? After all, it isn't natural for a man to be quite so fond of his own company."

"He wasn't particularly fond of his *own* company, sergeant. He had many companions—hundreds, in fact."

"Books?"

"Yes."

"You can't yarn with a book, or have a quick one with it at the little pub round the corner, or take it spooning on a moonlight night," Murphy pointed out drily. "But though it isn't my idea of life I suppose some people can remain satisfied with only books to keep them company without being otherwise soft in the top storey." He shook his head, angrily. "There's some aspect about this crime which we haven't begun to suspect. Of course, for two pins I'd make a guess that what was stolen from Harrison's library was the money itself—but if he wasn't a miser, which I take it he wasn't, what in the name of all the saints would he be doing with keeping all that money at home for six months?"

"What's your next move, sergeant?"

The sergeant made a groaning noise. "An interview with the Old Man, and that in the very near future, or me name isn't Tim Murphy."

"Which will probably mean—"

"The C.I.D.," Murphy exploded, as he emptied his glass with a gesture of indignation and disgust.

Chapter Five

Despite Murphy's pessimism, when he 'phoned Terhune up late the following Sunday night the C.I.D. had still not been invited by the Chief Constable to assist in solving the mystery of Harrison's death. But as Murphy ruefully pointed out, that move couldn't be long delayed now. Had Mr. Terhune seen the Sunday papers, bedad? Terhune had seen them—at least some of them—and the more sensational had not neglected the usual clichés regarding the inefficiency of modern police methods compared with those of the previous decade, etc., etc.

Terhune soon learned, to his disappointment, that Murphy had not 'phoned up with news of some fresh development. On the contrary, the sergeant's real reason, it seemed, was a vague hope that Terhune might have come across something to throw new light on the affair—although he did not say so in actual words, it was evident that he regarded Terhune as something of a mascot. With reason, for every case in which Terhune had held a watching brief, as it were, the sergeant had brought to a successful conclusion.

But Terhune had had no brain waves this time. He had given thought to the problem. Often. He had gone over the facts as he knew them time and time again. None but the most fantastic solutions had occurred to him, and to these he had given only as much time and thought as they deserved. Never mind along which track, new or old, his mind groped, always he arrived at the same conclusion—the one the sergeant had voiced—namely, that there was an aspect of the crime which, so far, had eluded them, the *conditio sine qua non*, the indispensable condition which had brought two "professional" criminals to Harrison's library.

Another remark of the sergeant's was equally true. Nothing concerning the crime made sense! It didn't make sense that Harrison should have realized half his fortune. It didn't make sense that he should have drawn out the entire seventy-five thousand pounds in £1 notes. It didn't make sense that he, whose only interest in life was books, could have used this money for the purchase of things other than books. It didn't make sense that the criminals found it necessary to kill Harrison to obtain whatever it was they were after. It didn't make sense that the murderers should have emptied the bookshelves of their contents unless they were searching for something hidden behind the books. And it didn't make sense that anything worth seventy-five thousand pounds (presumably) should have been hidden in such an inadequate hiding-place.

One obvious explanation to account for the withdrawal from the bank of seventy-five thousand £1 notes had, of course, occurred to him, Blackmail! But he could not make that explanation fit in with the circumstances of Harrison's death. Besides, why would a blackmailer search behind books? Surely not to look for further instruments of blackmail. Any evidence damning enough to exact seventy-five thousand pounds would be damning enough to run through the whole of Harrison's capital. And if anyone had to be killed as a result of a spot of blackmailing, one would expect the blackmailer to be—almost justifiably!—the victim. Unless death had followed a struggle of sorts. But there was no evidence that there had been a struggle. In fact, the murder had every appearance of having been damnably cold-blooded—a stab in the back while the victim's attention was being held elsewhere.

So Terhune had to admit to the sergeant that nothing of consequence worth passing on had happened, and Murphy, with an exclamation of disappointment, apologized for disturbing Terhune, and disconnected.

II

Excluding Thursday—market day—and Saturday, Monday was Terhune's busiest day in the week. In the first case it was usually a heavy day where correspondence was concerned, there still being many people left in the world, apparently, who retained the habit of writing all their letters on Sunday afternoon. Besides this batch of correspondence, he had also to deal with the many book-readers who finished their books over the week-end, and hurried along to the shop on Monday mornings to exchange the finished titles for new ones.

The morning after Murphy's telephone call proved to be no exception to the rule. Doctor Arthur Harris was one of the first to call in; he snatched a few moments between the end of surgery and starting off on his visits to run over from his house and ask for the latest John Dickson Carr. He was soon followed by Isabel Shelley, who was leaving for London, there to begin rehearsing for a new Noel Coward play—she did not want any book in particular but eventually chose Lady Eleanor Smith's *Magic Lantern*.

Then Mrs. Quilter, to snatch a few words with Anne; Thomas Hunt, from Farthing Toll, to know whether Raymond Bush had published any more Penguins; Jeremy Cardyce, from Great Hinton, to order a new book on Common Law, shortly to be published by Butterworths; Mrs. Tobin, to ask Terhune whether he would buy some books which poor dear Grannie had been so fond of reading—as two of the dozen which the young woman produced were first editions of Thomas Hardy, Terhune was very glad to have the opportunity of paying the twelve shillings which were asked for them.

People came in and went out in a never-ending procession. Some completed their business with reasonable speed; these were persons of quick decision, and no special inclination to talk longer than was necessary; others took their time about choosing a book, taking first one and then another off the shelves, and replacing each one in turn—usually in the wrong place—because a cursory dip into the pages failed to yield any hint of passionate romance. Others, again, were too undecided to choose for themselves, and insisted upon asking the advice of either Anne or Terhune himself, before making a final decision. Mrs. Moore, wife of George Moore, of *Three Ways Farm*, was a particular offender in this respect; she had to be told almost the entire plot of a book before she would risk taking it away. Then there were those others, and their name was legion, who wasted no time about choosing a book, but who obstinately lingered on, long after it was necessary, in the hope of a few minutes' conversation with Terhune.

One of these was Mrs. Lluellyn, the bank manager's wife. For more than five minutes she kept Terhune gossiping. When at last she did leave it so happened that only Anne and Terhune were present.

"Why are you so nice to people who seem to have nothing else to do all day but talk?" Anne asked primly. She had become very efficient and business-like, had Anne, and because she loved her work—and Terhune, with adolescent hero-worship!—it pained her to see his time wasted by chattering rivals.

"It's good business to be polite to one's clients, my child."

She made a grimace at him—she detested being called "my child" by him—as she usually was.

"You are more than polite. You are positively *nice*."

"It's still good business."

"Good business! One would think you thought of nothing else but business!"

"Well, don't I?"

"Of course not," she snapped. "I honestly don't believe you care whether the business makes money or not. All you care about is handling books."

"What about yourself, my child?"

"I've come to love books too, ever since I've been working with you." She gazed at his back with adoring eyes. Then she pursed her lips angrily. "But that doesn't make me want to be nice to people with peroxide-soaked hair, like Mrs. Lluellyn."

"Peroxide! Aren't you being just a little critical—"

"Of course I'm not, Mr. Terhune," she replied scornfully. "Anybody—any woman—can see that she dyes her hair."

He chuckled. "After all, her husband is the bank manager. I might need his help one of these days."

"That isn't why you were nice to Mrs. Lluellyn."

"Then why was I?"

"Because you can't help being nice. To everybody," she added, with a slight quaver in her voice.

Her reply disconcerted him. He had never known Anne talk like this. Was she beginning to grow up? He hoped not. He didn't want her to blossom too soon into mature womanhood, for when that happened some young gallant in the district would soon snap her up, and he would lose a most efficient and reliable secretary-assistant. Besides, this judgment on his own character embarrassed him. He wasn't in the habit of indulging in bouts of introspection.

He decided to change the conversation. Quickly. "Have you had time to look through the last Surrey Bookshop catalogue, Anne?"

"Yes, Mr. Terhune." She, too, became business-like. "There's a copy of Racine's *Œuvres* advertised for three and sixpence. That's one of the titles Mr, Graham Hicks asked you to buy for him."

"Fine! Write to Albert Turner and ask him to send the book to me as soon as possible. Are there any more we want?"

"Not *from* that list, but Charles J. Sawyer, Ltd. have a copy—"

The door opened, and a gushing voice interrupted: "My dear Theodore! How fortunate to find you all alone, for once." Alicia MacMunn floated across the shop—she usually created the impression of being slightly air-borne, rather than earth-bound, possibly because she wore so many accessories of fluttery material.

"I've just dropped in for a moment—only for the most fleetingest of moments, dear boy, because I know how busy you are on a Monday morning—but I want to tell you—" She interrupted with a shrill laugh of delight, as she picked up a book from his desk. "What fantastic dresses! How could women allow themselves to look so terrible? Do tell me, my dear, what country did those dresses come from? No, don't tell me; I can make a guess. Roumania or Bulgaria, or one of those Baltic countries—"

"Balkan," he corrected softly.

"Of course! How *silly* of me! I am always mixing up the Baltic with the Balkan countries. Isn't it stupid to have two names so much alike, I think they ought to rename one group or the other. It's so confusing. But you haven't told me which country. Or when, I am sure these were not worn after the eighteen-eighties."

The letterpress was there, beneath the illustrations, to answer both her questions; but Alicia could never be bothered to find out anything for herself if there were anyone handy to do the work for her.

"Those are London fashions of nineteen five," he told her drily.

"Nineteen five! I cannot believe that I ever looked like that!" She chuckled afresh as she gazed at the illustrations, and began turning over the pages of the book.

The door of the shop opened again. Two people entered. The first was Diana Pearson; a consistent reader, and regular Monday morning visitor. The other newcomer was a tall, stooping figure with thin, grey hair, and pince-nez guarded eyes. His face was familiar, but Terhune could not identify him.

"You came in to tell me something, Mrs. MacMunn," he prompted, a trifle impatiently—Sir George Brereton's car had just drawn up outside the shop: he would probably be the next to enter.

Alicia's forehead puckered. "*I* came to tell *you* something," she began in surprise. "Really, Theodore—" She paused, and began to giggle. "How *terribly* stupid of me! Of course I did, didn't I. But there, Theodore, you shouldn't leave such *fascinating* books about for people to look at. They make one so horribly forgetful."

Terhune became impatient. He saw that Diana had changed her book for another, and was edging up behind Alicia with the deliberate intention of joining her. Meanwhile, the newcomer with the familiar face—who the devil was he?—was obviously waiting to speak; he stood by a small table which displayed a selection of illustrated books published in the eighteenth century, and gazed expectantly through his pince-nez. Outside the shop Sir George was marching briskly across the pavement.

Terhune made another attempt to prompt Alicia to state her business. "Did you want to ask for a particular book, Mrs. MacMunn?"

"I didn't know you stocked children's books," Diana Pearson drawled from behind Alicia.

Alicia turned quickly, "Diana, darling! How nice to see you! When did you come back from Scotland?"

"We are not due to go until next week, Alicia, my sweet," Diana stated drily, in her deep, slightly husky voice. "And as you had tea with us only last Thursday—"

Alicia was no whit disconcerted. "Then it must have been somebody else who went to Scotland."

"It was somebody else," Diana drawled. "Mildred went to Edinburgh last Wednesday week. But, my dear, you're surely not borrowing or buying a book for yourself. I thought the only books you ever read were cookery books, and then only when you wish to impress cook."

"Diana, darling, your cattiness becomes more pronounced every time we meet." But this without malice on the part of Alicia MacMunn.

The grey-haired man's fingers began to beat out a tattoo on the polished table-top. The door opened; Sir George entered.

"Mrs. MacMunn!" Terhune exclaimed desperately.

"For Heaven's sake, Alicia, put poor Mr. Terhune out of his misery, and don't waste all his time," Diana urged. "I have something to ask him, too."

"I don't want to *ask* him anything, Diana. I merely want to *tell* him—"

"Hullo, Alicia! Hullo, Diana!" Sir George's voice boomed out. The two women turned quickly.

"Hullo, George," Diana drawled.

Alicia greeted Brereton with a shrill warning. "If you've come here to tell us one of your fishing stories, George Brereton, I'll walk straight out of this shop—"

"*Please*, Mrs. MacMunn," Terhune pleaded desperately, as he watched the unidentified man turn away from Sir George, pick up the handiest book, and pretend to be studying it most deeply, with an air suspiciously furtive.

Brereton was unperturbed. "My stories are too good to be wasted on unappreciative womenfolk," he retorted equably. "Morning, Terhune."

"Good morning, Sir George."

"Any news of that first edition of the *Angler's Sure Guide?*"

"Your manners, George, are, to say the least, not improving," Alicia said acidly. "Theodore is supposed to be telling me something—"

"Sorry, Alicia," apologized the unrepentant Brereton. "Carry on, Terhune."

"You were going to tell me, Mrs. MacMunn," Terhune told her despairingly.

Sir George laughed boomingly.

"Really, George!" Alicia's forehead puckered as she turned back to Terhune. "Did I really come in to tell you something?"

"So you said."

"Then I've forgotten what it was. Never mind," she continued brightly. "I'm sure to think of it again some time this morning. If I do I'll telephone you—"

"Was it about Julia?" he suggested tentatively.

"Of course it was. How *terribly* stupid of me to forget. Yes, dear boy; I had a wire from her this morning to say that she was returning home this afternoon, and asking me to let you know. Which means, I suppose, that she will be asking you to take her dancing one night soon."

"Thank you," Terhune muttered, not daring to glance in Diana Pearson's direction; he was sure there would be an expression of slight malice in her eyes—Diana's tongue could be almost as sharp as Julie's; the atmosphere when the two met, as they often did, was apt to be charged with impending disaster,

"There is one thing I like about Julia," Diana said sweetly, "She is so delightfully ingenuous. Are you coming, Alicia?"

With a nod for Terhune and Brereton, and a smile for Anne, Alicia and Diana left. Terhune glanced inquiringly at the man by the eighteenth-century book display, but he had his back turned towards Brereton, and his face buried in one of the books. Sir George boomed out: "Did I ever tell you, my dear Terhune, of the time I followed Pryce's advice to use a Silver Doctor to catch a spring salmon—"

The story droned on. Terhune had heard it on not less than three previous occasions, but he listened with an attentive face—if not an entirely attentive mind—which more than satisfied the teller. Meanwhile, a constant stream of people moved in and out of the shop, most of whom, becoming aware that Sir George was telling one of his notorious fishing stories, registered resignation in one form of another, and approached Anne instead of Terhune.

But the story eventually finished, and Sir George departed with a breezy: "'Bye, Terhune. Hope to see you, Thursday," whereupon the stranger replaced the book on the table and hurried over to Terhune's desk before anyone else had the opportunity of forestalling him.

He held out a long-fingered hand. "Good morning, Mr. Terhune." His pale lips parted in a dry smile. "You do not recognize me?"

The emotionless, scholarly voice jogged Terhune's memory in time. "Of course, I do, Mr. Howard," he said quickly. But there was surprise behind his smile of welcome. Howard was the senior partner in a firm of Ashford solicitors; perhaps not the biggest firm of solicitors outside the Metropolitan area, but certainly there was many a better-known London firm which, on financial grounds alone, would cheerfully have exchanged their practice for Howard's. What had brought Howard into his shop, Terhune wondered, and why had the solicitor gone to such pains to hide himself from Sir George Brereton, and Alicia MacMunn, both of whom were clients of his?

Perhaps Terhune's fleeting, puzzled glance towards the door, through which Sir George was to be seen stepping into his car, gave the astute solicitor a hint of what Terhune was thinking.

"I am glad neither Mrs. MacMunn nor George Brereton saw me here, Mr. Terhune. They would have insisted upon taking up my time, of which I have little to spare this morning." His sparse, grey eyebrows were raised in query. "Can you spare me a few minutes? I have some business which I wish to discuss with you."

Terhune nodded. "Anne will see that we are not disturbed." He called over to her, and gave her a sign which she acknowledged, then glanced inquiringly at the solicitor.

Howard coughed drily; a mannerism which reminded Terhune of his first meeting with the other man.

"I am on my way back from *Twelve Chimneys*, Mr. Terhune. The unfortunate Mr. Harrison was one of our clients, so you will not be surprised to hear that he made me his sole executor." He coughed again. "Er—I understand from Miss Baggs that you were acquainted with the late Mr. Harrison?"

"That is so. Mr. Harrison has purchased a number of books from me during the last few years."

"I am not surprised. You have a very pleasant shop here, Mr. Terhune, and to a person as ignorant as myself concerning books—a fine selection, I judge." His glance rested swiftly upon the collection of eighteenth-century books by which he had been standing; and Terhune judged by the suspicion of a twinkle in his eyes that Howard's precise legal mind had, for once, been titillated by something he had read or seen in one of the books.

The mood quickly passed; he continued formally: "Under Mr. Harrison's will, the residuary and principal beneficiary—after the payment of a few small bequests to friends, servants and local charities—is his only near relative, a nephew by the name of Thomas Harrison. Thomas Harrison is living on a small ranch which he owns not far from Calgary, Canada. As soon as I was told the news of Mr. Arthur Harrison's death I sent a letter, by air mail, to the nephew to give him the news of his uncle's death, together with the information that he is the principal beneficiary under his uncle's will, and asking for his instructions.

"This morning I received a cable from Mr. Thomas Harrison." He coughed, "A most extravagant cable, I should add. In it the beneficiary informed me that he was on the point of being dispossessed of his ranch as a result of being unable to meet certain financial obligations, but that my letter had arrived in time to prevent the legal processes from being completed. By which I judge that his creditors, in view of his inheritance and also, no doubt, for some financial consideration, have agreed to grant him a further period of time for the payment of his debts.

"Because of these rather unfortunate circumstances, Mr. Harrison's cable contained explicit instructions to me that I am to hurry through probate as quickly as possible, so that he can take over his inheritance as soon as all formalities have been complied with. Meanwhile, with regard to the property and personal effects of the deceased, these are to be realized by putting them up to public auction at the first convenient date."

"Including the library?" Terhune asked.

"Including the library," Howard confirmed drily. His sparse eyebrows waggled again. "The information *interests* you?" he continued, with a slight emphasis on the verb which implied that Terhune, as a bookseller, would probably welcome the opportunity of buying back some of the books he had sold to the dead man.

"On the contrary, I regret it."

"Regret?"

"Because a lifetime's work will be irretrievably ruined by the distribution of a fine collection of books, which had been brought together with what I can only describe as loving care."

Howard looked a little astonished. "Yes, yes, of course!" he muttered. Then, briskly: "From your knowledge of Mr. Harrison's library, would you say that it is worth—one thousand pounds? Two? More?"

"Easily more than ten thousand, Mr. Howard—if the sale is properly conducted."

"Ah! By which you mean?—"

"If the books are assembled in the right lots to produce the highest bids."

"As I thought! Then would it be an expert's job to arrange the books for sale?"

"Yes."

The thin head nodded. A pause. A dry cough. "Is that a task which you would undertake, Mr. Terhune?" Howard asked in his precise, formal way.

Chapter Six

Howard's proposal was a tempting one. To handle the many fine, and many rare books which made up Harrison's library, to examine them, classify them—all would be a labour of love which Terhune was inclined to accept without a second thought. How could he refuse such an opportunity? But, being of a cautious, and sometimes methodical nature, he gave a second thought to the proposition, and with a growing sense of disappointment, quickly realized that common sense dictated a refusal. There were hundreds of books in the library, nearly every one of which would need individual attention, to examine, identify and describe. The work would take many hours to complete. Too many, in view of his responsibilities to the shop. As it was there were some days when Anne and he found difficulty in coping with all the work which went to making the business so successful. There was so much to be done.

"I'm sorry, Mr. Howard——" he began, after a long pause.

"I have the authority to arrange for a fee to be paid for the work," the solicitor slipped in quickly.

"It's not a question of money."

"Then why are you refusing?" Howard asked, with more than a suggestion of irritation in his attitude.

"It will be quite a long job to prepare Harrison's library for an auction sale. I haven't the time to spare." Terhune indicated the small group of women who clustered round Anne Quilter. "You have seen for yourself what it is like. Although I don't pretend that the shop is always as busy as it is this morning, I should not care to leave Anne too much on her own at this time of the year."

"As you say, I have seen for myself what an excellent business you have built up. I congratulate you, Mr. Terhune. At the same time," the solicitor continued drily, "Your success was not previously unknown to me, so that it can be admitted that I anticipated your refusal."

"I wish I could——" Terhune began regretfully,

"Wait, if you please, my dear sir. I have not finished. Anticipating, as I have indicated, that pressure of work here would prevent your being able to visit *Twelve Chimneys* during the day, I have made arrangements—subject to your assent, of course—for you to visit the house of an evening, after your day's work is finished."

Terhune chuckled. "My day's work finishes when I fall asleep, Mr. Howard. In addition to my work as a writer, I have other booksellers' catalogues to study, and my own to make up and check, I have to work out what price to pay when offered a library for sale, I have——"

Howard laughed wryly. "Please! I have heard enough, and offer my apologies for underestimating the amount of work which has to be done. I should have realized that no successful business runs itself—even a solicitor's! I will telephone and let Miss Baggs know that she is not to expect you——"

"Miss Baggs!"

The solicitor nodded. "She has recovered from the shock of Mr. Harrison's death, and has agreed—and so has the maid, Mary—to return to *Twelve Chimneys* until the property is sold. They are sleeping there to-night, the police guard having been withdrawn from dawn this morning." He held out his hand. "I hope you will forgive my intrusion, Mr. Terhune, and allow me to express my regret that you are unable to undertake the work."

Terhune felt rueful. It hurt him to forgo the opportunity of browsing among Harrison's books—probably he would never again have the chance of handling a finer library——

He reached a sudden decision. He was busy, but was he too busy to pass up such a chance? That be damned for a tale!

"On second thoughts I'll do the job, Mr. Howard," he said eagerly. "Perhaps Anne won't mind a little overtime on my own routine work, which will give me time to prepare Harrison's library for sale."

Howard looked relieved. "I am glad you have changed your mind, If you had not done so I should have sent the library up to Sothebys, but I have a feeling that, as the library must, unhappily, be sold and dispersed, the proper scene for its demise is the house which has sheltered it for so many years. As for how long you take, this I must leave to you. Would two weeks be sufficient?"

"May I give you a ring after inspecting the library to-night?"

"An excellent plan," Howard agreed briskly.

I I

For Terhune the rest of the day dragged on wearily. Having made his decision to prepare Harrison's library for sale he was all impatient to begin at the earliest possible moment. He longed to caress some of the fine leather bindings which, hitherto, he had seen only from a distance—a short distance, it was true; no more than the thickness of the enclosing glass, but one too great for a bibliophile to accept with equanimity. He was impatient to inspect their contents; to experience the thrill of enjoying at first hand the painstaking skill of bygone illustrators, and the florid artistry of the old calligraphers; to recapture the joy of identifying a forgotten colophon, to chuckle over the vagaries of Tudor spelling, and the pedantic phraseologies of the Middle Ages; to envy and regret the dead, or dying, craftsmanship of the bookbinding guildsmen.

He would have to work long and arduous hours every evening to complete the task of cataloguing the library in anything like the two weeks Howard had mentioned, but joy would march hand in hand with labour. Then there was another aspect of the work he had undertaken which had only occurred to him halfway through the afternoon—in preparing the library for sale he would gain a very distinct advantage over his competitors when the sale began. Whereas they would have to rely upon the comparatively short period of the one or two days previous to the sale which, doubtless, would be allotted for the books to remain on view, he would have both the time and opportunity to calculate to a shilling the maximum amount which it was safe to bid, not merely on a handful of lots, but on every single lot in the sale. If some bargains, as distinct from good buys, did not come his way as a result of that foreknowledge, well, he was a pretty poor bookseller!

As closing-time approached Terhune became a 'clock-watcher.' With ten minutes still to tick away before the hour of five, he began fidgeting here and there, tidying, arranging and rearranging, collecting, and loosening the blind-cords. Then, precisely as the clock of St. James's Church struck the first note of the hour he let down the curtain of the left-hand window. Then, the right-hand curtain, and lastly, having bustled Anne out into the Square while she was still trying to slip her arms through the sleeves of her jacket, he locked and bolted the door, and ran upstairs for a hurried tea before leaving for *Twelve Chimneys*.

Presently he was ready to leave. He collected his walking-stick from the closet under the stairs, and let himself out of the private door which opened out on to Three Hundreds Lane—a narrow lane leading eventually to Three Hundreds Farm, where it finished ingloriously in the stockyard. But as he turned right, to face Market Square, a large sports-car swung round the corner, and came to an abrupt stop before him. A voice called out gaily:

"Theo!"

Julia, back from two weeks' visit to an uncle in Richmond. She looked ravishing. She wore a costume new to him; no need to ask where it came from; it bore the unmistakable hallmark of Grosvenor Square. A new hat, too, a creation in a shade of rich gold which seemed to give added warmth to her gypsy-black hair, and reflected itself in her dark, brown eyes. Her crimsoned-lips were parted in a welcoming smile, her eyes danced. Rarely had he seen her look less moody, more desirable.

"Julie!" He hurried towards the car. "It's nice to see you back again."

"It's nice to hear you say so, Theo."

"Did you have a good holiday—? Don't tell me, I know you did. You positively radiate the after-effects of a good time."

"Perhaps the reason for my looking happy is that I've returned home."

"You happy to *return* home!" He laughed loudly, and was blind to the shadow which passed across her eyes. "Not you, old girl. You're always too anxious to leave home and go gadding about all over the place to be pleased about coming back."

"Mother gave you my message?"

"To say that you were returning to-day?" He nodded.

"And asking about to-night?"

"To-night! She didn't say anything about to-night, Julie."

A sudden frown—and few people could frown so darkly as Julia MacMunn. "Don't be so absurd! She must have done so."

He chuckled. "You know your mother. As it was, I had difficulty in extracting from her even that much of your message." Them as an afterthought: "What about to-night?"

"I want you to come to dinner, and take me to Folkestone afterwards." She became suspicious. "Weren't you waiting for me?" she asked sharply.

"N-no! I—I was just on my way to do a spot of work at *Twelve Chimneys.*"

Apparently the name of the house conveyed little to her; for she asked: "Will you be long?"

"Any time up to midnight, probably."

"Theo!" Her eyes sparkled, as they began to reflect her frown. "Does that mean that you won't be able to take me out at all to-night?"

"I'm afraid not, Julie," he told her regretfully.

Her mouth hardened. "It's too bad of Mother," she exclaimed spitefully. "I had been looking forward to going dancing with you to-night, Theo. You could have helped to off-set the misery of coming back home."

"Just now you were trying to suggest that you were happy because you had returned home," he pointed out, with far too much gusto.

"Sometimes you are not as funny as you think you are, my pet," she snapped. "Then will you take me out to-morrow night?"

He shook his head. He had the uncomfortable feeling that Julia was not going to welcome his news.

"I—I don't think I can manage any night this week."

Now the expression in her eyes hardened in company with her facial expression. "Are you trying to tell me that you don't *want* to take me out?"

"Good Lord! No!" he exclaimed violently—pity that Julie had to fly off the handle whenever her blessed pride was touched. "But I've promised Howard to do a job of work in the shortest possible time, and two weeks won't be any too long."

"Howard! *Twelve Chimneys*! Why have you promised to do a job for that stuffy old idiot?" she stormed. "What sort of a job? What has Howard to do with Harrison?" Between disappointment and anger she was beginning to be dangerously spiteful. "I didn't realize that you were in the habit of hiring yourself out as an odd-job man!"

"But surely you've heard the news, Julie?"

"What news?"

"About Harrison's death—his murder."

"Oh!" She shook her head. "I hadn't. When—how—"

"A week ago. Some swine stabbed him in the back."

"Theo!" The last trace of her fury disappeared. "I didn't know. I didn't trouble to read the newspapers while I was away, and I only saw Mother for a few moments when I arrived home—" She paused.

"A murder! So that is why you are going to be busy? You can't resist being a detective, can you, Theo?"

He grinned delightedly. "That's just where you are barking up the wrong tree for once, old girl. I'm going to *Twelve Chimneys* as a book expert. Do you want to hear what's what?"

She nodded, so he told her. Towards the end her eyes began to smoulder with eagerness.

"Theo, my pet! I have an idea."

"Well?"

"Couldn't I help you? I mean, by writing down the titles of books as you examine them. Or—or in some other way—"

She could be of assistance to him, in several ways. With her help he might hasten the task by several nights at least.

"It will be very tiring work, Julie. Besides, you hate books—"

Her mouth tightened. "Am I to help you, or not?"

He recognized the danger signals. "Yes—if you promise to tell me when you get tired or bored."

"Promise."

"But—" He stared at her clothes.

"Well?"

"It's not a job for glad rags."

"I'll change." She opened the door. "Jump in, my sweet. I won't be five minutes changing."

He shook his head. "Be a pal, Julie, and meet me there. I want to walk. I need some exercise."

For a moment he was in doubt as to her reply; to his surprise she nodded eagerly. "If you'll see me home afterwards."

He felt inclined to tell her that she was a scheming little minx, but he withstood the temptation. One could go so far with Julia, but no farther. Her pride was intolerably sensitive.

"All right! I'll expect you there."

"I'll meet you half way, Theo. Where?"

"I thought of going by way of the short cut."

"Across Smugglers Farm?"

"Yes."

"Then I'll meet you by the stile."

She did not wait for any further word from him, but pressed the button of the self-starter; directly the engine purred she slipped the gears into reverse, backed the car into the Square, and with a sharp twist on the steering-wheel, swung the throbbing car along the short length of St. James's Road which bordered Market Square, and quickly disappeared left into the Willingham Road.

Terhune followed along the same route until he reached the stile which gave on to a public footpath leading across Farmer Chitty's fields to the Canal, not far from where it was crossed by the Toll Road bridge, just south of *Twelve Chimneys*.

No Julia was by the stile, awaiting him—he had not expected her to be there, for Willingham Manor, the MacMunn's home, was nearly a mile farther from the stile than Bray was. So he sat himself down on the top of the stile, lit a pipe, and contentedly surveyed the woods which stretched away in a slow, gradual rise north of the road until they reached the summit of Bracken Hill.

From time to time cars passed by, not many, for the district was one happily by-passed by the twentieth century, so the nearest main road, also all secondary roads which led from anywhere to anywhere, were many miles away. Bray-in-the-Marsh, Wickford, Willingham, Farthing Toll, the two Hintons, Great and Little—all these places were in a Kentish world of their own, avoiding, and by the world avoided. Only from the far side of Bracken Hill was the modern, restless world to be glimpsed, as represented by the roofs and chimneys of Ashford.

The cars which passed, one way or the other, were mostly local; from more than one waved a recognizing hand, or came a shouted greeting. Cyclists also passed, in greater numbers; and farm wagons, in lesser. Sometimes just a touched hat, sometimes a "Good-evenin' to 'e, Mr.

Terhune," sometimes just a smile, but few passed without acknowl-
edging him, for his ridiculously youthful face, with its engaging grin
in absurd contrast to his otherwise studious gravity, was as well-known
as its owner was liked.

Julia was not too long in arriving. He saw her almost as soon as
she had passed *The Hop-Picker*, and watched her progress. She walked
with a lithe, jaunty swing, although she disliked walking for its own
sake—in contrast to him—infinitely preferring to race about in an
open sports-car. But if she was not fond of walking, she lived for tennis
and dancing. Perhaps it was these recreations which kept her so slim,
he reflected. Slimmer, if possible, than Helena Armstrong, who did
like walking, and walked, when possible, in preference to driving. And
thinking of Helena he forgot Julia for the moment. He recollected that,
not a stone's-throw from the stile, was the place where Helena had
been waylaid and attacked one foggy night. He had blundered into the
scene, and so, as an indirect sequel, into an ugly world of crime and
criminals and detectives and police. And all because he had attacked,
two-fisted, the gang of garlic-breathing plug-uglies who had been trying
to rob Helena. In consequence, Helena had taken him—unconscious
by then—to *Timberlands*, Lady Kylstone's home. In consequence,
Lady Kylstone had encouraged him to investigate the strange attack
on Helena. In consequence, Alicia MacMunn had asked him to solve
her Famous Mystery. In consequence, he had met—and thoroughly
disliked—Julia. In consequence, proud, arrogant, sulky Julia was on her
way to accompany him to *Twelve Chimneys*, there to act, very humbly,
as his assistant.

A strange world!

Julia, proud, arrogant, sulky! With, others, maybe, but not when
he was with her. They were good pals, the two of them. Damn' good
pals who could speak frankly to each other, and quarrel with each other,
and respect each other. And what a pal to be proud of, too! Graceful,
slim, handsome—not pretty, nor beautiful, but downright classically

handsome—intelligent, athletic, fond of dancing—what more could a man ask of a pal—

He helped her over the stile, and they walked across the field. Ahead of them the sheep ceased their grazing, stared at them with suspicious, resentful eyes, and lumbered away as they approached. And still neither of them spoke, for they were strangely content to walk in comfortable silence.

Half way across the ten-acre field, however, this silence was broken by Terhune. He came to an abrupt halt, pointed to the ground, and exclaimed: "I'll be damned!"

She looked down. Close to his feet was a large turf, upturned, in which had been cut, clearly and unmistakably, the Cross of Christ.

Chapter Seven

"Have you ever seen anything like that before, Julie?" Terhune continued.

"I haven't, but then walking across fields isn't one of my normal recreations. What is it?"

"Heaven alone knows! I've never seen a piece of turf treated like that before. I'm not seeing things, am I? It is the shape of the Cross, isn't it, which has been cut out of the turf?"

She nodded. "Do you think Farmer Chitty has turned religious?"

"Not Chitty, the incorrigible old rascal. Besides, even if he had been unexpectedly moved to express his religion in such terms, from what I know of him I cannot see his spoiling this field by cutting out a large square of fairly good turf from it, and then turning the turf upside down. He's too much a farmer willingly to deprive his sheep of even a square inch of good grazing. It wouldn't have done so much harm if he had cut the Cross out of the right side. But to chop out a large sod—" He frowned, bewildered. He knew his Chitty.

"You don't think he's buried something beneath—a dead lamb, perhaps?"

This explanation, without being probable, was a possible one; Terhune had known lazy farmers who buried dead lambs and sheep where they fell, and Chitty had the reputation of being, like far too many of his contemporaries, a second-rate farmer, a man too mentally indolent to worry about the finer points of his work.

Terhune laughed shortly. "Even if I thought Chitty was capable of burying the lamb here, I can't imagine his being sentimental enough to mark its grave with a Cross. He's more likely to have damned it to perdition for robbing his pocket of a few pounds."

"Then maybe it's only a practical joke—or perhaps the shape of the Cross is only a coincidence."

"Maybe!" Terhune shrugged. "Coming, Julie?"

They walked on, and the sheep which had lumbered away from them once did so again, with protesting bleats. They had covered about twenty yards when she gripped his arm.

"Look, Theo! There's another turf turned upside down with a Cross cut in it."

The second sod was almost a replica of the first. It was certainly very strange. Terhune began to wonder whether Chitty was aware of what was happening to his field—and as though his thought was the farmer's cue to appear they saw him enter the field ahead of them, through a five-barred gate.

They hurried on, and presently came face to face with Chitty. The weathered, rheumy old chap touched his hat to them.

"Good evening to 'ee, Miss, and 'ee, too, Mister Terhune. A fine evening it be, but there's rain coming; me corns ache that turrible, and me knees are that stiff it bain't too aisy for me ter walk."

"Good evening, Mr. Chitty. I'm glad we've met you. I want to ask you about something we've just seen in this field."

"They sheep! A fine lot of beasties they be, this year. Right fine." He chuckled; a little avariciously, Julia thought.

"Not the sheep. I mean the dug-up sods."

"What sods? No sods ain't been digged up in this field that I knows of."

"The sods with a Cross cut in them."

The leathery, crinkled lips were not a pretty sight. "I don't know what 'ee is trying to say, Mister Terhune, but it don't make sense to me. No sods has been digged up in this field. Nor any of my other fields neither."

"I'm afraid there have been, Mr. Chitty. Miss MacMunn and I saw two, about halfway across, near the footpath—"

"And there's another." Julia pointed to their left.

Chitty did not waste time asking questions. He stumped heavily across to the spot, followed by Julia and Terhune. When he was able to see for himself what had happened he bent painfully down to pick up the sod, meanwhile muttering a series of profanities which Terhune hoped Julia could not hear.

"If I catch the beggar who done this—" he began threateningly. He straightened his rheumy back. "Damme, if I don't know who digged up this sod, Mister Terhune. I'll bet it were one of they mission fellows from Ashford. I met a bunch of them praying, psalm-singing chaps in the *Three Tuns* last night when they starts to try and tell we what us ought to do with our mugs of mild. So I upps and tell they what us would do with the mugs if they didn't beggar off out of the place. Then one on 'em threatens we with the wrath of God."

Terhune had met the earnest young missionaries of whom old Chitty spoke; enthusiastic, foolish they might be, but as sincere Christians they would not, Terhune was convinced, stoop to the mean-spirited and useless wantonness of upturning portions of healthy turf in order to leave behind the mark of the God whose wrath they so lightly dealt out. No, whatever the true explanation for the unusual treatment of the ten-acre field, the farmer's explanation was not the true one.

He tried to convince Chitty of this, but he soon learned how futile his efforts were; as soon as he could he drew Julia away from the old man, leaving him stumping about in a search for more maltreated sods, and muttering something to the effect that it wouldn't be the wrath of God which would visit the young missionaries if ever he met them again, face to face.

Julia and Terhune reached the far corner of the ten-acre field, passed through the five-barred gate into another field which looked at least half as large again, and lastly, by way of a footpath through a small copse, they arrived at the footpath which followed the Canal bank. There they turned left, and walked along the bank as far as Toll Road, where they again turned left, to pass Willow Bend, and finally to reach *Twelve Chimneys*.

Miss Baggs opened the door to them. "Good evening, Mr. Terhune. Mr. Howard told me over the telephone that you was coming to-night to see to the books. Everything is all ready for you." She permitted an elusive note of surprise to register as she looked at Julia. "Good evening, Miss MacMunn."

"Good evening, Miss Baggs."

"Miss MacMunn is going to give me a hand with arranging the books," Terhune explained. "Have you recovered from your shock of last week, Miss Baggs?"

To judge by the appearance of her round, rosy cheeks she had. Her words confirmed this impression.

"Yes, thank you. That's the best of having been a nurse. But I hope the police won't be long in arresting the murderers. I want to know that they are going to be punished for what they did to poor Mr. Harrison."

All this time Miss Baggs had been leading them across the hall in the direction of the library. As she opened the door of the room she continued: "I've filled the lamp with oil, Mr. Terhune, and trimmed the wick. And Mr. Howard asked me to see that you had a nice supper, so I've prepared a nice, cold chicken for you with salad, and a sherry trifle to follow. Will you have coffee afterwards?"

"Please."

"And you, Miss MacMunn?"

"If it's not giving you too much trouble—"

"Of course it isn't," Miss Baggs protested sincerely. "You'll need something after you've been working awhile with all those books, Mr. Harrison always did." Her large, china-blue eyes misted as she quickly turned away. "What time shall I bring in the supper tray?" she asked unsteadily.

"About nine-thirty?" he suggested.

She nodded, and closed the door behind her.

"And now, Theo?"

He approached the nearest bookshelf. Since the night of the murder all the books had been replaced on the bookshelves, but a glance along the contents of one shelf told him that they had been replaced anyhow.

He went over to the desk, spread open a thick pile of foolscap, ruled up in columns, and motioned Julia to sit down in the swivel chair.

"Look, Julie, we shall have to go through the books systematically, shelf by shelf. I shall examine each book in turn, and classify it into three categories, A, B and C. Category A books will include those which should be sold as single titles, B, those which can be included with one or two other titles, and C, the riff-raff, as it were, which can be sold in lots of six."

He went across to the window, and picked out a book at random. "Here's a badly rubbed, out-of-date *English Dictionary*. Not worth a shilling on its own, but it might get that, or even more, if put with this *Glossary of Architecture*, for instance, and this torn copy of the eighteen-seventy edition of Lübke's *Ecclesiastical Art*."

"But an architect wanting the glossary might not want the dictionary," she protested.

"I don't suppose he would, for one minute—but this is where the art comes in of making people buy books otherwise unsaleable, for the sake of buying at least one title which they want very much."

"It sounds an indecent way of selling books, Theo," she criticized reproachfully.

He grinned, unashamed. "It's my business to see that the estate benefits to the best possible extent." He placed the *English Dictionary* on the floor. "We won't waste our time making a note of the C category titles, Julie—we can do that when we arrange them in lots of six." He returned to the desk. "Books in the other two categories we'll classify in full. In the first column write in the title of the book as I call it out to you, in the next, the author's name. The third column is for particulars, which I'll call out as I examine each book in turn; the fourth column, for date and place of publication, and the last column, for the price I think the title should realize. Is that clear?"

"Perfectly."

"Right. Then we'll make a start" He went over to the door, and from the uppermost shelf nearest to it took down a book. "Here's the first, Julie. Title: *Enchiridion Preclare Ecclesie Sarisburiensis*. Author's name—"

"Theo!"

He glanced up, over the top of the book. "Yes?"

"You don't expect me to spell that terrible title?"

He chuckled. "Sorry, Julie. I wasn't thinking. It was a bit hot to start off with this one. I'll spell the title. Are you ready?" He slowly spelled out each word in turn. As soon as he was satisfied that she had finished he continued: "Author's name, leave blank. Particulars—as follows." He opened the book. "Printed on vellum in black and red—" He turned over some pages. "Rubrics in English, G. L.—"

"*GL?*" she interrupted.

"Gothic Lettering."

"Oh!"

He continued: "Contemporary purple velvet, worn; chased silver-gilt corner pieces; Tudor Rose in medallions in centre of each cover, broken clasp, morocco folder and case—" He stopped talking for awhile as he swiftly turned over the pages. Presently: "Fifteen sm. wdcts. at head of sections all cold and illumd.—"

"Theo, my pet!" she murmured softly.

"Yes, yes." He was a trifle impatient.

"What are smwdcts, and why is it cold?"

"Not smwdcts," he explained. "But sm full stop which means small and wdcts full stop—"

"Which means woodcuts," she supplied sweetly.

"You are learning fast," he congratulated.

"And illumd full stop means, I suppose, illuminated. But what does the fact of its being cold indicate?"

He laughed. "Not cold, old girl, but cold full stop. In other words, an abbreviation for coloured."

"Oh!" She scribbled away. Then: "Any more particulars?"

"No, but under date and place of publication put, Paris, Germain Hardouyn, fifteen hundred and thirty-three."

"Let me see it," she pleaded unexpectedly.

He passed the book to her. When she had examined it for two minutes she announced: "I think I should like to buy this book, Theo."

"Why?"

"Because I am just beginning to appreciate the romance of old books. Just think, my sweet. This book is well over four hundred years old, and yet we humans think we are wonderful if we live to be one hundred."

"Well, if you are willing to outbid Grafton, Maggs, Heffer and a few of the other hard-headed boys, you'll probably have to give up to forty-five pounds for it."

"Oh!"

"Have you changed your mind?"

"I think so. Is forty-five the figure to write in the last column?"

"No, leave it at forty."

He replaced the book on the shelf, and extracted its neighbour. A modern book this.

"Here's the next, Julie. *Woodcuts from Books of the Fifteenth Century shown in Original Specimens*, W. L. Schreiber, translated by André Barbey. Particulars: Illustrated with fifty-five illustrations from books ptd—sorry! printed!—in Germany, Switzerland, Bohemia, Netherlands, Italy, matted, text bound in wraps and enclosed with the original illustrations in linen case. Fo—folio, to you, Julie—Published in Munich, nineteen twenty-nine. Price, about twenty-five pounds, I'd say. No, make it thirty-three."

Terhune took down a third book. "Ah! Here's something to interest Sir George. William H. Schreiner's *Sporting Manual. A Complete Treatise on Fishing, Fowling and Hunting.* First Edition, too. Got that, Julie? Add, illustrations, a few hand-coloured, original cloth—"

His voice droned on, sometimes monotonously, but mostly, vital, enthusiastic, caressing.

II

As soon as Julia had mastered the abbreviations which Terhune rattled off with the ease of familiarity the work proceeded at a steady pace. Sometimes, of course, she was able to enjoy pauses lasting minutes while he counted illustrations, or examined colophons, looked for autographs, inspected annotations, looked for signs of stains and discolouring, or deciphered a monogram. Sometimes, after a prolonged inspection, he told her to add the letters w.a.f. at the end of particulars—with all faults—or n.p. which denoted no place of publication—or, quite often, rebkd. or reprd.—meaning, respectively, rebacked or repaired.

As the hours passed Julia gained her first insight into the mysteries of book-collecting, and her respect for Terhune increased enormously, as she realized how profound was his knowledge of the business. She was vaguely surprised; and a little annoyed with herself for her previous valuation of his character. She had always liked him; better than any other man, or woman, she knew, but this liking had come from the fact that he had a charming nature, an ingenuousness which made most women want to mother him, a sense of humour, a keen intelligence, and a forthrightness which even his ingenuousness failed entirely to conceal. Furthermore, he was a pretty fair athlete, an unequalled dancer, and a good conversation-alist. In short, as far as she was concerned he made an ideal companion. Now she began to realize that she had allowed herself to be deceived—or perhaps side-tracked was the better word, she reflected—by his whimsical manner, which had made her, as it had most people, think of him as an overgrown schoolboy rather than a keen business man.

Just before 9.30 Miss Baggs appeared with the promised, and very welcome, supper tray. They stopped work for thirty minutes. During that time Julia asked Terhune whether she could continue to help him with his work in Harrison's library. For her sake he refused, whereupon her tongue sharpened with annoyance. In spite of the fact that her hand was aching with the unusual strain of prolonged writing, she had enjoyed working with him in the intimate atmosphere of the library as much, quite as much, as some other evenings they had spent together in more public surroundings, dancing, dining playing tennis, driving. And being a wilful person, accustomed to having her own way in most things, she was determined to share other evenings with him like this one.

The argument was not protracted, and she was quickly her nicer self again, that nicer self whom few people in the district knew.

By the time they had finished the meal darkness was closing down upon the country. Before resuming work Terhune lighted the oil-lamp which stood on the corner of the desk, and closed the heavy velvet curtains across the French windows.

"A cigarette and then to work?"

She answered the query in his voice. "I shall be ready the moment you are, my sweet."

"Not too tired?"

"Of course not."

"What time shall we stop?"

"Eleven thirty?"

"If that's not going to be too late for you, Julie?"

"Not a moment too late. I'm enjoying myself immensely."

They smoked awhile until Terhune stubbed out his cigarette with a purposeful air, and went back to the bookshelves.

"Theo!" He turned. "I really would like to bid for one of the books, as a memento to remind me of at least one honest day's work. Can you find me one which I should be able to buy for a few pounds?"

"Any particular subject, period or type?"

"I leave the choice to you."

He went along the shelves, picking out a book here and a book there, which he collected together on one of the empty shelves. But presently he exclaimed his satisfaction. "Here's the very title for you, Julie: an uncut copy of *Aucassin and Nicolette*, with gilt top and edges, and illustrations on India paper. If you are prepared to pay up to four pounds for it I think you will outlast the dealers."

"I'll buy that if I have to pay double that price," she said with decision.

"And here's another. A collection of one hundred coloured reproductions of Frank Brangwyn's works. You'll have to pay up to two pounds for it, but one of these *days* your grandchildren will probably sell it for several times that amount."

"I'm not in the least interested in buying for my grandchildren," she retorted sharply.

He grinned. "I still advise you to buy it. Meanwhile, are you ready, Julie?"

"Ready."

He returned to the shelf upon which he had been working when Miss Baggs had interrupted with the supper tray.

"Josephus—" he began.

III

Round about eleven p.m. Terhune stopped dictating to examine Mersennus's book of engravings and woodcuts of musical instruments, published in Paris, 1636. Julia waited for him to continue. She had already learned not to interrupt him at moments of critical examination—he was apt not to hear, or, if he did, to express irritation. Besides, she was beginning to feel sleepy. Her heavy eyelids closed—

They opened abruptly. She was sure the French windows had rattled gently. Or had she just dreamed that she had heard the faint noise? She turned to ask Terhune, but even as she did so he leaned over her shoulder and snuffed out the oil-lamp.

"Duck below the desk, Julie—and not a sound," he whispered urgently.

She obeyed without question, to the accompaniment of the sound of wooden curtain rings sliding along their pole. Somebody was entering the library by way of the French windows.

Chapter Eight

For agonizing seconds nothing happened. Tension eased; as it did so Julia began to wonder whether anything more alarming had happened than that a gust of wind had blown open the door, and had made the curtains flutter. Then, without any warning, a white splash of light stabbed the darkness above her head. She started with the suddenness of it, then felt her hand grasped by strong fingers which sought to warn her to keep still and quiet.

She did so; the white beam travelled slowly round the room and remained in the vicinity of the window.

More tense seconds. She could not see properly what was happening, because of the intervening desk-table, nor hear much, but there was enough reflection from the strong electric torch to show her that Terhune, crouched down beside her, was cautiously peering round the edge of the desk.

Presently a scraping noise, followed a moment later by a slight rubbing sound, gave her a clue to what was happening over by the window. The scraping noise, she believed, had been caused by the lifting up and sliding into a groove of the glass panel protecting one of the bookshelves; the rubbing sound had been that of a book being pulled out of its accustomed place.

To account for this extraordinary occurrence she could think of only one explanation; surely one too incredible to be true—Harrison's library was being robbed for the second time! Before she had time to reflect further another sound disturbed the close silence—the muffled *plop* of something not too heavy, not too light, falling upon the thick-carpeted floor. For all the world as if the housebreaker had thrown the book down in temper.

Another period of silence, so quiet that only the dancing reflection of the light warned them that the housebreaker was still in the room. Then the rattle of the curtain rings again, and a soft whisper, which she could not properly distinguish, but which sounded like: "No way to earn me worsted," and a harsh reply, of which she could make nothing at all.

A fresh rattle of curtain rings, followed by silence, convinced her that the second man had left, but the light reflected from the torch was never still, and occasional sounds, left her in no doubt about the continued presence of the first. She wondered how long it would be before he worked his way round to a point from which he would be able to detect the presence of the two people behind the desk-table. Then what would happen? She was sure that Terhune would not wait to be attacked; more than likely he might not even wait to be seen, but would take advantage of the fact that his presence was apparently unsuspected by making a surprise onset on the housebreaker in the hope of making an arrest—in spite of the slightness of his wiry frame, Terhune possessed, where pluck and courage were concerned, a somewhat aggressive nature. As she had seen for herself in the past, Terhune was well able to hold his own in a rough-house. The possibility of either alternative happening made her wince with apprehension, for she remembered that Harrison had been cold-bloodedly murdered in this very room, just seven days ago. It was by no means certain, of course, that the burglary of a week ago was connected with the attempted burglary taking place at that moment, but Julia had very little doubt but that the men who had broken into the library then were in some way connected with the ones rifling it now. If so, it was not likely that they would hesitate to kill again, especially to save their own skins.

As though her thoughts had mysteriously communicated themselves to him, she felt the fingers which were still holding her wrist stiffen with decision, and then let go. Sure in her own mind that he was preparing to make a surprise attack she turned to restrain him.

A fatal move, as it happened, for her movement, slight though it was, caused something on the desk to overbalance, and fall to the floor with a dull thud.

There was a startled exclamation from the intruder; the torchlight flashed round the room, and rested momentarily upon the face of Terhune peering round the corner of the desk. In a succession quick enough to seem simultaneous to Julia's confused mind, several things happened. The housebreaker shouted in startled surprise, Terhune leaped to his feet and lunged forward, the room was plunged into darkness, there was a heavy thud on the floor, a gasped exclamation of pain, the curtain rings rattled, and from the far side of the French windows sounded a shrill whistle, followed by the distant sound of an automobile-engine spluttering into action.

Julia guessed what had happened, and barely repressed a sob of anguish. A moment of panic made her feel sick with fear—surely God could not be so cruel as to allow *two* men to die in this one room—

"Theo!" She stared into the darkness, debating frantically what to do, how to find matches—"*Theo!*"

"Steady on, Julie! I'm okay. I fell over a pile of blasted books." She closed her eyes with relief and tried, unsuccessfully, to will her beating heart to quieten down. A scraping match quickly made her open her eyes once more; through a misty haze she saw Terhune move towards the oil lamp, and light it. By the time its soft glow was at full strength she was herself again.

"Damn those books," he exclaimed with unusual viciousness, "Another step and I'd have grabbed him."

"And have been stabbed for your pains," she told him, angry now for his imprudence.

"Stabbed—" He began to chuckle, but unexpectedly, he sobered up. "That reminds me—" He picked up the lamp, and carrying it across to the window, began to search the floor.

"What are you looking for?"

"I knocked something out of the man's hand as I fell," he explained. "Probably his torch."

Julia found that "something." It had fallen, or been kicked, behind the curtain. But it was not the electric torch, but a lethal weapon, as nasty a looking stiletto as either of them had ever seen. The grey-blue steel reflected the light in the form of a malevolent, evil stare. Julia experienced a queasy sensation at the thought of what might have happened to Terhune had he not stumbled over the books, and so disconcerted the other man.

Terhune felt none too happy either. He looked down at the weapon with grave eyes.

"My God, Julie. They're killers."

"Theo! What are they after this time?"

"Whatever they didn't get last week, when they killed Harrison." He carefully kicked the stiletto farther into the room, then, leaving it where it lay, walked over to the telephone, and began dialling. "Murphy?" she queried.

He nodded. "You bet! I think he's going to have something of a shock."

I I

When Murphy slept, he slept. The telephone bell rang loudly and longly, but it failed to awaken the sergeant, or even to disturb him sufficiently to produce a twitch, a vague stirring, a turning over. He slept like a dead man.

Fortunately, his wife possessed greater sensitiveness. She smacked his pyjama'd posterior, which was turned in her direction. Smacked it good and hard—and many years of domestic work had produced a horny palm! He struggled into dim wakefulness, sat up in bed, switched on the electric light, turned his sleep-closed eyes towards the bedside table, fumbled about for the alarm clock, turned it right-about face, switched off the electric light, flopped back into a recumbent position, snuggled his head deeply into the pillow, and blissfully fell asleep again.

The bell continued its persistent, irritating noise. Mrs. Murphy began to feel annoyed. If the noise continued it could easily awaken the children.

"Tim! Wake up!" This, to the accompaniment of an even heavier smack on that rounded portion of his anatomy which now occupied a considerable salient into territory rightfully hers. "It's the 'phone."

Semi-consciousness returned to the unfortunate detective. For the second time he sat up and switched on the light.

"The 'phone, Tim," she urged, with a hefty push in the ribs.

He picked up the receiver. "Hu—" A terrific yawn interrupted, and there was silence. Then, at last, a long, rumbling: "Lo!"

"Is that you, sergeant?"

He answered automatically. "Detective-Sergeant Murphy speaking."

"Murphy, this is Terhune speaking. I'm at *Twelve Chimneys*. There's just been another attempted burglary—and maybe an attempted murder, at that."

The sergeant recovered full consciousness. "What's the time?"

"Nearly eleven twenty."

"Are you in any particular hurry, Mr. Terhune? Can you wait there until I can join you?"

"That was my idea in ringing up," Terhune informed him cheerfully.

"I'll be with you as soon as I can."

Murphy slammed down the receiver, and throwing off the bedclothes, uncovered them both. With an air of patient resignation Mrs. Murphy covered herself up again, and with a mental shrug, settled herself for sleep. For many years now she had realized that there were disadvantages in being the wife of a detective-sergeant—

III

Murphy made good time, and found Julia and Terhune waiting for him outside the front door.

"I believe Miss Baggs and Mary are asleep," Terhune explained in a low voice.

They entered the house and went along the hall on tip-toe, but directly the door of the library closed behind them the sergeant asked sharply: "What happened, Mr. Terhune?"

Terhune gave an account of what had happened. Murphy's face became grave when Terhune spoke about the knife.

"Where is it?" he demanded harshly.

Terhune revealed the stiletto by picking up the duster which hid it. "There you are, sergeant. I kicked it there from where we found it."

"You *kicked* it!" Murphy smiled grimly. "Then any fingerprints we may find will not be yours. Thanks, Mr. Terhune. I wish we always had to deal with people who know as much about the game as you do."

Terhune chuckled. "*Do* you, sergeant?"

"Perhaps not," came the admission. "Either us police wouldn't be wanted, or we wouldn't be able to do anything without being surrounded by a company of amateur detectives—which the Saints forbid!" He used his handkerchief to pick up the knife, which he then examined.

"If this isn't the brother of the knife which killed Harrison, then I'm a Dutchman. This fits to a T the type of weapon which Doctor Edwards described as having made the wound."

"It might even be the same weapon," Terhune suggested.

Murphy carefully placed the stiletto down on the desk, then stared inquiringly at Terhune.

"What makes you think so?"

"Look, sergeant, until now we've taken it for granted, haven't we? that the men who killed Harrison got away with whatever it was they were after."

"Yes."

"Why?"

"Why!" The detective pointed vaguely in the direction of the French windows. "You see those shelves on either side of the French windows, also those on the west wall, close to the window. More especially the third shelf up from the floor—" He walked across the room to the shelf. "This one! Well, only half of the books had been emptied from this shelf, while the shelves below, and all those either side of the window, hadn't been touched. Right! Now if the men hadn't found what they had been looking for, would they have stopped short half way along this shelf, and would they have left the others completely untouched?"

"Yes, if they had been interrupted."

A wicked-looking twinkle appeared in Murphy's eyes. "By whom?"

"Miss Baggs and Mary. Don't forget they arrived home about one hour earlier than expected, through having run into the Rector's wife, who treated them to a lift home."

"I thought you were going to make that point, Mr. Terhune. But have you remembered that Mrs. Rector drove the car up as far as the side entrance?"

"I have."

"If the men had been here when Miss Baggs returned either she or Mary would have seen another car standing outside the front entrance. The fact that no car was there proves that it must have been driven off before the others returned."

"Unless the men had parked the car somewhere else other than outside this house."

"I agree—but, in that case, where did they park it? As you know, I made exhaustive inquiries last week, and wasn't able to find anyone who had seen a car about at the time of Harrison's death."

"For the sake of argument would you be prepared to agree that the men could have parked the car say half a mile away, and have walked the rest of their journey?"

"I agree with the possibility, but not the probability. Thieves and thugs like to keep their cars handy, ready for a quick get-away. Besides, by walking through the village the men risked the chance of being recognized. Still, for the sake of argument, as you suggest, I'll allow that the men walked here. What difference does it make whether they came here by car or on foot?"

"Because, if they footed it here, the car wouldn't have been seen, which destroys your argument."

"That's true," the sergeant agreed slowly.

"But something else happened which I think supports my contention. From where I was, behind the desk, I could see everything the man did. He went straight to the shelves which had been left untouched during the previous burglary. Why? Coincidence? Or the knowledge that he was continuing where he left off?"

"Humph!" Murphy exclaimed non-committally.

"One last point," Terhune persisted. "If it's true that he did come back for something which he didn't find last time, because he was interrupted, why did he leave it until to-night to make his second attempt?"

"Why, Theo?" Julia asked.

"Because to-night is the first night since the murder that there hasn't been a constable on guard."

The sergeant was impressed. "There may be something in what you say, Mr. Terhune, and if so, we are back again where we started—what did the man come for?"

Before Terhune could answer Julia broke in, excitedly: "Theo—Mr. Murphy—is it likely that the man was looking behind the books for a wall safe?"

Murphy nodded his approval of the suggestion. "That solution had occurred to me, Miss MacMunn, but you must remember that all the wall space where one might reasonably expect to find a safe had been uncovered during the previous visit. The only space still, hidden by books when I got here last week was round about, and within reach of anyone at the window, the last place in the world where anyone in his right mind would build in a wall safe."

Julia smiled wryly. "Of course, how stupid of me," she murmured.

"But, in any case, Miss MacMunn," the sergeant continued, "I took the precaution of looking behind the books round about the window, just to make sure."

"Besides," Terhune joined in, "the man who came here to-night wasn't looking for a wall safe; he was looking for one particular book."

"How do you know that, sir?"

"I was able to watch him, sergeant. He directed the light of the torch on the titles of the books. Those whose titles he couldn't see properly he pulled off the shelves, and chucked on the floor when he found they were not what he wanted.'"

Murphy began to look worried. "Then, in spite of our theories, he was after a book and nothing else?"

"It would seem like it."

"But, Glory be to God! What book?"

"None that is on the shelves in this room, sergeant. While you were on your way here to-night I looked along the books which were not touched on the previous occasion. There wasn't a title among them worth risking a month's imprisonment for, still less a hanging. Practically all the untouched books have little or no individual value; they will be sold in lots of six, various, and if some of the lots make that number of shillings I shall be surprised."

"Why did I come to Kent to join the police force?" Murphy moaned. "I should have gone to Dorset, or Devon, or one of the quiet counties. Unless it's your influence, Mr. Terhune! You seem to attract the damnedest crimes—It's only three weeks ago that the people at the Yard were twitting me for not having produced one of those fancy jobs, as they called them. It was your Inspector Sampson who started that game. He's joined the Special Branch, by the way. Been seconded is his fancy way of describing the transfer." He swung round, and stared at the stiletto on the desk. His thin lips tightened in a grim line; he shook his head.

"I don't like this business, Mr. Terhune. I don't believe we're up against just a couple of armed thugs. Going back to what happened here to-night, you did say, didn't you, that as you tripped over the books you heard somebody outside the window whistle?"

"Yes, and the sound was quickly followed by that of a car being started."

"That's the point. How quickly?"

"Almost immediately."

"How far would you say is the nearest part of the drive to the other side of the French windows?"

"About fifty yards or so."

"Was the interval between you hearing the sound of the whistle and then the car long enough for a man to have sprinted fifty yards?"

"Nothing like long enough."

"I was afraid not. That means that there was at least one man in a car in addition to the two you saw in here, and that, in turn, means that this burglary was carefully organized. Organization plus numbers spells g-a-n-g."

Terhune nodded. "A foreign gang, in this case."

"Foreign?" Murphy queried sharply.

Terhune indicated the stiletto. "That's not usually the type of weapon carried by British crooks."

"Not usually, maybe, but I shouldn't care to make too much of that point. Officers in the Merchant Navy often carry stilettos on them." Murphy was sure he detected a mischievous grin on Terhune's lips. "You have something else up your sleeve," he accused.

"Yes. The two men who were in this room to-night spoke in a foreign language."

"The devil they did! What language?" the sergeant snapped.

"I'm not sure, but not French."

"Swedish?"

Terhune remembered Harrison's visit to Stockholm, and appreciated the reasoning which prompted the question.

"I don't know any Swedish, sergeant. But I don't think so. If I have to make a wild guess I should suggest one of the Latin root tongues. But for all I really know it might just as likely have been Greek, or Russian, or Arabic."

"That news doesn't please me," the sergeant said glumly.

The remark surprised Julia. "Why not, sergeant? Doesn't the knowledge that they are foreigners narrow down, to a considerable extent, the—the—how shall I put it? The—the field of search?"

"Yes and no, Miss MacMunn. In the first case there are probably more foreigners in this country than you believe. But the main trouble is this; the police make quite a large proportion of their arrests 'from information received.' In other words, from unofficial spies, 'noses' we call them sometimes, who hang about pubs, billiard-saloons, and other places where crooks are in the habit of meeting, and listen to 'careless talk' and keep an eye open for men or women spending more money than they should be. It's no secret that us coppers buy any likely information for a pint, or a dollar, or even a quid if it's very hot.

"Suppose a nose reports to me that Bill Smith flourished a wad at the *Red Lion* last Wednesday, and suppose I know that Bill Smith hadn't enough to pay the rent two weeks before, and suppose we know that a certain warehouse was burgled last Saturday week—warehouses being Bill Smith's speciality—why, we start putting two and two together, and that usually results in a friendly conversation with Bill. 'Where were you at one a.m. last Saturday week, Bill?' we ask, and if he can't produce an alibi to satisfy us we apply for a search-warrant. Ten to one when we search Bills' bedroom we find something hidden that can be identified as having come from the warehouse in question.

"Or perhaps the nose overhears Ted Brown say to Tom Jones, 'Is old Ikey in the market for five hundred bottles of gin?' That's all we want to know. So it was Ted Brown who pinched that lorry-load from outside Stowell's warehouse! Or if Ted Brown whispers: 'Know anyone wanting fifty quids' worth of penny stamps, Tom?' it doesn't require a Sherlock Holmes—or Mr. Terhune here!—to guess that Ted probably had something to do with that job at the Deptford sub-post-office a few nights before. Do you follow me, Miss MacMunn?"

"I think so."

"But what happens when these foreigners jabber to themselves in one of their own heathen lingos. Our noses can't understand a blooming word of what's said, and bang goes the one clue which might have put us on to Mr. Blooming Scraplewaffer, or Mr. Oily Macaroni." Murphy's face expressed deep indignation, but he was airing his pet grievance, and continued:

"It isn't only that that's against us, miss. Crooks have a habit of committing only one sort of crime, and that mostly in the same way, or by the same means. Some of 'em all but leave a visiting card behind. Five times out of ten when we investigate a crime we can see right away that it was done by one of four or five men. Well, after that, the rest is easy. But these foreign crooks when they first get over here, well, we don't know their trademarks, or their fingerprints, so we're stumped from the word go.

"What I hate about thim foreign crooks is, they don't play the game. An English crook, when he's cornered, he just says, 'Okay, Robert, it's a cop fair and square. I'll come quiet.' Not them ruddy foreigners. They're like rats, they are, and when they're cornered, they'll fish out a knife, or a gun, or a pair of knuckle-dusters, and scrap like the divil. Killers, many of 'em, especially since the war. As long as we knew they was genuine Patriots or Guerrillas we armed 'em and taught 'em every dirty, double-crossing trick under the sun. 'Unarmed combat' we called it, and didn't care what dirt they did as long as they did it to the blasted Huns. But they haven't forgot those tricks, many of 'em, and thim that have turned crook, they're killers, that's what they are." Murphy paused abruptly, and in a horrified voice exclaimed: "Mother o' God!"

"What's the matter?" Terhune asked, startled by the unexpected change in the sergeant's manner.

"It's meself that's made a ruddy speech!" the sergeant explained in astonishment.

Chapter Nine

Murphy's self-possession was not easily unbalanced, but when he realized how long he had been speaking, almost without interruption, he became embarrassed, and apologetic.

"It's sorry I am to be sure, Miss MacMunn, to be boring you with all the uninteresting part of police procedure—"

"Nonsense, Mr. Murphy. It wasn't uninteresting in the slightest. On the contrary, indeed. You should take up lecturing."

"Lecturing! Now you're making fun of me, miss," the sergeant accused reproachfully.

Terhune chuckled quietly. The last thing Julie ever did was to make fun of people. She was too cruelly forthright, and habitually used the sharper edged weapon of irony rather than the more genial, blunt-ended banter.

"I am sure Miss MacMunn meant every word of what she said, sergeant. You probably don't realize how interesting you were." Terhune saw the other man about to speak, and went on quickly: "So you believe the gang who are trying to rob this library have some dangerous members?"

The detective looked grim. His mouth hardened. "I do, Mr. Terhune. God knows what book it is they are after, but all the signs are that they'll stick at nothing to get it. At any rate, I for one am not taking any chances on their entering this house for the third time. Before I leave here I'm going to 'phone through to the Super to ask for the police guard to be restored right away. He'll curse me like hell for waking him up, but we can't afford to take any chances." He paused to glance quizzically at Terhune.

"Look, Mr. Terhune, I haven't kept secret from you the fact that we know no more about the murder of Mr. Harrison than we did five minutes after it had taken place. What has happened here to-night might lead us somewhere—there may be fingerprints on the knife which the people at the Yard will be able to identify—we may be able to trace the shop which sold it, and to whom, though not if it was bought abroad, of course—some local person might have seen a car loitering about in the road, and having taken a note of the number, will report it to the police to-morrow, which happens more often than you might think— one of half a dozen other unlikely things might have happened, which will give us a slight clue to get cracking with. But personally, I'm not too hopeful. That's why I'm wondering if you would care to give us a hand once more."

"Doing what, sergeant?"

Murphy touched one of the drawers in the desk. "There's a file in this drawer filled with receipts of money paid for books bought during the past few years. Most of 'em have come from firms in London. I've looked through the receipts to see if any of them were for some big amount, by which I mean a sum worth hanging for, but there was only one receipt for three figures, and that was for one hundred and five pounds."

"Well?"

"I was wondering whether you would care to visit the principal booksellers in turn, Mr. Terhune, and try to find out whether any of 'em ever sold a really valuable book to Mr. Harrison, a book valuable enough to make it worth the gang's while to commit murder for."

"But I thought you didn't think a pro. would steal a book which might possibly be traced back to him?"

"So I did, and I'm still of the same opinion," Murphy admitted obstinately. "But it's no use us just sitting on our seats waiting for the murderer to walk into the station and surrender himself. As usual methods aren't getting us anywhere we must try unusual ones."

"If he did buy such a book, where is it?" Terhune demanded. "I'm ready to swear it isn't in this room."

"It might be somewhere else in the house. Or he might have resold it—"

"Not Harrison."

"You don't make things any easier for me, Mr. Terhune," Murphy complained drily.

"Sorry, sergeant!"

"Not that I don't think you are right. But the point I'm trying to make is this. If Harrison did have a really valuable book he seems to have kept the fact a well-guarded secret, even from you, the one person you would have expected him to show it to. Now if he was keeping his possession of the book a secret, how did the gang find out that he owned it? Possibly from the person who sold it to Harrison. If we could trace that man, then it might be possible for us to work forward from that point. Of course, I could ask the C.I.D. to make inquiries, but I think you would have a better chance of making the booksellers, understand what we were after, because you know them and can talk their lingo."

Murphy's reasoning seemed sound enough. Terhune nodded, and agreed to make an early visit to London. "Wednesday, probably."

"Thanks," Murphy acknowledged briefly. He looked round the library with slow deliberation as if to make sure that he had not over-looked anything which might be of use to him in his investigations. Then he began to wrap up the stiletto.

"There doesn't seem anything more we can do for the time being, Mr. Terhune. Sorry to have kept you up as late as this."

Terhune did not reply, but stared, absent-mindedly, at one of the piles of books on the floor.

"Anything the matter, sir" the sergeant questioned.

"Nothing wrong," Terhune raised his head; behind his horn-rimmed spectacles his eyes danced with excitement. "An idea has just occurred to me. Two, in fact. The first is this. Remembering your theory that no professional gang would steal a valuable book because of the risks involved in disposing of it for money, I am now wondering if we aren't barking up the wrong tree altogether."

"In what way?"

"Suppose it isn't the book itself which the gang is after, but some information to be found in its pages. In that case the intrinsic value of the book mightn't be more than a few shillings."

"Information!" Murphy shook his head in perplexity. "I don't follow you, Mr. Terhune."

Terhune turned to Julia. "I'm sorry to drag up the past, Julie, but you remember how the man Lewis secured the information which enabled him, to trace and murder Jasper Belcher's son, so that he could claim Belcher's money for himself—"

"He stole some pages from Father's book." She looked at Murphy, and spoke in a voice not altogether steady: "Father's book wasn't of any value except to Mother and me, Mr. Murphy, but as a result of the theft Lewis came into possession of a small fortune."

"May the Saints preserve me from ever having the imagination of a writer!" Murphy exclaimed feelingly. "And what's the book to be revealing now—a pirate's treasure in the West Indies? Or maybe just another of thim secret rooms like 'twas found in the House with Crooked Walls? And if the information is to be found in one of the books in this room, then what's to prevent the men reading another copy of the same book in the British Museum, at all, at all?"

Terhune chuckled. "There might not be a copy of the book in question in the British Museum."

"Not a copy in the British Museum!" The idea shocked Murphy. "But, bedad! I thought the Museum had a copy of almost every book ever published."

"Not every book, Murphy. Besides, many were destroyed during the Blitz."

"That's right; they were now!" The detective began to give the idea more serious consideration. "But what sort of information would you be expecting to find now in one of these books?"

"Now you're asking too much, sergeant. But here's one suggestion. There might be a paragraph in one of the books containing information which would be of help to somebody trying to prove direct descent from the holder of a title which has become extinct. With such proof a man could apply for the Committee of Privileges of the House of Lords to investigate his claim, which, if substantiated, would entitle him to use the title."

"And there's many a man who wouldn't be above committing a murder for the sake of being called Me Lord this or Me Lord that." Murphy shook his head. "I see what you mean, Mr. Terhune, but glory be to God! if the information was to be had from one of these books, couldn't the claimant have bought the book from Harrison without murdering the poor divil?"

"Have you ever tried to make a bibliophile part with one of his precious books?"

"Then couldn't the other man have borrowed the book for a few minutes, and copied out the paragraph?" Murphy asked swiftly. "Mind you," he continued, "I'm not saying there's nothing in your idea, Mr. Terhune, and I'm not admitting there's something, but if there is, may the Saints help us! for then your visit to London won't help at all in finding the murderer. Your bookseller blokes might remember selling Harrison a book worth a few thousand pounds, but not one worth a few pounds or shillings."

"Agreed! Which brings me to my second idea, sergeant. You're convinced, aren't you, that somebody means to get possession of something in this house, presumably a book, by hook or by crook."

"It looks that way," Murphy agreed.

"Then if you could make absolutely certain that the book is not stolen in the meantime, you could set a trap for the murderer."

"A trap, eh!" Murphy brightened, and began to look interested. "Go on."

Terhune picked up a book from a pile near at hand. "You see this copy of Beatrice Fortescue's *Holbein*, sergeant? To anyone in the trade it is worth about seven pounds. To a private collector, well, use your own imagination, but say, for the sake of argument, up to fifteen or even twenty pounds. Now, although we don't know it, this is the book which Harrison's murderer wants at all costs."

Murphy nodded. "Go on."

"On the day of the auction sale of these books you can bet there will be a pretty big crowd of people here, most of them well-known book-collectors and booksellers, or their representatives. It is almost certain that a good many strangers will come along too, some out of curiosity, others in the hope of picking up bargains—not that there will be many bargains for others if I'm still alive to make a bid." Terhune chuckled, but quickly continued: "The odds are about one hundred to one that among the strangers will be Harrison's murderer, who will come here in the hope of buying what he has been unable to steal."

"Ah!" Murphy exclaimed significantly, as he began to appreciate Terhune's plan.

"My idea is this, sergeant. If you have failed to trace the murderer by the time the sale comes off I suggest that you and a couple of plain-clothes men attend the sale. Directly a bidder not known to me as a bona-fide book-collector or bookseller begins to bid more than a maximum amount for a book I'll make a signal—"

The detective interrupted impatiently: "You said yourself that a good many people not known to you are likely to be at the sale."

"I am coming to that. Don't forget I said something about a maximum amount, by which I mean the maximum amount which I should expect a collector to pay for the lot being bid for. This copy of *Holbein* for instance. Suppose it starts at three pounds, bid by a stranger, and that Henry Sotheran and the stranger then run it up between them to seven pounds. At that point the stranger, if he's in the trade, might retire. If he's a private collector, however, he might, and probably would, be prepared to carry on, in which case Sotheran's man would probably fall out. This is where I step in—If I'm not already in the bidding. I shall start bidding against the stranger. If he drops out at, say, twenty pounds, well and good; we shall know that he was a genuine collector. But suppose he carries on, to twenty-five, thirty, thirty-five—"

"Bedad! He's our man!"

"Well, anyone willing to pay five times the existing value of a book would want a pretty good reason for so doing, sergeant, so I shouldn't think any harm would come of your asking him a few discreet questions."

"The divil it wouldn't!" Murphy agreed enthusiastically.

It was left to Julia to see the disadvantage of the plan.

"Theo, my sweet, if you outbid every collector who attends the sale you will find yourself bankrupt by the time it's over."

Terhune rubbed the back of his ear and grinned his embarrassment. In his enthusiasm he had overlooked the point.

Murphy was equally disappointed. "Pity!" he muttered. "There were possibilities in the scheme." His mouth tightened. "Who's going to auction the books, Mr. Terhune? Tuttell?"

"I think so."

"Then something might be arranged."

"Such as?"

"Would it be possible for you to bid as two separate people, as it were, Mr. Terhune? For yourself as yourself, of course, but afterwards, when you dropped out on your own account, you could continue bidding on behalf of the police. Of course the Chief Constable would have to give his consent, and the arrangement would have to be agreed by Tuttell, also Howard, on behalf of the estate. But from what I know of them I think the two gentlemen would be agreeable if they were told the reason why."

"It would be easy enough for me to do as you suggest, sergeant, and to keep the business from being too complicated I could supply, before the sale, a list of the lots I intended bidding for, and the maximum of each bid. But would the Watch Committee thank you for using Police Funds to bid for a library of rare books?"

The sergeant chuckled. "I can guess *how* they'd thank me. But would there be much difficulty about your reselling the books later on, to the maker of the last genuine bid?"

"Not if I could find out the bidder's name and address?"

Murphy snapped his fingers. "That's what I mean could probably be arranged with Tuttell. You leave things to me, Mr. Terhune. I'll see the Chief Constable to-morrow, that I will, bedad!"

II

Late the following afternoon Murphy 'phoned up to tell Terhune that, after a certain amount of persuasion, the Chief Constable had agreed to the plan of setting a trap for Harrison's murderer. The detective also reported that, in spite of extensive inquiries, nothing further had been learned about the men who had made the attempted burglary at *Twelve Chimneys* the previous night, nor was there any news of the car they had used.

The following morning Terhune paid his promised visit to London, where he made a series of calls upon those booksellers from whom Harrison had been in the habit of buying books. First he called upon Francis Edwards, of Marylebone High Street. At first the atmosphere was frigid. The firm's business was confidential, he was told; surely Mr. Terhune had himself been a bookseller long enough to know that it would be a gross breach of confidence, to say nothing of its being a rather dangerous method of business, for one bookseller to reveal to another the names of clients, their purchases, and the prices paid?

Faced with this reasonable objection Terhune found himself obliged to reveal the reason for his inquiries. The other man's mood at once changed; he became both understanding and obliging—of course, Mr. Terhune had helped the police on one or two occasions, hadn't he? Indeed, he was becoming quite famous as an amateur detective, wasn't he? (Terhune winced.) In the circumstances, one was ready to co-operate within the limits of ethics and trade interests. But (the inevitable but!) unfortunately none of the books which they sold to poor Mr. Harrison could rightly be described as one for the possession of which one bibliophile might murder another. One regretted not being able to help more than that—

From Marylebone High Street Terhune walked south-east to Great Russell Street. There he called on Grafton & Co., but this time he took the precaution of stating the object of his visit before making his inquiries. He was at once promised any reasonable information—after all, with Harrison's death they had lost a valued and esteemed client; they would be only too happy to contribute anything to the murderer's arrest and punishment. Unhappily, their anything proved to be of very little use.

From Graftons, west to Sackville Street and Sotherans, and further disappointment. Thence, still westwards, to New Bond Street, where he made inquiries of Myers & Co., only to meet with the same result. So to Maggs Brothers, in Berkeley Square.

"Harrison certainly purchased a number of books from us, Mr. Terhune, and many of them were collectors' pieces, as it were. But surely nobody would commit murder for the sake of a book worth one hundred pounds or less?"

"Exactly!" Terhune agreed. "That is why, sir, I asked whether you had ever sold him a book so valuable that a man might risk hanging to obtain it."

An understanding nod. "Yes, of course; I follow your meaning, Mr. Terhune. The most valuable book which my firm has been privileged to sell to Mr. Harrison was an illuminated Bible—"

"Girard Desmoulin's translation of Comestor's *Historia Scholastica?*"

"Yes, indeed. The amount which Mr. Harrison paid for the manuscript is one which I do not propose to disclose, Mr. Terhune, but you may draw your own conclusions from the fact that I paid two thousand four hundred pounds for it. I think I could mention the names of two or three collectors who would gladly commit murder—in contemplation if not, perhaps, in fact—to obtain possession of such a treasure."

"So could I, but the manuscript is still in Mr. Harrison's library, undamaged, I am glad to say, although it was found on the floor."

"Sacrilege!" came an indignant exclamation. "In the circumstances, Mr. Terhune, has it occurred to you that a book was not the object for which the criminals killed poor Mr. Harrison? No bibliomaniac would have overlooked the chance of stealing Desmoulin's manuscript."

"Not unless they were after a far greater treasure."

"Ah! Yes, indeed. I follow your meaning. But surely the genuine bibliomaniac would have taken the Desmoulin's manuscript whether or not he found the greater treasure which he was hoping to steal. If it is not being too presumptuous for an older man to make a suggestion to a young man who has achieved a certain amount of fame, I should look for one of two people: either, one who has no knowledge of books, notwithstanding the fact that he was, presumably, in search of one specific book, or, one who was not looking for a book of any sort, but something entirely different."

The first alternative was a reasonable one, and Terhune felt a little chagrined that it had not occurred to him some time ago. The second alternative he ignored, being convinced, from all the facts known to him, that a book, and nothing else, was the object of the attempted theft.

"You may be right, sir, in believing that the housebreaker had no knowledge of books, but I am sure that he was after some particular book."

"Quite probably, though I cannot think of any book outside of a national museum which would tempt a man to commit murder to possess it."

So much for Maggs Brothers. Terhune walked back towards Piccadilly feeling not dissatisfied with his morning's work. If there was anything in the argument that nobody with any knowledge of rare books would have overlooked the chance of stealing the illuminated manuscript then it could well be that he was justified in his theory that the wanted book had no intrinsic value. Moreover, this theory agreed with Murphy's, that a professional crook would hesitate to steal a book which could be easily traced back to him. Take Desmoulin's MS. for instance! Once it was known to the world that it had been stolen no regular "fence" would dare to handle such a dangerous article.

After lunch, and having time to spare, Terhune visited some of the smaller booksellers from whom Harrison had occasionally purchased books. From none did he obtain any useful information, so at last he made his way to Cannon Street Station, where he caught the 5.00 p.m. train for Ashford. Less than three hours later he was once again in Harrison's library, together with Julia, who had insisted upon carrying on until his work was completed.

Outside the house two very disconsolate police constables patrolled round about, one in front, and one behind. Murphy meant to make quite sure that the bait was not stolen before the trap was sprung.

Chapter Ten

A t an exceedingly early hour on the day following Terhune's visit to London, a car drove into Bray from the direction of Ashford. It was one of many vehicles, not a few of which were farm wagons, for it was Bray's market day, and Market Square was already noisy, although the sun was not an hour's journey above the hazed horizon.

The man who had driven in from Ashford had his own work to do; quite disinterested in the bustling activity round about he carefully guided the bumping car over the cobbles towards that part of the square reserved for parking. Once there he shut off the engine, collected a bundle of posters, a large paste-pot, and a paste brush from the rear seat, and made his way towards a notice board which stood outside Higgins's, the newsagent. That board was the property of Tuttell, the estate-agent, and reserved for his announcements. A few minutes later the first announcement of the forthcoming auction sale to be held at *Twelve Chimneys* was being pasted up, and even as the bill-poster walked away to another of Mr. Tullett's announcement boards, early stall-holders began to cluster round the newsagent's shop to read the red and blue printed particulars.

Slick Sims was among the small group, and being the accepted wit of the market, wasn't slow to remark upon the bill—after all, he had a reputation to maintain!

"Take a look at that, me lads and lassies," he began in his fruity, Cockney voice. "Unfair competition; that's what I calls it. Unfair competition to yours truly."

This sally was greeted with the anticipated laughter, for Slick Sims was by way of being an auctioneer himself—of the so-called "Dutch" variety, be it admitted. Each market day he was to be seen in Market Square, bellowing, blarneying, chaffing, laughing, cajoling, but always selling, selling, selling; trousers, socks, stockings, bloomers, shirts, blouses, plain, stout, hard-wearing clothes to stand up against country wear—"Come along, mates, who's going to be the first to snap up this bargain? Generosity's me middle name, so I'll say two pun' ten for this 'ere pair of trousers what'll see yer own life out, and still be good to cut down for the nipper. Two pun' ten, and that's ten bob less than it should be. Two pun' five, then, two pun', Gor' blimey! Ain't none of yer got any bees and honey? Yer breaking me 'eart. One pun' fifteen, then, one pun' ten, twenty-five blooming bob. Who wants it for twenty-five blooming bob? Going, going—All right, me lads and lassies. Ruin me. I don't care. Ruin me. Take the money right out of me blooming pockets. One pun'. One pun'. For the last time, one pun'. Seventeen-and-a-tanner—That's yours, mate, me lucky lad. You know a bargain when you see one. Now, who'll have another pair? Two pun' ten—two pun' five—"

Oh! yes, there wasn't a more likeable character than Slick Sims, and if he had a few thousand "pun'" tucked away in the bank, nobody outside the bank suspected the fact. A few thousand "pun'," and all amassed from, microscopic profits, for Slick Sims was only slick with his tongue, and not with his financial transactions. Anyone buying goods from Slick Sims bought good value for little money.

"What's this 'ere Tuttell bloke got what I ain't?" he continued loudly. "That's what I ask you, me lads and lassies. What's 'e got—"

"Modesty," called out old Thomas Hobby, whose country wit and sagacity matched Sims's Cockney wiles—Hobby was the bane of Sims's auctioneering existence, even if they often shared a pint at the *Three Tuns*.

The morning continued fine; with that intoxicating promise which forces even the most obstinate stay-abed to savour the warming air, dewy still from the sharpness of the night. On such mornings Market

Square at Bray usually became the hub of the local community; thither proceeded all who had the slightest excuse, be it of no greater importance than changing a book at the Bookshop, or drinking a cocktail at the *Almond Tree*. Mr. Tuttell, who was a shrewd observer of life, was well aware that a large number would be visiting the small, old-world market town; hence the earliness of the bill-poster's arrival.

How justified the auctioneer was in his judgment was soon obvious. In front of all three announcement boards which faced Market Square from different directions small groups of people began to cluster. The news was travelling quickly, and even those few who normally had no interest whatever in an auction sale were anxious to read the poster through from top to bottom, not because they wished to find out what was for sale, but merely on account of morbid curiosity.

Reactions to the bill varied greatly. Mrs. Chancellor, from Farthing Toll, who was there to take her turn at the Women's Institute stall, read the bill and changed her mind about buying a new ten-inch mower from Pratts, the ironmonger, whose shop stood alongside Collis's, the grocer—among the items listed on the bill under Outdoor Effects was a ten-inch mower, as good as new. In view of the exciting possibility of saving a few shillings by buying what she wanted at the sale, there would be the thrill of attending the sale, a sensation which few country people are able to resist—all of which was hard luck on the ironmonger. On the other hand Pratt had already decided to attend the sale to snap up any likely bargains in ironmongery, including, he hoped, the ten-inch mower.

Mildred Hetherington was another who made a mental note of the dates of sale, and there and then determined not to miss one hour of it. An excuse?—why, she wanted some new chintz curtains, didn't she, and wasn't it likely that a pair or so of curtains would be offered, which her clever and ever-ready needle could adapt? And if Mr. Terhune didn't buy *all* the books there might be one or two travel books which would be knocked down for an odd shilling or two.

Lady Kylstone, an early visitor to the market, read the bill, and forthwith called upon Terhune.

"Good morning, dear boy. So poor Harrison's library is to be scattered to the four winds! What a pity! I do not have to ask whether you will be at the sale. Will you execute a commission for me, Theodore?"

"Of course."

"I have always wanted that copy of Thorogood's *Kent Muniments*—it contains a chapter on the first Piers Kirtlyngton."

Naturally! Sir Piers Kirtlyngton was the ancestor and founder of the Kylstone family. But Terhune shook his head doubtfully.

"Is anything wrong with my wanting to buy the book?" she asked sharply.

"On the contrary," he assured her. "Unfortunately, there's a steady demand for Thorogood's *Muniments*. Dowell's of Edinburgh auctioned a copy less than a year ago for twenty pounds. Puttick and Simpson sold one about the same time, in quarter morocco, for twenty-two or twenty-three pounds, I forget which."

The light of battle began to smoulder in Lady Kylstone's eyes. "I am not a poor woman, Theodore, so I am not going to let anyone from London outbid me. You are to buy it for me whatever it costs. Do you understand? At whatever cost, even if it means giving double the sum you have mentioned. The book ought to have been included among the family records years ago."

Sir George Brereton entered. "Hullo, Kathleen," he boomed. "How's the head? Better?"

"Head! What's the matter with my head?" she snapped.

"You were complaining of it the last time we met."

"What a ridiculous man you are, George. That was nearly a week ago. Besides, I was *not* complaining. I just wasn't feeling strong enough to listen to another of your fishing stories."

He grinned amiably. "I can't keep track of time in these days. Well, Terhune, so Harrison's library is to be sold up, I hear." He chuckled with anticipation. "I'm going to enjoy myself; Harrison had a least half a dozen books which I want."

"You're not going to bid for them yourself, are you, George?"

"Why shouldn't I, my dear?"

"Because you'll have every bookseller in the country bidding against you."

"Don't worry about me. I can be as cute as they, Kathleen."

She laughed scornfully. "As if a big baby like you could be."

"But why shouldn't I bid for the books? I want them, and am willing to pay for them."

"Let Theodore bid for them. He should be able to buy them more cheaply than you."

"Nonsense. Why should you have all the fun, eh! Terhune, my boy? Besides, I don't doubt you will be busy enough on your own account."

"I sincerely trust so, Sir George, but I am not too hopeful. I can't expect to compete against all the big people."

"Well, if it's fishing books they're after I'll shew 'em that they've come to the wrong neighbourhood for bargains," Sir George boasted.

Lady Kylstone's eyes twinkled. "If that's your mood, George, you must make sure that your bank balance can withstand shocks."

Market Square became ever more crowded. The glorious morning was attracting everybody to Bray. Godfrey and Patricia from Wickford; the two neighbours, and antagonistic rose rivals from Farthing Toll, Captain James Forbes, R.N. (retired) and Col. Terence O'Malley, once of the Inniskilling Dragoons, the Rev. Septimus Andrews, vicar of St. Agnes's at Great Hinton, accompanied by his daughter, the Pemberton brothers, Gary Jones, Lady Kylstone's nephew from Athens, Alabama, with Helena, his fiancée—from every point of the compass they came, in Rolls, Daimlers, Austins, Morrises, Fords; in governess carts, traps, heavy farm wagons; on bicycles; afoot. Before long the three inns, the *Almond Tree*, the *Wheatsheaf*—and round the corner, the *Three Tuns*—were almost as crowded inside as out. Inside the saloon bars, and the public bars, outside on the pavements, in front of Tuttell's bills, round about the market stalls—in all directions were to be heard snatches of conversation referring either to the forthcoming sale or to the murder of Harrison. Only the farmers and the farm workers were in the minority. They discussed farming.

Oh yes! Tuttell had undoubtedly chosen a good day for his first announcements of the *Twelve Chimneys* sale.

11

The next day the weather broke, and for a full week remained undecided. As the days passed by it seemed almost certain that the weather would continue unsettled—and what a difference that would make to the final amount he would inherit was fortunately not realized by Harrison's nephew in Canada, who was impatiently awaiting news of the sale. But evidently he was looked upon with a friendly eye by the Clerk of the Weather; on the Saturday morning preceding the week of the sale, the heavy banks of clouds slowly drifted south, and the bright, sparkling sun began to warm the earth again, and make life seem so infinitely more cheerful.

By mid-afternoon not a cloud was anywhere to be seen. By six o'clock the B.B.C. news-reader was able to start off the latest weather forecast by announcing that an anti-cyclone was moving south from Iceland, and that the following day would be fair and warm.

For once the weather forecast was truly prophetic. The day *was* fair and warm. Even hot, indeed. So countless wives and mothers living in the neighbourhood of Wickford began to plan their time for the next few days. Monday—well, Monday was washing-day. Sacrosanct! Particularly with weather conditions, ideal for quick drying. But Tuesday, now! Ah! Tuesday was View Day, a day only a little less exciting than the actual Day of Sale. As for the Wednesday, well, what about a few sandwiches, and a bottle of lemonade, and make a picnic of the sale? It might be very pleasant, weather permitting, to pass the luncheon interval in a quiet spot somewhere in the lovely grounds of *Twelve Chimneys*. Besides, there wouldn't be any need to hurry back to the sale during the afternoon, for only the silly books were to be sold during the afternoons of the three days' sale.

Monday was as fine as the preceding day. Monday was also a View Day for those for whom a Monday had no special significance. From ten a.m. onwards a succession of people passed through the rooms of *Twelve Chimneys*. Isabel Shelley was one of the earliest; accompanied by Diana Pearson she called there on her way up to London. She ticked off three items on her catalogue—a French bracket clock, a Shirvan rug with an ivory medallion *motif*, and a pair of Bristol Delft plates. Diana had less expensive, and more mundane tastes; her fancy was fixed on a set of copper saucepans which had been the pride of Miss Baggs's life, and which Miss Baggs had determined to buy whatever the cost. As Diana's requirements were not competitive she was there and then commissioned by Isabel to bid for her three lots.

Everard Winstanley was another early caller. His interest in the sale was purely academic. He had no money to spare for buying any of the lots—unless the silver cigarette case which used to stand on the library desk should go for a less than reasonable sum, he reflected—but like the Mrs. Smiths, the Mrs. Browns, and the Mrs. Joneses, who, at that moment, were bent over their scrubbing boards, he, too, intended to enjoy himself at the sale. For one reason, among others, Patricia Hutton would, for certain, be among the bidders. Pat Hutton rarely missed a local sale at which anything worth-while was being sold; she was wealthy enough to buy what, when and where she wanted, but the only pleasure she had from buying was in open competition at auction sales. Winstanley could not appreciate the psychology of this particular trait, but he could and did appreciate her company at such times. For years past Pat and he had shared a clandestine, but extremely harmless, flirtation. Besides, even if Pat should, by some mischance, stay away, Joy Fawcett from Great Hinton was sure to be there. A good second-best, Joy Fawcett, when she was in the mood—which wasn't always. A nice filly, but moody. And just a *leetle* too middle-aged in these days.

Before long the house hummed with little activity, but much conversation as more and more people arrived—old friends, new friends, neighbours, acquaintances—Alicia MacMunn, whose cheerful, high-pitched voice could be heard from almost every room in the house; Alec Hamblin, Thomas Pain, the veterinary surgeon—a busy man, but not too busy to snatch an hour for a "look-see" at *Twelve Chimneys* and its contents. And the two local doctors' wives, of course: Vera Harris, and Ann Edwards. Bobby Hicks, from Bray Tap Farm; Olive Brereton; Edward Pryce; Nicholas Harvey with his daughter; Miss Tucker, the retired, and faded schoolmistress, grimly determined to use the event of the sale as material for an article to be published in one of the local newspapers; the Bulletts, Max and wife—

Monday afternoon was almost as busy. Tuesday being Market Day at Ashford, the local farmers chose Monday afternoon as the most convenient time to visit *Twelve Chimneys*. To see whether there were any articles for sale to appeal particularly to them? Scarcely. But farmers are not less curious than ordinary folk when it comes to peeking into other people's homes.

Tuesday was still busier. The Mrs. Smiths, the Mrs. Browns, and the Mrs. Joneses, having disposed of their washing the previous day, flocked towards *Twelve Chimneys* in their half-dozens. Bert Binks, of the garage at Great Hinton, with his wife, and his sister-in-law, George's Adelaide. Mrs. Newman, Joy Fawcett's cook-housekeeper; Betty Wrong from Maid of Honour Farm (her name was really Wright, but the Wrights were Wrongs to the local wits); Bacon and his blousy, blonde better-half from Cooper's Cottage; Hilda Hughes, from Farthing Toll, old Thomas Hobby, of course—as if anything could happen anywhere without the old shepherd hobbling about nearby!—Mrs. Mann, looking superior in the knowledge that her Mr. Terhune was giving a hand with the sale—she was a little obscure as to the precise nature of the assistance—

So to the next day, the first day of sale, with Terhune cycling up the short, curving drive to the house a full hour before the advertised start of the sale. But Murphy was already there.

"Good morning, Mr. Terhune."

"Good morning, sergeant. No trouble last night?"

"Not a suggestion of any. There hasn't been since the night you were interrupted."

"Then we can take it for granted that the book which those men were so anxious to secure is still in the house?"

"Certainly. And what is more—" Murphy paused to allow a meaning smile to pass across his lips. "We can take it equally for granted that if our men come here with the intention of buying instead of stealing it—or, for that matter, if they still attempt to steal it—they will walk straight into our trap."

Terhune had a quick glance about him. Three men in plain clothes were standing together in a group near the front door, smoking and yarning; these, he suspected, were detective constables. This supposition was immediately confirmed by Murphy, who had followed the direction of Terhune's gaze.

"Thompson, Hutchins, and Pritchard," the sergeant said, with a motion of his head in their direction. "There's another man due—Wilkins—who should be arriving at any moment."

"Four will be enough?"

"Four should be more than enough, but I'm not taking any risks, so, in addition to those four and myself, there will be a uniformed constable at hand, and those two."

Another quick nod of Murphy's head indicated two porters, in shirt-sleeves and green-baize aprons.

Terhune was vaguely astonished at the idea of Murphy's making use of Tuttell's porters, until the sergeant offered an explanation.

"They are two of my best men," he chuckled. "To keep up appearances they'll give the regular porters a hand with shifting the furniture about, but they'll be keeping their weather-eyes open for any signal from you or me, or for any suspicious move from anyone else."

Terhune grinned. "Seven men and yourself should be able to tackle anything that happens."

The sergeant's face turned grim. "Put that way it sounds blasted foolish, Mr. Terhune, and the Chief Constable wasn't too polite when I told him how many men I needed. He asked me whether I would like to call the army in as well while I was about it.

"But if you want the truth, sir, I'm ready to admit that I'm worried. Perhaps it's the Irish in me, but I've a feeling that we're up against something really big; something bigger than anything I've ever had a hand in. I didn't think so on the night Harrison was butchered. I laughed then at the idea of habitual criminals risking their hides for the sake of a book. I don't now."

"Has anything else happened to make you change your views? Bar the second attempt, of course."

Murphy's glance was a little reproachful. "I should have passed the information on to you if it had, Mr. Terhune. No, it's just me Irish blood saying to me: 'Tim, me boy, there's something more in this than just the theft of a ruddy book. Something you don't begin to suspect. So watch out for yourself, keep your eyes skinned, and don't let thim thugs put a fast one across you.' That's what meself is saying, Mr. Terhune, and don't ask me what's at the bottom of it, for it's meself that couldn't be telling you why."

Terhune was startled. The realistic sergeant was the last man in the world to be susceptible to psychic influences; he was so essentially of the earth earthy in his outlook on life, and particularly, matters criminal. To hear him admit that he was being influenced by intuition was somewhat of a shock.

"What have you in mind, sergeant? A smash-and-grab—or a hold-up of sorts?"

Murphy's chin stuck out defiantly. "Maybe!"

"They couldn't hope to get away with anything like that in these days."

"They can't hope to in face of our preparations, but the idea isn't quite as fantastic as you seem to think, Mr. Terhune. Listen. The sale is proceeding. The auctioneer says: 'What will you give me for this lot, ladies and gentlemen? A fine copy of Hans Andersen's *Fairy Tales*.' Two men pull out revolvers. 'Gimme that book,' says one of them. What do you think is going to happen?"

Terhune grinned. "That's easy. The porter hands over the book, *tout de suite*, and as I doubt whether there would be any Hollywood heroes at the sale, the stick-up men would quietly vanish. But wouldn't that be the easiest part of the theft? How far would they get before the Mobile Police cars were on the lookout for them?"

"Not far, but it's not very difficult to change cars, especially along one of the quiet roads round about here."

Such a plan would be daring, even desperate, but a few moments reflection warned Terhune that it was not quite so fantastic as he had at first believed. He could easily imagine the confusion into which the unsuspecting people at the sale would be thrown in the event of a sudden hold-up, and if the men had taken the precaution of cutting the telephone-wire, many precious minutes might elapse before the police were advised of the crime. By that time the robbers could have driven the car to an agreed spot, and in case its number and description had been noted, had there abandoned it, to drive back home in a different, unsuspected car. How could they be traced, except by mischance?"

He nodded. "Certainly, it's possible, even if it isn't probable."

"Mind you, Mr. Terhune," Murphy continued earnestly. "I don't say that that is what I think they'll do. I've an idea they would be more subtle. Like bidding for it straightforward-like, as you suggest. That's why I like your plan. But, as I told you just now, I'm not taking any chances.

"Meanwhile, the men all know what they have to do. Perkins, the uniformed constable, will do nothing; he will hang around in case of trouble. So will the two who are helping the porters. But the three men over there, and Wilkins—here he is, by the way—will pretend to be bidders. Their job is to take orders from you and me. They've learned the signals which either you, Tuttell or I will give them, and that will let them know which men are known to any one of the three of us, and which are strangers. They will keep an eye on all strangers, and will make inquiries about them while the sale proceeds.

"They also know what to do immediately you give the signal that somebody has made a bid for any book that's far more than its real value. Anyone who does that will thereafter be a marked man. If there's only one, Thompson and Hutchins will be responsible for shadowing him to his destruction, but in case, by a coincidence, there should be two extra-high bidders—I don't like to overlook the possibility of coincidence—Pritchard and Wilkins will look after the second. Is that clear, sir?"

"Quite."

Murphy beckoned the four detective-constables to meet Terhune. The criminals would have to be more than super to lay their hands upon the book they wanted so desperately, he reflected.

If the article which the criminals were after were a book—whispered the voice of nagging doubt. But Murphy would not listen to it. Life was already sufficiently complicated.

Chapter Eleven

P eople began arriving at *Twelve Chimneys* long before the sale was due to begin. The majority of the earlier arrivals came by bicycle— local people, these, who had come for the specific purpose of bidding for one or more of the lots listed under Outside Effects, with which the sale was to begin, or for Kitchen Equipment, which was to follow Outside Effects. By opening the sale with these two categories Tuttell was reversing the customary procedure, but his purpose in doing so was to enable the people from London to arrive in time without having had to catch trains at an uncomfortably early hour.

In an astonishingly short while there were straggling lines of bicycles radiating from the house in several directions; for the most part they were propped up against the trim hedges which were a characteristic of the garden lay-out. Almost as soon came the first cars. They filled up the curving drive which led to the front entrance of the house, and all who arrived thereafter had to park their cars on the grass verge, bordering the road. Soon the line of cars stretched beyond the church in the one direction, and almost as far as the Canal bridge in the other.

Then the first bus from Ashford, packed to overflowing, stopped outside the house. When the conductor at last signalled to his driver to go on, only three passengers were left in the bus.

A crowd milled in and out and round about the house. Many more waited on the back lawn, where the auction was to be held, and sat themselves down upon the chairs as quickly as the porters carried them out, and placed them in position. Once seated the lucky ones gazed about them with triumphant eyes, and some pulled out knitting to while away the time until the fun began.

Children and dogs rapidly multiplied. In one part of the garden an energetic game of "he" was begun; the excited shouts of the players soon drowned all other noises. And as was only to be expected, they were not long satisfied to remain in the open spaces—the temptation to dodge in and out of the chairs, and the perambulating sight-seers, was too strong to be resisted. They rushed hither and thither, falling over feet or baskets, or sometimes an excited dog, and generally annoying all but their complacent mothers, who were relieved to be temporarily rid of the little worry-guts, even if it were at the expense of some degree of noise. All this time the porters cursed roundly, and not silently, but their adjectival wrath, tempered in consideration of the company about them, made no more impression upon the players than drops of water upon a patch of sand. As for the dogs, they were in paradise; they left innumerable visiting cards, and even sprayed the legs of the table upon which the auctioneer's rostrum had been mounted. It was a colourful scene if viewed dispassionately; one that seemed to have borrowed something from a circus, something from a Sunday school treat, something from a garden party and fête.

In the meanwhile Terhune, Murphy, Jameson—Tuttell's clerk—and Detective-Constable Hutchins, stood together in a discreet group at one of the bedroom windows, from which the drive below was visible, and inspected all who entered the house. As each comer, or group, came into view one or another of the watchers in the window identified, when possible, the person or people concerned. This they had been doing already for some thirty minutes, and so far Hutchins had written down in the ready note-book the descriptions of only three people whom none of them had recognized.

A man and woman cycled along the curving drive into view. Jameson spoke.

"Okay, sergeant. They're Mr. and Mrs. Dodds; second-hand dealers from Tenterden."

A man on his own; a small, short-legged man looking like an ex-jockey.

"Okay" said all four men, roughly in those words, and almost simultaneously. They chuckled. The man was Ted Shore, landlord of *The Dusty Miller* at Great Hinton.

A woman. "Mrs. Rowlandson, from the house opposite," Terhune supplied.

Another woman. "Mrs. Edwards," Murphy said crisply.

Two men. For awhile, silence.

"Well?" the sergeant snapped.

"I think I know the one on the right," Jameson ventured. "Ah! yes. Now I remember. He lives in Willesborough. I think his name is Raymond."

Next, an elderly man and woman. "The Perkins, from Bracken Hill," Terhune said promptly.

Hutchins himself knew the next comer. He chuckled. "Okay, sergeant. Bill Potter. He lives down our street. He has that second-hand shop along the High Street."

So it continued, until Jameson looked at his watch and saw that it was time for him to wait for his employer. By then only four unknowns in all had arrived, but Murphy was not disappointed. He had not expected the preliminary check-up to yield any different result, for it was not likely that the book-buyers would be arriving before the afternoon, when the first of the books would be offered.

Ten minutes later the loud clang of a handbell announced that the sale was about to start. Everyone began to move in the direction of the back lawn. By now every seat was occupied, also every inch of available sitting accommodation, such as tops of tables, chests-of-drawers, commodes, and the like. Many sat on the grass. Those who arrived in answer to the bell found themselves compelled to stand. Soon the lawn was crowded.

Tuttell appeared at the French windows which opened out on to the lawn, and made his way towards the rostrum, followed by Jameson. Having first stepped on to a kitchen chair, thence on to the table, which was protected by a thick carpet, Tuttell sat down, and beamed at the people before him.

"Good morning, ladies and gentlemen. As usual I apologize for being ten minutes late in starting, but in doing so I know that if we were to start on time some of my esteemed friends, whom I see about me, would be too startled to bid."

This sally produced the desired chuckle, and from Mrs. Bacon, a burst of high-pitched laughter—this was her first sale, so the familiar excuse was fresh to her.

Tuttell gave Mrs. Bacon a quick nod of thanks—a ripple of laughter now and then usually had the tonic effect of producing higher bids.

"Thank you, madam. Now, ladies and gentlemen, as you know, to-day and the two following days we are selling the entire contents of *Twelve Chimneys* by order of the executors of the late Mr. Arthur Harrison. The goods are to be sold without reserve, and subject to the usual terms and conditions, an extract of which you will find inside your catalogues. Well, we have a lot of work in front of us so I shall waste no further time in preliminaries.

"Lot one, ladies and gentlemen, consists of two three-prong Canterbury hoes, leaf broom, bass broom, and a rammer."

"Showing here, sir," one of the porters shouted, drawing attention to the goods in question, which, with others, were propped up against a nearby wall.

"What am I bid for this useful assortment of garden tools? Will somebody start me at five shillings. Two shillings. Thank you. Two shillings. And sixpence. Three shillings. And sixpence. Four shillings. And sixpence. Five shillings. Six. Seven. Eight. Nine. Ten. Ten shillings. Any more. Ten shillings I am bid, on my right. Going for ten shillings—" The hammer rapped sharply. "Mr. Harvey, is it not?"

Nicholas Harvey nodded. A smile played on his lips. He was more than satisfied.

"Lot two, an iron frame Folding Garden Seat and two Deck Chairs. Will somebody start me off at ten shillings? Mrs. Fawcett, will you—you will! Thank you. Ten shillings I am bid for lot two. Ten. Twelve. Fourteen—"

II

During the next hour and a half Tuttell disposed of some 150 lots which consisted of Outside Effects—41 lots—and the Contents of the Kitchen, which numbered 112. The 153rd lot was an hors-d'œuvre dish with six containers.

"What am I bid for this? Five shillings? Five shillings in two places. Six. Seven. Eight. Nine. Nine. Does anyone say ten?"

Lady Kylstone unexpectedly nodded. "That reminds me, Theo," she murmured. "Biddy broke mine two weeks ago."

Tuttell's quick glance at Lady Kylstone was a shade deferential. "Ten it is. Ten. Eleven." He looked inquiringly in Lady Kylstone's direction. She nodded.

"Twelve on my left. Thirteen. Fourteen. Fifteen. Sixteen. Seventeen. Eighteen. Nineteen. One pound. One pound. Two. Four. Six. One pound six. Going for one pound six shillings." A slight pause. A hearty rap.

"Lady Kylstone," he announced. "And now, ladies and gentlemen, there will be a break for one hour for luncheon. At two-thirty sharp the sale will be resumed, when the only items to be put up will consist of books from the late Mr. Harrison's famous library."

Tuttell rose, whereupon there was a discreet scurry towards the line of parked cars. Within two minutes the morning was noisy with the exhaust from a dozen cars all jockeying to be the first to get away. Apart from those motorists, some twenty cyclists or so, who were within easy distance of *Twelve Chimneys*, and a small minority who had no interest in books, and were not affected by curiosity, morbid or otherwise, the majority of the people remained behind. The porters found themselves convenient resting-places in what had once been Miss Baggs's sitting-room, and there produced brown-paper packages, and sundry bottles containing cold tea. The detectives borrowed some of the deck chairs which had been sold earlier in the morning, and placed them just inside the open French windows of the library; they, too, produced picnic luncheons. So, also, did a number of the bidders. Others preferred to walk the short distance into the village, where they overcrowded the two rooms at *The Hop-Picker*, and kept the two Houlden brothers hard at work for the best part of forty-five minutes.

For Terhune and Murphy the break for luncheon was a brief one; even as they opened the attaché case which each had brought with him, the first of the London book-buyers arrived: a tall, iron-grey haired man, dressed in grey.

Terhune nodded at the oncoming figure. "Here they come."

Murphy chuckled. "One of your hated rivals?"

"Yes, curse his bank balance! He's buying for Quaritch. Wait until he and Maggs start bidding against each other! Then I and my ilk fold our tents and silently creep away!" Terhune took a quick bite, then almost choked as he swallowed hastily. "Talk of the devil—"

The sergeant stared at the small figure with slumberous eyes, white hair, and a white Captain Kettle-like beard.

"Maggs?" he questioned, his mouth full of ham sandwich.

Terhune nodded. His mouth, also, was impolitely filled.

For the next five minutes the curving drive remained empty. Then two men arrived together; short, thick-set, swarthy-complexioned men dressed in loud ties, and broad pin-striped suits.

Murphy made a sucking noise with his lips. "Know these two birds, Mr. Terhune?" he asked sharply.

Terhune didn't, and said so.

"Bit foreign-looking, aren't they?" the sergeant went on.

Terhune agreed. "Italian-looking. Or Southern Frenchmen."

"Italian or French, I'm going to keep my eye on those birds. I ask you, do they look like book-buyers or collectors?"

The two apparent foreigners were followed by a fat little man with a big corporation, black hair, and a diamond tie-pin.

Terhune remained silent.

"Him?" Murphy asked succinctly, ungrammatically, but effectively.

"No."

"Bedad! We are going to have a jolly time watching everybody if this continues."

The next three comers somewhat relieved Murphy's gloom. They arrived separately, at short intervals, but Terhune recognized all three.

"Sawyers," he said of the first one. Then: "Joseph" and later: "Foyles."

Then a stranger; an insignificant-looking man with a droopy moustache, a perpetual dewdrop, and mousy-coloured hair plastered over a whitish dome.

"Don't know him," Terhune told the sergeant. "But he looks like a book-collector."

Murphy was more critical. "Don't like his eyes," he grunted.

People began arriving at ever-lessening intervals. Terhune reeled off the names of the firms: Reeves, from Bournemouth—Sotheran—Myers—the George Gregory Bookstore, from Bath—Stevens and Brown—Heffer—Steedman, from Newcastle—

Then: "By Saint Patrick! Another foreigner."

This one, however, was known to Terhune—even at a distance the smart cut of the black jacket, the inevitable red carnation, the trimness of the black hair and moustache were unmistakable.

"He's the real McCoy, sergeant. I've sold him quite a number of expensive books during the past few years."

"Who is he?"

"Francisco Perez, of Charing Cross Road. He's the London representative of Sánchez Hermanos, of Buenos Aires, the largest firm of booksellers in South America."

Perez was followed by a shortish, chubby-faced man with keen eyes.

"Francis Edwards," Terhune announced, adding: "Okay the man just behind him, too. From one of the booksellers up north—either Young of Liverpool, or Godfrey of York, I can't remember which."

So it continued. The odd comers presently increased to a trickle of people, and the trickle, a stream, especially when the bidders from *The Hop-Picker* joined the fresh arrivals from London. The majority of the fresh faces Terhune was able to identify, while some he recognized without being able to give them a name. But there were others—too many for Murphy's peace of mind—who were complete strangers to Terhune.

"I hope we've taken enough precautions," the sergeant commented uneasily.

"Don't you think you have?"

"I've done everything I could think of, Mr. Terhune, as you know."

"Well?"

Murphy tapped out the ashes of his pipe—Tuttell had just made an appearance round the far end of the drive. "If the bees slip one across us in spite of everything, what the Chief Constable will have to say I don't even dare to think. Coming, sir?" Taking Terhune's agreement for granted he led the way through the house to the back lawn.

The lawn was little less crowded than it had been during the morning, but the character of the people had changed considerably. True, the greater number of those present had been there in the morning, but whereas during the morning's sale women had predominated, now the balance had been more or less adjusted by the influx of the book-collectors and booksellers, ninety-six per cent of whom were men.

Tuttell appeared from the house, and after a swift, satisfied glance at the crowd in front of him, he made his way quickly to the rostrum, and forthwith opened proceedings.

"I wish to say a word or two of welcome to the many gentlemen who, I see, have come along here since the luncheon interval. Now, ladies and gentlemen, during this afternoon, and the afternoons of the next two days, we are selling the entire library of the late Mr. Arthur Harrison. To those of you who neither live locally, nor are connected with the highly technical business of the purchase and sale of antique and modern books, I want to say a very few words about the library which it is my privilege to offer to you in convenient lots.

"During forty-three of his sixty-eight years Mr. Harrison was an ardent collector of fine and antique books. He specialized in three types of book rather than in subjects: *Incunabula*, books with superfine bindings, and lastly, illustrated books of outstanding excellence. With reference to his collection of *Incunabula* I do not think I exaggerate if I describe it as world-famous; if it was not the finest private collection in the world, at least it was among the first dozen.

"I have no need to enlarge further on the general excellence of the lots which I am shortly to offer you, but I wish to add one more word. Even if he did not specifically collect, Mr. Harrison also possessed a smaller and interesting library of general subjects and works of reference. These reference books total some two hundred and eighty, and will be sold in approximately ninety lots, thirty of which are being offered at the beginning of each afternoon's sale.

"Ladies and gentlemen, I now offer you Lot one hundred and fifty-four, *Cassell's German-English and English-German Dictionary*, *Weseen's Dictionary of American Slang*, and *Bartlett's Familiar Quotations*. What am I bid for this lot? Will anybody start me at five shillings?"

"One shilling," said a voice.

"Two."

Terhune nodded.

"Three, I am offered three. More than three?" Bang! "Terhune. Lot one hundred and fifty-five. A *Nouveau Petit Larousse Illustré*, and its Spanish equivalent, *Pequeño Larousse Illustrado*. The same? Three I am offered. Four. Five. Six. Seven, Seven, on my right." Bang! "Terhune."

"Lot one hundred and fifty-six. Six assorted novels. Five shillings, Mr. Terhune? Thank you. Five. Five." Bang! "Terhune. Lot one hundred and fifty-seven. A similar lot. Five shillings? Five, it is. Five." Bang! "Terhune. I suppose, Mr. Terhune, you wouldn't like to make a bid for the entire library, to save time?"

A ripple of laughter.

"Certainly," Terhune agreed promptly. "If the other gentlemen present will allow me?"

Tuttell beamed. "Do you all agree? Apparently not, so we must continue. Lot one hundred and fifty-eight. Eight assorted titles. What am I bid? Eight shillings? Then somebody start me at five? Somebody start me? Mr. Terhune, surely you will?"

Terhune shook his head.

"Then we will pass it unless somebody will make me an offer." He looked about him.

A young girl pulled at her father's arm. "Buy 'em, Dad."

"What for? What do 'ee want wi' a passel of dratted books?"

"I want to read 'em, Dad."

While Dad considered his gaze crossed that of the waiting auctioneer.

"One sillun," he called out nervously.

Bang! "Mr. Gates. Lot one hundred and fifty-nine. The Hon. A. Amherst's *History of Gardening* in England, Ralph Strauss's *Carriages and Coaches*, and three others. What am I bid? Five shillings? Ah! Five in two places."

"Ten," called out a voice.

"Fifteen."

"Twenty."

"Twenty," announced Tuttell. "I am bid twenty. Against you, Mr. Terhune. Ah! Twenty-five. Thirty. Thirty-five. Two pounds—"

"Five pounds," bid Foyle's buyer.

Terhune shook his head. He had reached his limit for that lot. Bang!

"Foyles. Lot one hundred and sixty. A complete Shakespeare and four others. What am I bid?"

Tuttell was bid nothing. "Somebody start me," he urged. "Surely a copy of the complete works of Shakespeare should be worth a few shillings to the studious-minded, or to a prospective Romeo. Come, Mr. Terhune, may I say one pound?"

"As a prospective Romeo?" Sir George called out loudly, with a fruity chuckle.

Laughter—save from the impatient London book-buyers.

"Certainly you may say one pound, Mr. Tuttell. I only say one shilling."

More laughter.

"Two," said Mary Harvey.

"Against you, Mr. Terhune. Three? Thank you. Three. Four. Five. Six. Seven. Eight. Against you again, Mr. Terhune."

Terhune hesitated. He did not want to bid against Mary Harvey, but the lot was worth up to a pound. He nodded.

"Nine. Nine it is. Any more."

"Ten," said the man with the droopy moustache and the mouse-coloured hair.

Terhune nodded. "Twelve," bid Droopy Moustache. Terhune nodded. "Fourteen," said his rival. Terhune nodded. "Sixteen." Terhune nodded. "Eighteen," said Droopy Moustache in a mournful voice. Terhune nodded. "One pound," the other man bid sadly.

Terhune looked at his rough notes. In addition to the *Complete Works of Shakespeare* in one volume, there was *A Grammar of the English Language*, *A French-English Dictionary*, *Cruden's Concordance*, and lastly, *Brewer's Dictionary of Phrase and Fable*.

As far as he was concerned 20s. was really the outside price he was prepared to pay for the lot. Yet he nodded.

"Twenty-two," said Tuttell.

"Twenty-four," said Droopy Moustache.

"Twenty-six," said Terhune, tight-lipped.

"Twenty-eight," said Droopy Moustache.

Terhune made a signal to Tuttell. Tuttell returned an inconspicuous signal—Droopy Moustache was not known to him.

"Two pounds," Terhune bid abruptly.

Droopy Moustache looked mournfully at the auctioneer. "Three," he mumbled.

Three pounds bid for books worth, to the trade, less than one-third that price! Terhune looked at Murphy, and gave the prearranged signal of warning.

Chapter Twelve

"Three pounds on my left. Against you, Mr. Terhune," tuttell urged.

To make quite sure that he was not mistaken, Terhune glanced again at his notes and checked the contents of Lot one hundred and sixty. The writing was Julia's; she had selected the five books from among those which he had put aside after a quick glance at the titles. *The Complete Shakespeare* was a copy of an edition published by John Stockdale in 1790. Its condition was bad; the front board cover was broken, the back missing, the spine was dropping off, the title page and frontispiece were stained. Its worth, well, 10s. would be a generous estimate. The second title was a modern publication: *Curme and Kurath's Grammar of the English Language*, published in 1931 by A. M. Heath & Co. Its present second-hand value, say, 4s. Then, *Cruden's Complete Concordance*, published by Frederick Warne in 1889. There was usually a market for a reference book of this nature, at 7s. 6d. or 10s. Say 10s. Next, *Spiers and Surenne's French and English Pronouncing Dictionary*, published by D. Appleton & Company in 1879. 5s. perhaps? Probably less. A useful volume, but very much out of date. Say 3s. 6d., at the most. Lastly, *Brewer's Dictionary of Phrase and Fable*, published by Cassell's in 1896. 5s.? Maybe.

He mentally totalled up the retail selling value of the five volumes. £1 12s. 6d. Was it reasonable for a bookseller to offer £3 for goods which he was not likely to sell for more than £1 12s. 6d.? If as much, indeed. More especially for books which might sell only in the course of time. The *French-English Dictionary*, for instance, and *The Grammar of the English Language*. The answer was a negative. The price offered was not a reasonable one. *Ergo*, Droopy Moustache was not a bookseller. But was he a book-collector, determined, like Lady Kylstone with regard to *Kent Muniments*, to obtain the Lot, regardless of cost, for the sake of one of the five books?

"Going for three pounds," Tuttell said with a suspicion of regret. He directed the remark specifically at Terhune who, abruptly realizing that the auctioneer had lifted his hammer, quickly nodded, at the same-time giving Tuttell the signal which was meant to convey the information that he was no longer bidding on his own account.

"Three pounds five," Tuttell announced with satisfaction.

A sepulchral: "Four pounds."

"Five," said Terhune.

The background noise of whispered conversation (and sometimes of conversation far from whispered), the shuffle of restless feet, the rustle of catalogues, the scraping of furniture, the shout of porter to porter— all the noises which are the despair of an auctioneer, while apparently inseparable from an auction sale—these noises began to subside as the people realized, telepathically, that a duel was beginning—one of those rare moments which make auctioneering history.

Among those most interested in the duel were the booksellers from London and elsewhere. With keen, surprised eyes some began to look first at Droopy Moustache, then at Terhune, as if to try and learn what lay at the root of the unexpected flare-up. Others, equally perplexed, but somewhat worried, turned to their catalogues as if annoyed at the possibility of the discovery of a bargain whose value had been over-looked by the majority.

The local people, equally excited, were unmistakably partisan: even those who did not know Terhune personally quickly learned that he was a local resident, and from that moment were at one with him, while being set against Droopy Moustache, who, as an unknown, was considered an interloper.

"Six," said Droopy Moustache.

Terhune countered promptly. "Seven."

Droopy Moustache sighed. "Ten," he muttered with a display of reluctance.

£10! A sum far exceeding that which even the most desperate bidder might be expected to offer for Lot 160. For the second time Terhune exchanged a meaning glance with the sergeant, and seeing the grim, determined set of the other man's mouth, appreciated that the detective was already convinced that their carefully set trap was sprung.

Terhune was scarcely less optimistic. The price offered by Droopy Moustache could bear only one construction—that one of the five books comprising the Lot was the volume for which Harrison had been murdered. But which one? Whatever the answer, one fact was emerging from the duel—whatever its title might be, Droopy Moustache was not trying to buy it for its intrinsic value. That had long been exceeded. In consequence, it was becoming increasingly obvious that the book was wanted for some other purpose, as he had himself suggested to the sergeant might be the case.

He nodded. Tuttell beamed. "Eleven," he said. "Eleven offered on my left."

"Fifteen," said Drooping Moustache.

"Fifteen," repeated Tuttell, looking at Terhune. "Sixteen it is."

"Twenty," said Droopy Moustache.

The booksellers were engaged in agitated, and low-voiced conversations. One of them... Francisco Perez... waved his arm, and called over to the porter who was standing by the rostrum, stolidly holding the bundle of five books.

"Let me see those books again."

"Yes, sir."

The porter carried the books across to Perez, around whom the nearer booksellers clustered in an inquiring group. Other worried buyers, too far off to see over the shoulder of Perez, called out or motioned to the porter that they, also, wanted to see the books.

Perez untied the string which held the books together, and after a quick glance at the other four titles, seized hold of the Shakespeare and opened it at the title-pages. A puzzled look passed across his expressive face, then he turned back to the flyleaf as if hoping to find an inscription there, which might be responsible for the high bidding. A shrug of his shoulders expressed his apparent failure as he passed the Shakespeare on to a curious, beckoning buyer. Then he picked up the remaining books, one by one, and gave each the quick, informed examination of a book-expert. As he placed each one in turn on the table before him it was eagerly seized by one or another of the group behind him, whereupon there were other similar, if somewhat less ostentatious exhibitions of mystification, or amusement, or irritation, according to personality.

Tuttell was quite content to wait until the booksellers had satisfied their curiosity, in case examination might encourage competitive bidding, but as soon as he noticed that the majority of the bidders had seen all they wanted he faced Terhune.

"Against you, Mr. Terhune, at twenty pounds."

Terhune nodded. "Twenty-five," Tuttell said.

"Thirty," said Droopy Moustache.

Tuttell's head turned. Terhune nodded. "Thirty-five," announced the auctioneer, turning to the other bidder again.

"Fifty," mumbled Droopy Moustache.

Terhune began to feel worried. What would happen if Tuttell had failed to catch the signal, and held him, Terhune, to his bid? Or, if the heir should get to hear of the episode through the Press—a possible contingency, if the local reporter's expression, and his swift-moving hand was any indication—and refuse to countenance the arrangements agreed between Tuttell and the police? It would be something of a minor disaster to be compelled to pay £50 or so for a lot worth considerably less than the same number of shillings.

Meanwhile, the other booksellers were beginning to enjoy themselves, as they sat back in their chairs and grinned, like Cheshire cats, at the spectacle of two mugs venting what must surely be personal spite, at the expense of their pockets. This was entertainment after their own hearts.

"Fifty on my left," Tuttell repeated significantly. "Fifty-five, Mr. Terhune? Ah! Fifty-five. Sixty, sir?" This to Droopy Moustache, who twitched a sparse eyebrow. "Sixty-five. Seventy. Seventy-five. Eighty. Eighty-five. Ninety. Ninety-five."

"One hundred pounds," Droopy Moustache bid tearfully.

"One hundred pounds. One hundred pounds." Tuttell looked at Terhune. "One hundred pounds on my left."

Terhune began to lose his courage. Suppose—suppose something went wrong! Suppose he had to pay £100 for five books worth no more than a few shillings each! It was too much to ask of any man. Besides, hadn't he proved his point already? Why force the price up any higher? One hundred or five hundred pounds! What was the difference—as far as the five books were concerned? The trap had sprung. Now it was up to Murphy to do the rest.

He decided to let the man with the droopy moustache and mouse-coloured hair have the Lot. Unfortunately, he glanced automatically at Murphy, as if to let the sergeant know that he was retiring. But Murphy nodded, not agreement, but a command to continue the bidding.

"One hundred and five," Terhune said hoarsely.

"One hundred and twenty-five," bid the other man.

Someone gasped his amazement. One of the booksellers laughed openly; others chuckled their contempt. One, indeed, went to the extent of discreetly tapping his head. A child called out shrilly: "Mum, what's that man paying all that money for?" Mum did not answer; she was thinking of all the things which could be bought for that amount, things she had wanted for years and years—all her married life—£125 for five books! Somehow, it didn't seem quite fair. She wasn't a Communist; not even a Socialist, but £125 would keep her old man employed for more than six months—

Sir George called out: "Stick to him, Terhune, my boy."

But Lady Kylstone, who was nearer, asked sharply in a low voice: "Surely the books cannot be worth that much money, Theo?"

"But the other man thinks so, too," Helena pointed out, defensively.

Terhune felt damp and sticky. He was sure he was sweating. And no wonder! £125! It was time gracefully to retire from the absurd contest. But he didn't! Instead:

"One hundred and fifty."

A sigh travelled across the lawn. What a moment! What a scene. One should thank one's lucky stars for having decided to stay! But what were the two men bidding for? Not just five ordinary books!

"Has the dear boy gone mad?" Alicia MacMunn asked in her penetrating voice. "Or are the books printed on gold leaf?"

"Please don't shout, Mother," Julia said testily. "I am sure Theo knows his own business best."

"Hey, porter, let me have another look at those books," snapped a buyer from London.

"One hundred and seventy-five," sighed Droopy Moustache.

Terhune took out his handkerchief, and mopped his forehead. It was all very well for Murphy to nod his head encouragingly, but the local reporter was fidgeting with excitement. Ten to one he would be telephoning Fleet Street within the next few minutes.

Lady Kylstone misinterpreted his expression. She leaned forward and whispered in his ear: "If you really must have the books, Theo, I will lend you the money."

Terhune hesitated, not because of what Lady Kylstone had said—he was not consciously aware of hearing a word—but because of Murphy's grim expression. Go on, it commanded. Go on. See how high the other man will go.

There was something to be said for seeing how much Droopy Moustache would give—not only would the measure of that limit convey to the police the extent of the man's urgent desire to possess the books, but also the measure of the financial strength of the gang.

"Two hundred," Terhune gasped.

There was a long pause.

"Two hundred and fifty," Droopy Moustache mumbled.

Terhune sighed—with relief! For one ghastly moment it had seemed as though the other man meant to leave him to carry off the prize. In any event, it did appear as though it might have been Droopy Moustache's last bid. It would be to tempt Providence to increase the last bid.

"Two hundred and fifty," Tuttell said loudly, "Two hundred and fifty on my left. Any more? Two hundred and fifty. On my left, two hundred and fifty." He waited, expectantly. "Mr. Terhune?"

Terhune shook his head, and Tuttell looked really disappointed. He suspected that the high-spot of the sale was passing on, and he regretted the fact. He looked at the other, booksellers.

"Two hundred and fifty," he said suggestively.

Two of the booksellers laughed.

"Two hundred and fifty for the last time," Tuttell said regretfully.

Silence. Then—Bang! Lot 160 was sold.

"Name?" Tuttell asked briskly.

"Cash," Droopy Moustache replied sadly. He walked towards Jameson.

"Lot one hundred and sixty-one," Tuttell began. "*Julius von Sachs's Lectures on the Physiology of Plants—*"

Droopy Moustache paid over to Jameson £250 in one pound notes, collected the five books which comprised Lot 160, and made his way through the bidders towards the path which led round to the front of the house. He soon disappeared behind a clump of lilac trees. At a sign from Murphy Thompson and Hutchins casually wandered off in the same direction—

I I

As far as Terhune was concerned, his duel with Droopy Moustache represented the highlight of the afternoon; the subsequent hours seemed tame in comparison. Excited at the prospect of news from Murphy later on, he found it difficult to concentrate on the bidding until, in a moment of abstraction, he nearly forgot to bid for one title which he had been trying to buy for a Canadian client for the past six months. He came to just as Tuttell was lifting the hammer. He secured the Lot—at a price, for Maggs was also after that particular title—but the moment had been sufficiently critical to ensure that, for the rest of the afternoon, he attended to the business on hand.

The first day's sale finished about four-fifty. Terhune looked about for Murphy, but was unable to see him. Before he could move Perez came up to him.

"Good afternoon, Mr. Terhune. I must speak with you for a moment, for I do not want to leave without presenting my apologies to you."

Terhune was surprised. He could think of no reason why the South American should apologize.

Perez smiled: his teeth were almost too perfect to be his own—though they were—and he had an expansive smile. A handsome devil, Perez, Terhune reflected. Unmistakably foreign, of course, with his dark complexion, and his black hair; somewhat exotic, too, but striking, all the same. Bet women look at him twice, he went on thinking.

"You cannot think why I should want to apologize to you?"

"Not really," Terhune confessed.

"For outbidding you on what your soccer football fans would call your home ground, no?"

Terhune chuckled. "Home or away, I can't pay eighty pounds for a first edition of *Adventures of Tom Sawyer* and three thousand eight hundred for an autographed first edition of *Alice's Adventures in Wonderland.*"

"But I thought I saw you bidding for both titles."

"You did—until the pace became too hot for me. I can't afford to lock up my capital for too long; I have to keep it turning over all the time. If it were not for that necessity I shouldn't have let you get away with Charnock's *History of Marine Architecture* for fifteen pounds."

"Ah! That was a bargain, I agree." Perez pulled out his cigarette case, and offered it. "If you will forgive unpardonable curiosity, Mr. Terhune, were you not being—er—rash in bidding so high for Lot one hundred and sixty? Or can it be that I am not quite the expert I have so far believed?"

His smile relieved the question of any suggestion of rudeness or impertinence, but none the less Terhune did not appreciate the necessity of having to give a reason for bidding up to £200 for books worth only a few shillings. The truth, obviously, was out of the question; to lie, equally so. His fellow booksellers would immediately become suspicious of him if, for instance, he were to try and bluff them into believing that one of the books in the Lot had a value unknown to, or overlooked by, them.

Yet what was the alternative between truth and lies? He could think of none, not at that moment, at any rate, so he began to feel damned annoyed.

Once again his expression was rightly interpreted by the South American.

"No, no, Mr. Terhune; do not answer, if you would rather not do so. I can see that the answer is a trade secret—"

Why not a half-truth? Terhune thought. "Not at all," he replied aloud. "I have no more idea than you what I was bidding for, Mr. Perez. As a matter of fact I was merely acting as a buying agent for Lot one hundred and sixty. If I had been bidding for myself I should have dropped out round about the pound mark."

"Ah!" The explanation appeared to satisfy. "As I have heard my friends in the United States say: 'There's a fool born every hour.' Or is it minute? Obviously your principal wanted the book for his own purposes, yes? Maybe the Shakespeare was a family heirloom!"

He smiled, but whether understandingly, or mockingly, Terhune could not decide.

"But now I must find a porter," the other man continued. "That one with the grey hair looks intelligent."

Terhune nodded. "Hoskins is still the quickest in spite of his age. Are you going back to town to-night?"

"No. I was lucky in booking a room at the *Saracen's Head* in Ashford. There are some Lots being offered to-morrow in which I am interested. I shall see you here, then?"

Terhune grinned. "D.V."

The South American held out a slim hand. "Until to-morrow, Mr. Terhune," His teeth flashed. "And more good hunting."

Perez and Murphy passed each other at the door.

"Our bird is at the police station in Ashford," the sergeant announced brusquely. "If you have the time to spare, Mr. Terhune, I should be obliged if you could come along to take a look at the books."

"I'm ready, sergeant, if you can strap my bicycle on your luggage grid—"

"I'll bring you back here. Coming?"

The two men were soon moving towards Ashford at a fast pace.

"The man's name is Smithson," Murphy explained. "He had kept one of Crouch's taxis waiting for him outside *Twelve Chimneys*, which took him direct to the railway station. He was waiting for the London train when Thompson requested his presence at the police station."

"Did he raise a rumpus?"

"He wasn't very obliging," Murphy said drily. "But Thompson has a persuasive manner, so Smithson went along to the station. Thompson then 'phoned me, and I went back to Ashford to interview our man—"

"I didn't see you leave."

"You were too busy bidding for one of Lewis Carroll's books."

"Which I didn't get. What did Smithson have to say?"

"Too much, damn him! The moment I began questioning him about his identity he pulled out a card. Here it is." Murphy passed over a large-sized trade card. "Do you know the firm?"

Terhune glanced at the card which bore the name: Henry Smithson, Representing Messrs. Langbridge & Co., Booksellers, Charing Cross Road, W.C.1. 'Libraries purchased. Speciality: Books in Foreign Languages.

"I know them; they have a small shop just off Cambridge Circus."

"Have they been established very long?"

"Ten years at least."

"Oh!" Murphy's exclamation was part puzzled, part disappointed. "When I asked him why he had bought Lot one sixty he looked at me with those ruddy, mournful eyes of his and asked me what business was it of the police what books he bought. Damn his nerve! If you ask my opinion, Mr. Terhune, that man isn't half as daft as he looks."

"What did you say?"

"I asked him if he didn't read the newspapers. When he said he did I asked him if he didn't know that the late owner of the books had been murdered not many weeks previously."

"I suppose he told you that he wasn't in the habit of reading crime stories."

"By God! that's just what he did say, almost in them very words. 'All right,' I says. 'That's as may be, sir, but it is because Mr. Harrison was murdered that the police are interested in finding out why you paid two hundred pounds for books worth only a few shillings apiece.'

"'Who told you they are worth only a few shillings apiece?' he asked. I told him that that was my business, so he shrugged his shoulders and said that a book was worth exactly what anyone was willing to give for it—"

"That was a nasty one," Terhune interrupted, "because it's true in essence."

"I know it is, blast the fellow! What's more, he didn't give me a chance of thinking out a snappy reply, because he went on to ask me whether there was any law to forbid a man paying a hundred times a book's reputed worth if he wanted it desperately enough to be that much of a mug."

"And then?"

"I told him that as he was so keen on law it might interest him to know that there was one which could deal with people who obstructed the police in the execution of their duty. But it didn't work; the blighter laughed in my face and said that he'd like to get back to London to-night, if I *didn't* mind. I told him he was free to go back to London any time he pleased, but that I should be extremely obliged to him if he would drop me even the merest hint as to his reasons for paying two hundred and fifty pounds for that particular Lot."

Terhune smiled; he thought Murphy's account of the interview was beginning to stray away from the strictly truthful.

"Did he oblige?"

"He told me to ring up his boss if I wanted any information. I had intended doing so in any event, just to check up our bird's credentials, so I got on the 'phone there and then. Langbridge himself answered me, and willingly answered my questions. It seems that last Friday a man who called himself George Collinson telephoned him, and saying that he had to go up to Scotland for a week or more, asked whether Langbridge could undertake a buying commission. Langbridge said, Yes, certainly, he would be only too pleased, etc., and what was it Mr. Collinson wanted bought? So Collinson spoke of the sale of books at *Twelve Chimneys* and said that he was willing to pay up to five hundred pounds for Lot one hundred and sixty."

"Five hundred!" Terhune whistled. "Do you mean to say that Langbridge undertook a commission like that, right out of the blue, and presumably from a complete stranger?"

"Yes and no. He wasn't a fool. He asked for cash before delivery. Collinson was willing. He said he would send the money, by registered post. Which he did, by the next post."

"What about collecting the books?"

"Ah! When Langbridge asked, at the time of this talk, where Collinson would like the books sent, the other man said, nowhere, he would call for them when he returned from Scotland, which would probably be some time this week-end. That's the position up to date. How does it strike you?"

Terhune did not reply immediately. The story was a mixture of the credible and the fantastic. It was credible that the man Collinson should get someone else to bid for Lot 160, particularly if he really were going to Scotland, Quite a number of book-collectors preferred to appoint other people as buying agents. He had himself bought for Mr. Justice Pemberton on more than one occasion. Also once for Edward Pryce, when the artist was abroad. It was equally credible that Langbridge took the precaution of asking for the money first, and that Collinson should send it by post, in one pound notes in case time precluded the clearing of a cheque. Indeed, the one, the only unlikely detail of Langbridge's story was the sum he was prepared to pay.

Five hundred pounds for Lot 160! If that amount were not incredible then his name wasn't—incredibly!—Theodore Ichabod Terhune!

Chapter Thirteen

"Well, what do you think of the explanation?" Murphy prompted impatiently. "Do you think it holds together?"

"I'm afraid it does, sergeant. From Langbridge's point of view it is quite an accepted custom of auction sales for men to bid for clients on a commission basis. Often the auctioneer himself is instructed to bid, sometimes his clerk, sometimes the porters. Langbridge would have had no reason for being surprised by a request to send a representative to bid for Lot one hundred and sixty."

"If he's in the trade, wouldn't the price have made him think there was something suspicious about a man—a stranger at that—being willing to pay up to five hundred pounds for a pound's worth of books?"

"Of course."

"Then that means he's no innocent, blue-eyed boy."

"Not so, sergeant. Most people connected professionally with any of the collector's trades—by which I mean antiques, stamps, old coins, pictures and so on—know that the world is full of amateur fools who can be persuaded, bluffed, or tricked into paying many times its worth for a reputed Old Master, or a Cape of Good Hope two-penny, or what would you."

Murphy laughed sourly. "Give me a nice, clean housebreaker."

"I agree, but I don't say that reputable dealers would take that much advantage of a mug. As far as Langbridge is concerned he probably thought that if Collinson were ready to fling so much good money away it was the man's own lookout, and that Langbridge & Co. might just as well have the commission as the next man."

"Humph! Maybe you're right, Mr. Terhune. I had already come to that conclusion myself, but I was hoping you wouldn't agree."

"Why?"

"Because a man in hand is worth two in the bush. If Smithson is an innocent party we shall have to let him go. I suppose you don't think that Collinson is equally innocent?"

"I don't," Terhune agreed with emphasis. "As far as can be judged at the moment Collinson's playing a wily game."

"He is that. He's sitting pretty, blast him! First, he wasn't taking the chance of coming down here to bid for the book himself just in case he might be seen, and recognized as having been in the neighbourhood about the time of Harrison's death. Secondly, he has used Langbridge as a cover, so that, if during the next few days he has reason for thinking that the police are on his track, he'll just not turn up to collect the books, and that'll be the end of any hope of trailing him."

Terhune shook his head. "I don't think the explanation is quite as simple as that, sergeant."

"Why not, sir?"

"Because Collinson restricted his maximum bid to five hundred pounds."

"Glory be! and wasn't that four hundred and ninety odd pounds more than the books were worth?"

"Listen, sergeant, we've already agreed, haven't we? that a book that's worth the risk of hanging is probably worth a hell of a lot more than five hundred pounds. Now, if Collinson were Harrison's murderer that must mean that he was willing to go to any lengths to get hold of a certain unknown book. He failed on two occasions. Do you think he would risk losing it on a third occasion by limiting his maximum bid to five hundred pounds?"

"You certainly have a way of complicating life," Murphy exclaimed protestingly.

"I haven't finished yet," Terhune retorted cheerfully. "If the book Collinson is after—I'm still assuming him to be Harrison's murderer, by the way—has an intrinsic value I don't think he would have taken the chance of appointing Langbridge, or any other bookseller or collector for that matter, to bid for it."

"In case the other fellow bought it on his own account?"

"Yes."

Murphy turned curiously. "So?"

"Collinson doesn't want the book for itself but for some other reason."

"By which you mean information, I suppose, along the lines you suggested some weeks ago?"

"Yes, Otherwise it is impossible to make any sense of the murder, the attempted theft, and the bid of two hundred and fifty pounds."

The sergeant made a growling noise. "Bedad! It still doesn't make sense to me."

By this time they had reached the outskirts of Ashford. The conversation ceased, for want of anything further to discuss, As soon as they reached the station Murphy took his companion into a private room, and pointed to the five books on the table.

"There's your two hundred and fifty quids' worth, Mr. Terhune. I examined them earlier on, but couldn't find a damn' thing suspicious about them. See if you have any better luck?"

Terhune sat down before the books, and picked up the uppermost volume, which was the *Grammar of the English Language* by Curme and Kurath. He thumbed fee pages over quickly, to find out whether any were stuck together, but they were all as they should be. Conscientiously, he repeated fee test, more slowly. At the same time he checked the pagination, to make sure that there were no missing pages. About two-thirds of the way through he found that he had jumped from page 175 to 180. He began to feel excited; as usual his expression reflected his emotions.

"You've found something?" Murphy asked anxiously.

"Some pages stuck together." He gave a short, thrilled laugh. His bubbling enthusiasm, in conjunction with his round, youthful face, and his complete ingenuousness made Murphy wonder, not for the first time, whether Terhune were really as old as he admitted: he had so much zest for life.

Terhune pulled a penknife from his pocket, and with one of its blades carefully parted the stuck pages. Inside was—nothing!

"Damn!" Murphy exclaimed viciously.

Terhune pointed to the stain which discoloured pages 178 and 179. "Toffee!" he guessed. "I think Smith Minor must have dipped into this book."

None of the other pages was stuck to its neighbour so he turned to the end papers—those pages which conceal the insides of the covers. A long shot, but the trick of concealing a thin document beneath an end paper was not an unknown one. The end papers of the grammar, however, though bearing traces *of* thumb marks, had quite obviously never been tampered with since the original binding operation; the binding tape was visible, also the edges of the cloth which covered the front of the boards; even the boards themselves.

Then he opened the covers to their fullest extent, and squinted along the inside of the spine. Again with no result. He returned to the body of the book, opened it at random, and peered through a magnifying glass at the printed page on the chance of identifying cypher marks. Nothing. He turned to another page. Nothing. And another page. Still nothing. He thumbed through the pages once more, still looking for any sign of pen or pencil marks—marks no larger than microscopic dots maybe. But in the end he had to put the *Grammar to* one side.

"Nothing?" Murphy asked.

"I don't think so."

Next, the *Concordance*. No pages missing; none stuck. End papers, stained with use, but apparently untouched. Spine also undisturbed. Lastly, examination of a page, opened at random.

Murphy was watching Terhune's face. "Well?"

Terhune indicated the open page. The sergeant stared down at it from behind a slim shoulder. A tiny ink-marked tick indicated: *John i, 1. In the beginning was the Word—*

The thin lips tightened. He needed no prompting to realize the possible significance of the tick. It might refer to *John*, to *one*, to the phrase: *In the beginning was the Word*—or even specifically to one of the six words: to *in* or *the* or *beginning* or *was* or *Word*. It might be "in clear," or in cypher. Or the phrase itself might not be of significance, but only its position on the page—113th line. Or maybe the pertinent clue was neither the phrase nor its position, but the page number: 564 in the Concordance. Or the number of the page on which begins the Gospel according to St. John in some specific edition. The possibilities were legion.

Lastly, the tick might bear no significance at all save as evidence that a previous owner had turned up, or proposed to turn up, the verse of St. John in which the phrase appeared.

"Turn over," he ordered brusquely.

Terhune did so. The next few pages were unmarked, but on page 572 another phrase was ticked. *Job i, 16: Yet he shall perish for ever, like his dung.*

"Go on, sir."

More clean pages, then another tick. And elsewhere, more and more ticks. Twenty or more in the space of less than three times that number of pages. Presently Terhune gave up turning over the pages and glanced up at his companion.

"A code message—or the work of a Bible student?"

Murphy shrugged. "When you've finished with the book I'll get Baker to copy out every ticked phrase—we can test for codes later."

"He had better have it right away; I'll be looking through the other three while he is working on the *Concordance*."

Murphy took the book and vanished; Terhune picked up the *French and English Pronouncing Dictionary* and began to test it as he had done the other two books. While he was doing so the detective returned, and watched without saying a word.

In neither the *French and English Dictionary*, nor Brewer's *Dictionary of Phrase and Fable* did the two men find anything that was in any way suspicious, but in the *Complete Shakespeare* they again found themselves faced with the problem of whether certain passages from *Hamlet, King Lear* and *The Merry Wives of Windsor* had been marked—this time by vertical lines instead of ticks—by a lover of Shakespeare, or by the writer of a cypher message. In case the answer might lie in the second of the alternatives Terhune copied out the lines, together with details of page numbers, act and scene numbers, and so on. He had just finished when a young, sharp-faced man in plain-clothes—Baker, no doubt—returned with the *Concordance*, and a sheaf of papers which he passed over to Murphy.

These, as soon as Baker had gone, the sergeant threw down on the table with an annoyed gesture.

"Exit Tim Murphy from the Great Book Mystery," he announced.

Terhune guessed what had happened. "The Chief Constable has called in the C.I.D.?"

"Not yet, but he will, bedad! as soon as I give him the latest information," the sergeant commented, sourly.

II

Mrs. Mann, the big-hearted, big-busted woman who "did" for Terhune, was in a hurry.

"Get on with your meal, do," she told Johnny, the eldest of the numerous progeny who sat round the breakfast table. "As for you, Bert, if I catch you teasing your sister again I'll not give you your penny this week."

"He's just pinched me again, Ma," Alice called out tearfully, as Mrs. Mann turned her back.

"Tell-tale Alice! Tell-tale Alice!" chanted Alfred, the youngest.

"You shut your mouth, young Alf; it ain't none of your business."
Mrs. Mann slapped some slabs of bread down upon the table as she faced
Bert. "Did you pinch Alice after what I said?"

"Nasty Alice made a face at Bert," Alf supplied in his baby treble.

"Did you, Alice?"

"She did, Mum——" Bert began.

"You shut up. Alice can answer for herself. Did you, Alice?"

"I only looked at him."

"You fibber, Alice," Bert exclaimed indignantly. "You put your
tongue out."

"I didn't."

"You did."

"I didn't."

"Be quiet! Both of you!" The harassed mother poured out cups of tea.
"Just for worrying your poor Ma when she's in a hurry neither of you
won't have a penny this week. Johnny! How many times will I have to
speak to you. Put that Sexton Blake down, and get on with your meal."

"But, Mum, the murderer's just going to blow up a house with
Sexton Blake in it."

"I don't care if he's going to blow up a dozen houses. You hurry up
or you'll be late for school again, and next time teacher reports you for
being late it won't be my hand you'll feel on your bottom but your Pa's."

"Pa doesn't hurt nearly as much as you do, Mum," Johnny announced
cheekily.

"Don't you give me none of your sauce, Johnny," Mrs. Mann ordered
wrathfully as she scraped some margarine across six thick slices of
bread; one for each child.

"Why are you in such a hurry to-day, Mums?" asked Peggy—not
without difficulty, for her mouth was full.

"I'm going to the sale."

"Are you going to buy some more of them nice cups?"

"I don't know what I'm going to buy, so don't start asking questions. Perhaps a nightshirt for Dad."

"Mum?"

"What is it now, Johnny? Haven't you finished your porridge yet?"

"Are there any Sexton Blake stories among the books? If there are would you buy some for me?"

"What nonsense you talk. As if a nice old gentleman like Mr. Harrison would have filled his head with that kind of reading!"

In her haste to pack the children off to school so that she could have her own breakfast, and get away to Market Square to prepare Terhune's, it seemed to Mrs. Mann that her children were even more troublesome and obstructive than usual. However, with little more than seconds to spare she bustled them out, and then swallowed a few mouthfuls as she moved back and forth from table to sink, and drank cups of black tea in between washing up successive bowls of dirty crockery. Soon all was moderately ship-shape in the small council house which the Mann family occupied, so she dressed herself in best hat and coat, gathered up shopping basket and purse, and bustled out to repeat the performance—in miniature, as it were—at 1, Market Square.

She soon reached the shop, which she went to enter by way of the private door overlooking Three Hundreds Lane. She inserted the key in the Yale lock, which she tried to turn. When it did not move she exerted more force—of which she had more than the average, for she was a large, big-boned woman. To her surprise instead of feeling the key turn in the lock she heard a faint click as the door swung open.

For a moment or two she stood and stared through the open doorway. A worried expression disturbed the usual serenity of her big, flat-featured face. In all the years she had "done" for Mr. Terhune she had always found the door properly closed in the mornings. Untidy he might be in his rooms above, in matters concerning the ground floor he was always scrupulously tidy and careful—meticulously so she might have added had she ever heard of the word, or known its meaning.

Then her eyes twinkled, and her big, thick lips parted in a mischievous smile. Naughty, naughty, she reflected magnanimously, and wondered where he had spent the late hours of the night before, and with whom. Not with Miss Julia, that was certain. Miss Julia wasn't no blue-stocking; she could take drink for drink with anyone; but she couldn't abide anyone who got even the least bit tiddly. So meandered her thoughts as she entered the tiny hall whose only excuse for existence was to enclose the staircase leading up to the floor above. She took off her coat—the morning was warm enough to make the garment unnecessary, but it offended against her code of respectability to walk through Bray without a coat. This she hung up on one of the pegs inside the tiny clothes-closet under the stairs, but the hat remained on her head, not to be taken off before settling at home for the evening.

Back to the foot of the stairs, which she had nearly reached when she saw that the door connecting the hall with the shop was half open. This fact was so definitely contrary to accepted custom that she became uneasy. From early childhood she had been burglar-conscious. She faltered, fearfully hesitating to approach any nearer to the ominous—to her it was very definitely ominous—gap between door and surround, beyond which all was shadowy.

A French clock in the dining-room above chimed sweetly. The noise restored her courage to some extent; it reminded her that she was not in the dark world of night, but in the sparkling, sunshiny world of day. Little more than an arm's-length from her people were going about their accustomed business, the postman, the milkman, the baker. She had only to lift her voice to summon help. Especially if she left the street door open.

She half-opened this door. The early sunshine streamed in, and made a golden carpet on the floor for her to step on. A bicycle bell tinkled. Both sight and sound were so commonplace as to be comforting. Without more than a little trepidation she moved forward into the shop.

In spite of the sunshine behind her which dispersed some of the nearer darkness, and enlarged her elongated shadow into elephantine proportions, the rear part of the shop remained shrouded in gloom. She switched on the electric light, but with a readiness to shriek and run at the first sight of anything tragical—Heaven alone knows what she expected to see, but as a fairly frequent visitor to either the Odeon or the Cinema at Ashford she had developed an appetite for sensation.

Her first glance revealed nothing unusual; everything was in its customary apple-pie order. Was she vaguely disappointed that her courage was wasted? Possibly. At any rate a second glance gave her some satisfaction. In the farthest corner of the shop was a convenient space, camouflaged with bookshelves, which Terhune retained as the packing and unpacking "department." She saw there something she had never seen before in her memory—a pile of books heaped on the floor.

She had no further doubts. Something unusual *had* happened. Mr. Terhune never, never left books on the floor. He fussed far too much over the silly things. So, as there were books on the floor—and worse, in an untidy heap—she was sure that he had had nothing to do with leaving them there. The only possible solution was, that the shop had been burgled. She had known it from the first; now she was surer than ever.

Fear developed, flourished. Everything was quiet overhead. There wasn't a sound to be heard, yet by now he should be in the bathroom, bathing and shaving. Had—had something happened to him? Something terrible? Had the—the thieves attacked him and left him unconscious? Even—even dead? Her fears returned. Her thoughts chattered even if her teeth didn't. She stepped back from the door leading into the shop— leaving the electric light still burning—and hurried back into the sweet sunshine. She stood for awhile by the open street door, debating whether or not to find companionship, but once again the familiar aspect of the street scene eased her sensational fears. Mr. Terhune couldn't have come to any harm. It wouldn't be right on such a lovely day. Besides, what would he think of her, taking some neighbour into his flat?

She pressed her rather thick lips together in decision. Although she couldn't persuade herself to close the street door she went upstairs, stamping loudly, and coughing. She arrived at the upper landing, and looked in at the kitchen, which faced her. All there was in order. She turned the corner. The bathroom door was open, the bedroom door closed. Farther along the passage the door of the den was closed; at the far end, the door of the dining-sitting-room was open.

The sight of the two closed doors did nothing to ease her mind, but now that she had ventured so far she wasn't going to turn back for anyone or anything. She stamped along the passage, and rapped loudly on the bedroom door.

"Mr. Terhune!" she shouted.

A moment's silence and then, sleepily: "What is it?"

She could almost have wept with relief. "Can you come out?"

"Coming."

She heard a short series of indistinct noises. The door opened. A tousle-haired Terhune, in pyjamas, slippers and dressing-gown, joined her.

"Do you want me, Mrs. Mann?" Then, as an afterthought:

"Why are you so early? Is anything wrong?"

"I'm later than usual, but—"

He did not let her finish. "Lord! I have slept."

"Mr. Terhune, you've been burgled," she told him breathlessly, excitedly.

"The devil!" He glanced towards the dining-room.

"Not the flat; the shop! Books all over the floor—"

He did not wait to hear more. He ran downstairs, the ends of his dressing-gown flapping behind him. Mrs. Mann followed as closely as she could.

He dashed into the shop, halted, looked about him—and due to his having moved farther into the shop than she had, failed to see anything out of place. He waited for her, wondering whether she was out of her mind, or merely playing a joke upon him.

"Mrs. Mann, are you quite sure——"

"Over there in the corner," she replied, pointing a red hand, swollen from washing. "Behind that there bookshelf. Besides, the side door was open."

He crossed to the farther corner, and looked down at the untidy collection of books which littered the floor.

"I'll be damned!" he muttered feelingly, for the books were those which he had bought at the auction the previous afternoon.

Chapter Fourteen

He knew better than to touch anything. He hurried over to the telephone, dialled O and asked for Murphy's number. Within a few seconds he was speaking to Murphy.

"Bedad, Mr. Terhune, you're up early. You'll not be telling me anything fresh has happened?"

"It has. Another burglary—"

"Not *Twelve Chimneys?* There was a man on guard there all night. Has anything—"

"Not *Twelve Chimneys*, sergeant. My place, this time. The shop."

"The shop! You don't mean *you've* had some books stolen? Bedad! This book stealing is becoming a mania."

"I don't know yet whether anything has been stolen; I'm not touching anything until you come along—that is, if you're free."

"I haven't had breakfast yet, Mr. Terhune, but as soon as I've swallowed a bite and 'phoned through to the Super, I'll be along."

"Fine. And just to give you an extra appetite—the only books which have been touched are those which I bought at the sale yesterday."

"I—I—you—what!—Bedad!—" Murphy was still stuttering as he rang off.

Something less than an hour later Murphy arrived at the shop. By that time Terhune had bathed, shaved, dressed and breakfasted.

It was not a normal sergeant who entered the shop. Usually upon meeting Terhune for the first time in a day his expression was homely and warm with a broad, friendly grin. To-day his lips were tight-pressed, his face worried.

"I don't like your news," he began without preamble. "It has me worried. You didn't buy any really valuable book yesterday, did you?"

"Forty-five pounds was the highest price I paid for a single book, and eighty pounds for one Lot containing three titles. The majority of the Lots I bought were in the ten to thirty shillings class."

The detective looked quickly at the neatly arranged shelves which surrounded him. "None of the other books missing?"

"None, And none touched so far as I can judge without stocktaking."

"Where are the books from *Twelve Chimneys?*"

"Over there." Terhune led the detective over to the far corner.

Thin-lipped, Murphy stared down at the pile of books. "The untidy bastard!" he muttered. "If you want any circumstantial evidence that the man who broke in here last night was the one who killed Mr. Harrison, there it is. Housebreakers aren't the tidiest of people, damn 'em! but this swine seems to ruddy-well take a delight in emptying everything on to the floor." He pointed to some small, empty packing-cases. "Were the books in those?"

"Every one of them. Wilson didn't bring them along until just after seven last night, so I didn't trouble to unpack."

"How did the man or men break in?"

"Through the private door."

"Did they force it?"

"No. They must have found a key to fit."

"The lock's a Yale, isn't it?"

"Yes."

"Then they didn't just find a key just like that. Take it from me, Mr. Terhune, they must've got hold of one of your keys long enough to cut a duplicate. How many have you, by-the-bye?"

"Three. One on my chain, a spare in the desk upstairs; the third Mrs. Mann keeps."

"Ah! A quid to a tanner that's the key they borrowed. Is the woman to be trusted?"

"Implicitly."

"Then you'll probably find out that she had a visit from a man calling himself the sanitary inspector, or something of that sort." Murphy sank on one knee beside the books and carefully examined the pile, and the space about it, for clues. Later he stood up; his face expressed resigned disappointment.

"Nothing, blast 'em! Now, if you'll begin checking off to find out what is missing, I'll have a look around."

For some time the two men did not speak again, each being too busy on his separate task. For his part Terhune proceeded methodically with the work of checking his purchases. He went through the list backwards, for the earlier lots had consisted mostly of miscellaneous titles, to give latitude for possible late-comers to arrive in time to bid for the more expensive titles. He had not finished by the time Anne arrived, so he enlisted her help, and the work of sorting out the lots went more quickly.

Presently Murphy returned. "Not a damn' thing to be found," he told them gloomily. "How are you getting on?"

Terhune was beginning to feel worried lest he had brought the sergeant out to Bray without good cause. "All the named titles are here, sergeant."

"You mean, there isn't a book missing?"

"I mean that we've only the odd Lots to sort out now, those containing several miscellaneous titles because none was worth listing separately."

"The ten bob Lots?"

"More or less."

The sergeant was alarmed. "If the titles weren't catalogued how can you check which ones, if any, are missing?"

"Fortunately Miss MacMunn listed them when we began work on the inventory that first night." Terhune picked up another book from the pile, now considerably smaller, and turned to Anne. "*A Shorter Oxford Dictionary?*"

She looked down a list of titles. "Lot one hundred and eighty-two."

"*Hall and Steven's Geometry*."

"The same Lot."

As the check continued the books were transferred, one by one, from an untidy heap on the floor to neat stacks on nearby shelves. At last only one remained.

"*Letters of Queen Victoria*," he announced.

"Lot one hundred and sixty-nine." She went on breathlessly:

"Every title is ticked off except one, Mr. Terhune."

"Well?"

"*A German-English Dictionary*, part of Lot one hundred and seventy-seven."

The two men exchanged glances, The thin lips all but vanished, so tightly did the sergeant press them together in exasperation. He turned abruptly in Anne's direction.

"Are you certain?" he rapped out.

She nodded. "Yes, Mr. Murphy."

"Let me look." He snatched the papers from her hand and began to examine them. As he turned over the pages of the lists his frown became more marked. Finally he reached the last page, and soon thrust the bundle back into her hands.

"There's no mistake. If those lists are reliable the only book taken last night was a copy of *A German-English Dictionary*, Bedad! sir, if that poor devil Harrison hadn't been deliberately murdered I should begin to think there was a group of damned lunatics at large. Why should anyone have wanted to pay two hundred and fifty pounds for a lot of junk yesterday afternoon and then, a few hours later, risk being sent to prison for the sake of stealing a two-a-penny dictionary?"

Terhune took off his horn-rimmed spectacles, and began, in an absent-minded manner, to polish the lenses with his breast-pocket handkerchief.

"Do you know, sergeant, I'm beginning to think that we are the lunatics, not they."

"If I'm soft it's this book-stealing business that's made me. What's making you feel so blue, sir?"

"Because it's just beginning to dawn upon me that we've been made fools of."

Murphy respected Terhune's opinions. His glance sharpened. "Go on," he ordered.

"Suppose that bid of two hundred and fifty for Lot one-sixty was merely a blind—a red-herring—"

No need to say more; Murphy had an intelligence which did not require prodding.

"Bedad!" he burst out, "And I'm thinking it's right that ye are, sir. By all the Saints! they've tied us up in knots. They must have heard of the trap we set for thim, so they set their own bait, and it's only ourselves that walked into it. Because that ruddy fool yesterday paid two hundred and fifty pounds for a lot of tripe of course we had to jump to the conclusion that the book the murdering divils had tried to steal must be one of Lot one-sixty. And all the time they laid low, and didn't even bid for the real book but watched out for him who did, so that while we poor fools were keeping an eye on that shop in Charing Cross Road they could break into the home of the buyer, and steal the book. The cunning devils!" he raved. "May their perishing necks stretch from here to high Heaven!"

Terhune considered the sergeant's explanation to be an oversimplification of the circumstances. How had the thieves come to hear of the trap being set for them, for instance? How could they have been sure that they would have the opportunity of stealing the book from the purchaser? How could they be sure that the buyer would not examine his purchase as soon as he had taken delivery of it, and so discover its secret? Yet he could think of several simple explanations, which would supply a more or less satisfactory reply to his questions, so he was inclined to agree, in principle, with the sergeant's deductions. As for the sentiments expressed anent the stretching of necks, with those he was in utter and entire agreement.

Meanwhile, what was the next move? This time, it would seem, the book really had been stolen. Its recovery was now, disappointingly, simply and solely a police matter. So, too, identification and arrest of the thief. A matter, he suspected, not of genius, deduction, intuition, but of monotonous drudgery, and patient waiting.

"Have you found anything worth while?" he presently asked, in a toneless voice.

"Not a damn' thing. As far as I can judge, the thief, or thieves, having entered by way of the private door—a simple enough matter when one has a key to fit—came straight into the shop here, looked about for the books which you had bought at the sale, found them, tipped the whole lot on to the floor, searched among them for the title they wanted, and then left by the way they had come. Just like that! As easy as pie!"

"A pro. job then?"

"It bears all the hallmarks of being a pro.'s work, just the same as that job at *Twelve Chimneys*. Except for one fact, of course. I just don't see pros. taking chances for the sake of a ruddy dictionary. So there's one thing the burglary here has done, it's finally convinced me that your theory is right, Mr. Terhune. In some way or other that dictionary conceals information that is worth a hell of a lot to somebody. So much so that that somebody was ready to chuck as much as five hundred pounds down the drain just to distract police attention from the real objective."

"What's happening about the books Langbridge bought?"

"The Chief Constable telephoned to the C.I.D. last night. They have agreed to watch the shop in Charing Cross Road and arrange with Langbridge that he should give them a signal when the man arrives to collect the books and the balance of the money! But after what happened here last night, it's rotten apples to a peanut that the man never will collect. At the same time they are going to check up and keep an eye on both Langbridge and Smithson. Personally, I don't think that will do any good. I haven't any doubt now about them being innocent parties. The cunning devil who organized the theft of the dictionary is too subtle to have made use of anyone who could be traced back to him."

"What's the next move, sergeant?"

The other man grinned unhumorously. "Now that the horse has bolted I'm going to make sure that the stable door is shut."

"The sale?"

Murphy nodded. "I want to see that everything is ready in case the burglary here was a sort of double-double bluff to hide the pulling off of another smart-Alec trick. I don't plan to be staying there all the time to-day; I have some work to do roundabouts. But I'll join you at *The Hop-Picker* during the interval, to give you any news, if you'd like to be there. For my own part I shall be more than ready for a drink."

So it was agreed, and presently the two men went to *Twelve Chimneys* in Murphy's car. The second morning's sale proceeded without incident—boringly so where Terhune was concerned. Having no interest in the bidding his thoughts constantly reverted to the previous night's burglary. Even though he knew himself to be normally a sound sleeper he was particularly annoyed at having slept so well the previous night. Housebreakers, he knew, did not make a habit of being noisy while committing a burglary, but the knowledge that the thief, or thieves, went about their business almost directly beneath his bedroom seemed to add insult to injury. If only something had awakened him—why not the unease of intuition, for instance?—by now the mystery of the *German-English Dictionary* might have been solved, and the identity of Harrison's murderer known.

The time passed slowly, but at last the hammer fell for the last time before the luncheon interval. After a word to one of the detectives Terhune started off for *The Hop-Picker*, which he reached just before

Murphy. Murphy's expression, as he entered the bar, was all the advance information Terhune needed to realize that the sergeant had no good news to report.

His first words confirmed this, so Terhune ordered drinks, to make the occasion a little more cheerful, and changed the conversation; beer and gloom, he considered, did not make good companions. The conversation somehow drifted from a cert. for the 2.30 the next day to cricket. Kent was shortly to play Sussex at Canterbury, so they began to discuss the prospects of Kent's winning the match. Murphy had begun to express a readiness to bet two to one in ten shilling notes that Kent would win when he was interrupted by a burly-shouldered, red-faced man who had just thrust his way to the bar.

"Well, well, well! This is a stroke of luck, Mr. Murphy. Dinged if it isn't. You're just the man I want to see."

Murphy's attitude was not over genial. "What do you want to see me about, Mr. Pyke?"

Pyke glanced doubtfully at Terhune. "I've summat dinged funny to tell you about if you've a minute to spare."

"Is it anything that mustn't be said before Mr. Terhune here? If so you'd better see me later."

"The Mr. Terhune of Bray?"

"Yes."

Pyke held out a huge hand. "Pleased to meet you, Mr. Terhune. My name's Pyke, Fred Pyke, of Dew Pond Farm. I've heard of you, You're getting to be quite famous, dinged if you ain't." He leaned forward confidentially. "You being a clever man, Mr. Terhune, if you don't mind me saying so, blow me if you won't be just as interested in what's happened on my farm as Mr. Murphy here."

In spite of his preoccupation Murphy became interested. "What has happened?"

The farmer was not slow to accept the invitation to begin a story which he was obviously bursting to tell.

"You remember Grey Dawn," he began, his voice hoarse with fury, "I mean, that there grey mare what you recovered for me two year ago. Well, she foaled this year; as nice a filly as any farmer in this district has set eyes on. Sunshine Susie, I calls her, 'cause she was out of Grey Dawn by Black Knight, see!" For a moment it seemed as though he were ready to chuckle appreciation of his own sense of humour, but between his anger, and his eagerness to continue, he checked himself.

"Ding me! if last night, when I was going across the fields I didn't see the animal galloping round and round in a circle. I knew what that meant so I telephoned the vet.—"

"What did it mean?" Murphy interrupted.

"Meningitis, ding it!"

"I didn't know foals suffered from meningitis. Go on."

"Well, I 'phoned the vet. as I was telling you, 'cause I didn't want to take no chances of losing a valuable animal, but the ruddy man had gone to Dover for a day or two to see his old ma, and wasn't expected back home till to-night.

"I didn't want to do nothing without old Hyde, for there isn't a better man for horses from the North Foreland to Land's End, but I didn't sleep none too easy last night thinking of Sunshine Susie. As soon as I could this morning I went to see how she was faring." The anger in his voice deepened; his expression turned thunderous. "And, by God! I found out that somebody had been messing about with her. If ever I lay my hands upon him—" He banged one of those hands on the bar, and as Terhune glanced at the coarse, muscled hand he felt certain that he would not care to feel himself within its clutch.

"Messing about in what way?" Murphy asked.

Blue veins in the farmer's red face throbbed with passion. "Some blasted swine had branded Susie behind the right ear."

His companions were startled. "Branded?"

"That's what I said, Mr. Murphy, and that's what I mean."

"For what would anyone be wanting to brand the foal for, Mr. Pyke? To steal it?"

"Steal it be dinged! If the ruddy man wanted to pinch the beast why didn't he do so there and then. No, I'll tell you what it was done for, Mr. Murphy. I'm too successful a farmer for some of the people heres-about, so somebody's out to ruin me through my stock, that's what! And it's up to the police to find out the swine that dared to muck about wi' my Susie, and right quick, too, because I don't want no other animals to be mucked about with."

"All right, all right, Mr. Pyke," Murphy urged soothingly. "Let's get this business straight. Are you quite sure the animal was branded overnight?"

"It wasn't branded yesterday at this time, and that's sure. Do you think I don't know nothing about my own beasts?"

"You also say that, when you went to bed last night, the animal was developing meningitis?"

"That's right, she was."

"And as far as you know none of your employees branded the foal?"

"They'd know I'd half kill 'em if they did, so they wouldn't be likely to."

"The animal was branded behind the right ear?"

"It were."

Murphy nodded. "One more question. Is the brand mark a definite one—I mean, is it identifiable?"

"By God, it is and all, and d'you know what? A cross, Mr. Murphy, that's what. As sure as I'm a living man, Sunshine Susie's been branded with a cross."

Chapter Fifteen

Of the two men listening to Pyke's story Terhune was the more startled, for the mention of a cross brought back to his mind something which he had quite forgotten.

"That's funny!" he exclaimed, with a significance which caused the sergeant to turn abruptly.

"What is?"

So Terhune told his two companions of the upturned sods which Julia and he had found some weeks previously.

"If I see anyone digging up sods in my fields I'll shoot the bastard," the farmer burst out. "Look here, Mr. Murphy, it seems to me that it's time the police got busy—"

"All right, all right!" Murphy interrupted testily: "Are there any loonies living in this neighbourhood?"

Pyke's expression was blank. "Loonies?"

"Somebody a bit soft in the head," the sergeant explained with scarcely concealed impatience.

"I knows what a loony is," Pyke retorted, aggrieved. "But I don't know as how I can call anyone to mind."

"Or anyone who might have developed a religious mania?"

"There's the rector, Mr. Murphy. Real religious he is—"

"Of course he is. Isn't that what he's supposed to be. But you don't think the rector goes round branding horses with a cross, do you? Or carving crosses in sods?"

The farmer was somewhat reproachful. "I don't think the rector would do that."

"That's what I'm trying to tell you. But is there anyone else you know who can't keep away from the subject of religion?"

"Not that I knows of."

"Well, I'll report the matter at the station, and inquiries will be made, Mr. Pyke. Is that all?"

The hint could scarcely have been more obvious, but Pyke was either thick-skinned or slow-witted. He lingered on.

"I hope you catches the man soon; I don't want Sunshine Susie mucked about wi' any more—"

"By the way, I forgot to ask you—is the animal dead?"

"Susie dead! Naw, that she ain't. She's as well as ever she was, but that's no fault of the bastard who branded her."

"What do you mean, as well as ever? What about the meningitis?"

Pyke chuckled. "Believe it or not, without a word of a lie, that filly has no more meningitis now than what I have." He became angry again. "But it's no thanks to the man who branded her, and I'm warning you, Mr. Murphy, if ever I sees him mucking about wi' my Susie or my fields my old twelve-bore will give him a peppering in his backside."

"I shouldn't be too free with that gun of yours if I was you," Murphy warned the other man. "You might find yourself in trouble. And now, if you don't mind, Mr. Terhune and I have some business to discuss." This time the sergeant discarded subtlety altogether by turning his back on Pyke, The farmer moved away, and joined a friend who was watching a game of darts.

"I know Mr. Pyke. He would keep us jawing here for the next hour if we gave, him half a chance. All the same, it's funny, this business of branding Susie with a cross. What do you make of it, Mr. Terhune?"

"The same as you; a form of religious mania. I can't think of any other explanation."

Murphy's face expressed his disgust. "As if we haven't enough trouble on our hands as it is. But getting back to the business on hand, there's one point that's occurred to me since I left you this morning. The books in Lot one hundred and seventy-seven weren't listed separately, were they?"

"No. The only description was *Six Works of Reference*."

"Then the man who's organized the theft of the dictionary must either have come down himself, or sent somebody else, during one of the View days, to look over the Lots and find out which one contained the book he was after?" He didn't wait for the obvious reply to his question, but continued gloomily: "I wish I had anticipated that move; I should have seen to it that we kept some sort of a check on everybody who entered the house to view."

"By asking for names and addresses?"

Murphy smiled thinly, "And invite a false name and address? No, sir, we should have asked to see some proof of identification—a driving licence, for instance. But I'm wasting time, talking of ifs and ands."

Terhune nodded. "Your speaking of the man's coming to find out which Lot the dictionary was in makes me realize that we've overlooked a fact which may have some significance—though I don't quite see why."

Murphy was eager. "Well, sir?"

"I suppose we can assume that, as the dictionary was the only book to be stolen, the thief must have had previous knowledge that that particular title was the one he was after?"

"Yes," the somewhat puzzled sergeant agreed.

"But I don't think he had that information on the night Harrison was murdered. It seems possible, therefore, that he has only recently learned which title he was looking for."

The puzzled expression became more pronounced than ever. "I don't follow you, Mr. Terhune. How could a man look for something without knowing what it was he was looking for?"

"Listen, sergeant. The book which was stolen from my shop last night was a *German-English Dictionary*, probably one of an edition of several thousand, and not worth more than a few shillings at the most. Now, if you broke into a library for the specific purpose of stealing a dictionary, would you expect to find it on the shelves among books which anyone with half an ounce of common sense could see were of some value? More especially when it must have been quite obvious that other shelves were kept only for reference books."

"Bedad! I shouldn't, and that's a fact!" Murphy's eyes became anxious. "Does that mean that the theft of the dictionary is a red herring after all?"

"Maybe, but I don't think so. I have an idea that, on the night Harrison was murdered, the thief didn't know the title of the book he was looking for, but that he did so when he broke into the house when Miss MacMunn and I were starting the inventory. I noticed that he went straight across to the shelves each side of the window, but at that time I concluded that he was merely continuing at the point where he had left off when he was interrupted. But as I've said before, I don't think that that knowledge, even if it is true, is going to be of any help in tracing the thief."

"Don't be so sure of that, sir. If your theory is right it means that another party's involved in the crime, and the more people there are mixed up in the business the more chance there will be of us getting on the track of one of them." The sergeant turned gloomy again. "Not that we've started to get on anybody's track yet. It's cars that have us beat. By having cars they can come here from London, and clear off back there again all within a few hours. If only they had had to put up for the night somewhere in the neighbourhood that would have given us something to work on, but they didn't, and that's that."

"Then you're sure they didn't stay anywhere in this district?"

"Absolutely!" Murphy stated definitely. "I mean, of course, not at any of the hotels. We've checked up on everyone who stayed at any hotel within a radius of ten miles on the night of Harrison's death, and on the night *Twelve Chimneys* was broken into for the second time." He shrugged his shoulders in a disconsolate manner. "Now we are making a check on last night, but I'm not hopeful at all, at all."

The two men were silent for a time. Heedless of the cheerful buzz of conversation which filled the small bar they stared mournfully at the rows of bottles, pewter and glass mugs, cartons of cigarettes, and all the other items which lined the shelves behind the bar. Consequently they were startled when a metallic but vaguely familiar voice behind them said:

"Are you two attending a funeral this afternoon?"

They turned quickly, to gaze into the sardonic face of Detective Inspector Sampson, of the C.I.D.

"Bedad!" Murphy exclaimed. "Inspector Sampson!"

Terhune grinned sheepishly. "Hullo, inspector. What's brought you down to this part of the world?"

"Your activities, Mr. Terhune."

Murphy groaned. "I thought it wouldn't be long before a C.I.D. man came poking his nose into our business." It was not Sergeant Murphy speaking now to Inspector Sampson, but Tim Murphy, to John Sampson, for the two detectives, so oddly contrasted in every way, were firm friends.

"What did you expect? You shouldn't have begged your Old Man to call us in to finish the job."

"Bedad!" Poor Murphy nearly choked. "The only begging I did was to beg him to keep you out of it. One would think we weren't capable of doing more than catch an odd poacher or so, or charge a wife-beater. 'We must call in Scotland Yard, he moans, the silly old bee, every time something a little juicy happens. What I say is—"

Sampson chuckled. "We know what you would like to say, sergeant. But if it's any consolation, you might like to hear that if your Old Man hadn't called us in we should soon have been suggesting it ourselves."

Murphy's jocular mood vanished as he appreciated the significance underlining Sampson's words.

"What's to do, inspector?"

"Did you know that I had been temporarily seconded to the Special Branch?"

The sergeant became tense with interest. "Bedad! And I did now, for wasn't it yourself that told me? But in that case for what were you sent down here to help us with this book-stealing business? You'll not be telling us that the Special Branch is interested in the theft of a ruddy dictionary?"

"That's why I've come down, to find out whether we are or not."

Murphy rubbed his hands gleefully. "I'm thinking this calls for a round." He saw Terhune make a slight move. "And I'm the chair, Mr. Terhune," he added quickly, "So what's yours? The same?"

"Please."

"And yours, inspector?"

"Half a bitter, for me, sergeant."

The drinks were served and sampled. Then Sampson's scarred face looked towards his companions in turn. "I only arrived back in England from Belgrade last night so my knowledge of what has happened is almost nil. Before I start talking I'd like an account of everything that has happened to date, sergeant."

"Very good, inspector." Without further preamble Murphy gave the C.I.D. man a full account of Harrison's murder, and subsequent events. Sampson listened intently, and only interrupted when he wanted a point made clear. As soon as he had heard everything he offered cigarettes.

"I suppose you've both heard of the Inter-Allied Committee of the Institute of Art and Design? In case you've forgotten, this is its brief history. When Germany overran Europe in nineteen-forty she started looting its treasures on a grand scale, officially and unofficially. Pictures, statues, tapestries, books, manuscripts—all was grist to the German mill. In Poland, Norway, Denmark, Holland, Belgium and France, national and private museums were robbed of famous masterpieces and works of art, which were sent to Germany. Many of these—perhaps the majority—were despatched to German museums. Others found their way into the private homes of the Nazi leaders—Goering, Goebbels, old Ribbontripe, and the other rats, but were subsequently hidden in caves, coal-mines, and other underground hiding places. Still other treasures were pinched, surreptitiously, by the lesser lights, and sent back to Germany as private loot.

"In the two following years other countries were similarly robbed of their treasures—Greece, Yugo-Slavia, Russia, and later, Sicily and Italy: it didn't much matter to a German whether they robbed friend or foe so long as they robbed somebody. Anyway, by the middle of nineteen forty-four Germany had amassed enough treasures to fill Aladdin's Cave two or three times over.

"By that time, however, the United Nations were already anticipating final victory. But that wasn't all. Some bright spark, bless his white hairs, foresaw the chaos which was likely to arise at the end of the war when all the unfortunate victims of the German gangsters began to clamour for the return of their precious art treasures. To prevent the possibility of some first-class squabbles, and to see that justice was done, it was resolved that an Inter-Allied Committee should be set up, whose work it would be to do these things: *a*, to compile a list of all looted treasures from all the different countries, *b*, to trace and recover as many treasures as possible, and *c*, to identify same and restore to their rightful owners— or, at any rate, their nineteen thirty-nine owners."

Terhune grinned. "Is that a crack at Napoleon?"

Sampson nodded. "More or less. It might make an interesting question for a Brains Trust—when does a treasure *de facto* by military loot become a treasure *de jure?* A decade? A generation? A century? Or by right of might? All of which being by the way I'll return to the Inter-Allied Committee.

"When the idea of the Committee was first thought of it was realized that the work would be difficult, but I doubt whether anyone anticipated that it would be quite so difficult as it is being. This is due to an unfore-seen complication. Towards the end of nineteen forty-four, when the knowledgable Germans realized that eventual defeat was inevitable, the dyed-in-the-wool Nazis began to think of the future. Just as the Germans of the First World War began planning the Second World War as early as nineteen eighteen, the Nazis of the Second World War began to make their plans for the Third World War in nineteen forty-four."

Murphy shook his head. "I can't swallow that, inspector!"

"Swallow what? That the Germans began planning the next war in nineteen eighteen, or that the Nazis did so in forty-four?"

"Both."

"Then you are ignoring historical facts, sergeant. The naval revolt, and the so-called civilian collapse in nineteen-eighteen were deliberate, cold-blooded manœuvres to create the fable of the stab in the back of the invincible German army. Ask Mr. Terhune here if I'm not right."

Terhune nodded. "There's plenty of evidence for that theory."

Murphy was shaken but still obstinate. "Maybe there is, but what plans did they make during the Second World War for the Third—which God forbid!"

"For one thing they began to put the blue-prints of the later V-weapons into cold storage."

"Are you telling us the Germans still have some secret weapons which we don't know anything about?"

"I do," Sampson replied harshly. "Though I didn't say that we don't know *anything* about them. Nor did I say they had reached the stage of being actual weapons. I said blue-prints, and I mean blue-prints. Of an atomic rocket bomb, for instance."

"You're very cheerful," the sergeant said despondently.

"I'm very realistic. Still, you needn't be too gloomy about the future—our own Intelligence aren't sitting on their seats doing nothing about anything. Nor are our scientists—Back Room Boys to you! But hushing up future V-weapons was not the only Nazi move towards preparing for the next war. They believed that, if there was to be a Third and Final World War, it was necessary to send the Nazi organization underground, and to maintain it while it was there. To do that money was needed. And one way to ensure a future supply of money was to send underground, with the Nazi organization, some of the art treasures they had looted."

"How would they get money by hiding art treasures?"

"How do you think? By selling them from time to time."

The puzzled Murphy shook his head. "I suppose I'm dense, but how could they be sold? The moment any well-known treasure was put up for sale wouldn't this Inter-Allied what-not say: 'Hey! Nobody can buy that picture. It's stolen property, and anyone who buys it does so at his risk. It belongs to the Thingamy Museum, and is to be restored'?"

Sampson smiled, but the effect was to make his scarred face appear more saturnine than usual.

"To some extent you are right, but there are some collectors in this world who have no scruples about buying stolen property, and who would readily take the risk of doing so."

"What for?" the sergeant persisted. "What would be the use of anyone buying a stolen picture—the *Mona Lisa*, for the sake of argument. He would never dare to exhibit it, even to his own friends, for fear of being reported and punished."

"That is where you are wrong, Murphy. There are some characters whose ego thrives on the knowledge of possessing something which nobody else has. To a slight degree that feeling is responsible for the ceremony of marriage. The man takes a woman to be his own, so that nobody else may share her—"

"Quite right, too," Murphy exploded indignantly. "A fine world we should have if no man could be certain he was the father of his children."

"Of course, but that is not the sole reason for marriage. Suppose that your wife were incapable of having children, would you then not have any objection to your wife having a love affair with another man?"

"Bedad! What do you take me for?"

"Don't mistake me, Murphy. I'm not trying to make out a case for free love; I'm merely trying to prove that man has an inherent desire to possess something—or somebody—which is his alone."

The sergeant made a grudging admission. "I see what you mean about wives, and even about goods. It wasn't so long ago that Mr.

Terhune was saying something of the same sort about stamps and books and so on. All the same——" He hesitated.

"Well?"

"I can understand a man liking to have something rare which he can show off, but what ruddy satisfaction would anyone get from owning something which he wouldn't dare show to anyone?"

"Only the state of mind induced by an abnormal form of egoism. Like that millionaire in the States, for instance, who possesses one of the finest collection of pictures in the world. If he can help himself he won't let anyone else enjoy the pictures. Occasionally he gives way to the extent of allowing a few chosen art students to look at them, but that's all."

Murphy muttered something unintelligible under his breath.

"Now that you see what I mean——" Sampson grinned sardonically, "you will understand what the Nazis had in mind when they hid a selection of those art treasures which could most easily be smuggled in and out of countries. They knew that sooner or later they would find private people who would be willing to pay high prices for them just for the sake of owning something of international repute. And that, briefly, is the problem which has been facing the Inter-Allied Committee ever since the war finished. They have already obtained some evidence that this sort of traffic has been going on. To check it, and to recover as many of the stolen treasures as possible they have co-opted the assistance of nearly every police force in the world."

"Is that what you've been seconded to the Special Branch for?"

"It is."

Murphy whistled. "Lucky devil!" he muttered with a suspicion of envy. Then his expression became puzzled again. "If you're doing special work on this art-treasure business why were you sent down here?" he questioned.

The inspector did not answer directly. Instead, he turned to Terhune.

"Have you ever seen the Little Bible?" he asked.

Chapter Sixteen

T erhune shook his head, "I've not had that luck, I've seen illustra-
tions of it, of course; Hazelbrouch has a picture of it in *Ecclesiastical
Treasures of Europe*. So has Fuller in *Craftsmanship*. But the only travelling
I did before the war was to the Isle of Wight."

"What's all this about a little Bible, inspector?" Murphy asked.

"One of the most valuable treasures in the world is a Greek minuscule
Bible, known in antiquarian circles as the *Codex Johannis*, or sometimes
as the *Eltzbacher Bible*, but more popularly, as the Little Bible. It was
written, in the tenth century, by a man who was born Franz Eltzbacher.
As a boy he joined one of the monastic orders, from which moment until
the day he died he was known as Brother Johannes. On the eightieth
day of the year nine hundred and eight, which was the eve of Brother
Johannes' twenty-first birthday—so the story runs—Our Lord visited
him in a vision, commanding him to devote his skill to the service of the
Holy Father by making, with the help of no other pair of hands than his
own, a Bible that, on completion, should be no larger than the Prior's
pocket missal and yet miss out no word of the accepted scriptures.

"The following morning Brother Johannes related the story of his
vision to the Prior. The Prior immediately interpreted the vision as a
sign that Our Lord looked with favour upon the Priory, and he ordered
Brother Johannes to begin the work that very day, invoking God's
blessing upon the project.

"During the next thirty years Brother Johannes worked constantly
to produce a Bible that should be worthy of Our Lord, yet be no larger
than a pocket missal. On his fifty-first birthday the work was completed. The then Prior officiated at a Solemn High Mass, after which

the Cardinal blessed the Bible. As he did so Brother Johannes fainted with excitement. Upon recovering consciousness he found that he had been stricken with blindness."

"A cheerful little story!" Murphy commented.

"Brother Johannes and his fellow monks thought so, sergeant. His blindness was construed as a sign that he was in a State of Grace—he that had executed such an exquisitely beautiful work should no more be saddened by having to look upon the ugliness of life; henceforward he would live in a beautiful world of memory, of his own making, in which only his Bible should exist. When he died, exactly ten years later; it was said of him that no man had ever known happier years than those last ten. As a consequence, when it was suggested, in the middle of the eighteenth century, that Brother Johannes should be canonized, this supreme honour was denied his memory because he had not suffered in the service of Our Lord.

"However, to return to the Little Bible. This, naturally, became a treasured possession of the Priory. When the Priory was destroyed by an earthquake in the spring of eighteen-fifty eight the Little Bible was miraculously preserved. The stones of which the Priory had been built were subsequently transported to the town of Lamos in Greece, where they were used to build Holy Trinity Church. As soon as the new church had been built and consecrated, it housed Eltzbacher's Bible. And there it remained, in spite of the many offers to purchase it which were made—the last being for a sum rumoured to have been in the neighbourhood of nearly a quarter of a million pounds, in nineteen twenty-five, by the Metropolitan Museum in New York."

Murphy whistled. "Quarter of a million!"

The inspector nodded. "It's a big sum. But the Patriarch refused to sell. In nineteen forty-four, on the night when the retreating German army passed through Lamos, the Oberst in charge of the rearguard was ordered to enter Holy Trinity Church, remove the Little Bible from the crypt in which it was safeguarded, and despatch it under guard to Berlin.

"The Little Bible reached Berlin—and disappeared. We still do not know where it was hidden. What is known is this. Nearly six months after the cessation of hostilities in Europe the Little Bible was sold to a Roumanian book-dealer, living in Paris, for thirty thousand pounds. The transaction was reported to the French police, who sent detectives to his address to interrogate the man. They arrived too late; somebody had tipped him off that the Inter-Allied Committee were on his track, so he had cleared out of the country, together with the Little Bible. What happened subsequently to either the dealer or the Bible we don't know.

"Last night, when I was told that a man had been murdered during the attempted theft of a book, I began to wonder whether the Little Bible had travelled to England." Sampson stared at Terhune. "Well, sir?"

"Every piece fits into the pattern," Terhune murmured. "The sale of seventy-five thousand pounds of shares for cash, in one-pound notes, the journey to Stockholm, the murder of Harrison— For my part, inspector, I should say at once that your theory is right, but for one fact."

"And that, sir?"

"I looked at every book in Harrison's library, and I'm ready to take an oath that the Little Bible was not one of them."

"Perhaps it's in a hidden safe of sorts," Murphy suggested.

The inspector ignored the sergeant's remark. "You looked at every book, Mr. Terhune, but did you *open* every one?"

"All except what Sergeant Murphy calls the tripe—odd volumes not worth listing on their own."

Sampson nodded, tight-lipped, eager. "Were any of the odd volumes on the large side?"

"Some of them, of course. Especially the older works of reference; the dictionaries and so on."

"Large enough for a space to have been hollowed out of the middle pages—"

"Bedad!" Murphy exclaimed. "You'll not be telling me that you could hide one book inside of another?"

"That's an old trick, Murphy. All you have to do is to glue the inner pages together to make them solid, and then hollow out a space in the middle, leaving the pages loose at either end. Until or unless one tried to open the book out flat nobody would take it to be any different from any other book,"

"So that accounts for thim thieving devils stealing that dictionary from Mr. Terhune's shop last night. It wasn't the dictionary they wanted, but what was inside."

"I'm afraid so, but don't let's jump to conclusions too soon. This dictionary that's missing, Mr. Terhune, was it large enough to hold the Little Bible?"

Terhune grimaced miserably. "I don't remember it in detail, inspector. You see, what I did on the first night Miss MacMunn and I set to work on Harrison's library was to divide the ordinary books into two piles, one consisting of books which were worth mentioning by title in the catalogue, the other, of books which, not being worth more than a shilling or two on their own, were to be sold in miscellaneous lots. I didn't trouble to open and examine books in the miscellaneous pile; I left it to Miss MacMunn to tie them up in bundles, list them separately, and allocate Lot numbers while I classified the more valuable books."

The inspector nodded understandingly. "If I'm permitted a guess I'd say that the binding of the dictionary was pretty badly rubbed—isn't that the proper term, Mr. Terhune?—on the principle that the more dilapidated it looked the less likely anyone would be to handle it.

"Anyway, for argument's sake let's assume that the *German-English Dictionary* contained the Little Bible inside it. As a rough reconstruction of what led up to the burglary last night I'd say that something like this happened. When the Roumanian dealer left France he possibly went to Stockholm. As his purpose in buying the Little Bible was to make money he probably started casting about him for a likely buyer, maybe by making inquiries among other book-dealers, maybe by writing direct to likely buyers—maybe he had had previous dealings with Harrison. In any case, Harrison was a famous collector of old books—"

"*Incunabula!*" Murphy interposed with sly patronage.

"What?"

"Isn't that the right term for pre-sixteenth century publications, Mr. Terhune?"

Terhune chuckled. Sampson glared at the sergeant. "I'll bet you had never even heard of a word like that before Mr. Terhune gave you the low-down! Anyway, this Roumanian fellow—I can't pronounce his name—is sure to have heard of Harrison, and probably guessed that such an ardent collector would give his right hand to possess the Little Bible. Probably as a result of correspondence Harrison determined to try and buy the Little Bible, even if it cost him half his fortune."

"I think that he did buy it eventually—"

"Why so cheaply?" Murphy asked. "I should have thought that a book worth a quarter of a million pounds to the Metropolitan Museum in New York was worth more than seventy-five thousand pounds."

"That's not a bright remark, sergeant. Are you forgetting that the Bible was stolen property? No reputable purchaser would have bought it at any price."

"I was thinking of some of thim millionaires in the States. I'm sure one of them would have sprung as much again."

Sampson nodded. "Probably, but if I'm allowed another guess, then I'd say that the Roumanian may have had the wind-up, because of the activities of the Inter-Allied Committee, and was willing to accept less for the sake of making a quick sale. Besides, as far as can be judged, he didn't do so badly—he more than doubled his money."

"I still think that a man has to be crazy to pay seventy-five thousand pounds for something he wouldn't dare to show off to anyone." Murphy had the manner of a man who would never, to his dying day, understand such egoism. "But if Harrison was willing to do it I suppose there are other equally crazy people in the world only too eager to do the same, which is why the poor devil was killed."

"What's on your mind, Murphy?"

"Suppose this Roumanian fellow didn't write only to Harrison! Suppose he sent to some other European book-collectors, say! Harrison was the first to reply, and got the goods. But suppose one of thim others goes along to this Roumanian bloke and says: 'I'll buy the Little Bible from you.' What happens? The Roumanian answers: 'Too late, me boy. I've already sold it.' 'Damn and blast it!' says the first chap. 'I wanted it that bad. Tell me who bought it. I'll buy it from him.' So this other flaming idiot hears that Mr. Harrison has the book. Over he comes to this country—seeing we're sure that Harrison was killed by a ruddy foreigner—and says: 'Look here, Meester Harrison, you hava da Leetle Bible. I want her. You paya beeg sums of money for it, no. Well, I giva you as much and a lot more if you sella da Leetle Bible to me.' Then Harrison says: 'Go to the devil. I'm not selling.' So the other fellow says: 'Very well, if you no sella da Leetle Bible to me my friend he keel you,' and the second dirty swine sticks a flaming knife into Harrison's back. Doesn't that sound something like, inspector?"

"Perhaps," Sampson's manner was non-committal. "And then?"

"Then the two men began looking for the Bible, but were forced to skedaddle before they had finished their search. Probably they didn't go far away, meaning to return and finish the job as soon as the coast was clear. Unfortunately for them we set a police guard, but they must have been keeping a pretty close watch on the house; for, on the very first night we took the guard away they broke in again, not knowing that Mr. Terhune was there."

Terhune shook his head. "I think you are almost right, sergeant, but not quite, I don't think they waited for the police guard to be withdrawn before making the second attempt to steal the Little Bible—personally, I think they would have been capable of dealing with the policeman without much compunction."

"What do you think was the cause of the interval between the two attempts, Mr. Terhune?" Sampson asked.

"I think the answer to that lies in the answer to another question—how did the murderers know that the Little Bible had come into Harrison's possession?"

"I suppose the Roumanian gave them the information."

"Yes, but in doing so he probably didn't say anything about its being hidden inside another book—he may have taken it for granted that, once he had got the little Bible back home Harrison would keep it in some other hiding-place. What may have happened is this: when the murderer failed to find the book in the first place somebody returned to Stockholm to question the Roumanian—perhaps it was suspected that he had double-crossed them. The Roumanian may then have suggested that the Bible was still inside the *German-English Dictionary*, though, of course, we've no proof that it was the Roumanian who put it there—"

"Most likely it was, though," Murphy broke in. "I wouldn't mind betting that most people who travel about on the Continent carry some kind of a dictionary about with them."

Sampson joined in with: "Especially a German-English dictionary, in this instance, because it was probably a German who carried the Little Bible from Berlin to Paris, or wherever the Roumanian was when he bought it from the Nazis."

Murphy nodded. "I think you're right, Mr. Terhune. As soon as the murderers were told that the Bible might be inside the dictionary they returned to *Twelve Chimneys* for a second shot at stealing it. Luckily you were there; after that there was always a double police guard on the house, which didn't give them a third chance. That's when they decided to use cunning instead of brute force. As soon as the library was on view somebody went along to the house, found out which Lot the *German-English Dictionary* was in, and then invented that ruddy silly business of bidding two hundred and fifty pounds for another Lot, which they didn't want, to lead us up the garden path." Murphy's anger returned at the thought of the trick which had been played upon the police.

"Doesn't that presuppose that they knew that a trap was being set?" Sampson questioned in a dubious manner.

Murphy frowned. "I suppose it must, inspector, but I'll be damned if I know how."

"Well, that's your business. Meanwhile, between the three of us I believe we're not a long way away from the real facts, which means that the men who killed Harrison now have the Little Bible in their possession, which is very much my business. Whatever happens it mustn't leave this country."

"It would be a feather in your cap if you were able to restore the Bible to that thingamy church in Greece, wouldn't it, inspector?"

"It would, Murphy," Sampson agreed simply. "And if I'm to put it there, there's no time to waste. You're quite convinced, aren't you, that there are foreigners mixed up in the killing?"

"I am that. First, there's the method of death. A stab in the back isn't a British way of killing a man—"

"I hope you're not going all Little Englander, Murphy," Sampson interrupted sharply. "I've helped to send two people to jail for stabbing, and they were both British."

"I'm not saying it never happens," Murphy protested. "But more often than not if there is a stabbing job there's a ruddy foreigner mixed up in it somewhere or other. But as I was starting to say—" He paused pointedly, though a friendly grin robbed the rebuke of any offensiveness.

The inspector laughed. "Sorry, sergeant. Go on."

"First, the stabbing. Second, the weapon. It looked foreign; you know, dangerous enough but all fancy-like; the sort you'd expect to buy in Sicily, or Africa, or some place like that. Third, when the house was broken into on the night Mr. Terhune was there he heard one man shout out something that sounded like something in a foreign lingo."

"That's right, inspector."

"You didn't recognize the language, Mr. Terhune?"

"I'm sorry I didn't. I'm no linguist. But for what it's worth I'd say that it sounded more sibilant than guttural."

"You mean, it was either Italian, or French, or Spanish?"

"Not French. I think I should have recognized a word or two."

"Even Parisian argot?"

"Not that, of course. But I think you would be wrong to concentrate on the three Latin-root tongues. Some of the Slav languages sound sibilant to the English ear. At least, they do to mine."

"It couldn't have been Greek you heard?"

"It could have. It could also have been anything else."

"We'll leave it at that for the moment. The main fact is that you are convinced that you heard a foreign language being spoken?"

"Absolutely."

"Right! Were there any foreigners at the auction sale?"

As the last question had been addressed to him Murphy answered it. "Three that we know of—by which I mean, that Mr. Terhune knows of. A book collector from Denmark, and two dealers with offices in London, one a South American, the other a Pole."

"He was naturalized English during the war," Terhune explained. "The Pole, I mean."

"I'm beginning to think our man wasn't' one of them three, inspector."

"Why?"

"If it was only a question of finding out who bought the Lot with the dictionary in it he could have paid any Tom, Dick or Harry to be at the sale to do that for him."

Thin-lipped, Sampson stared at the sergeant. "You have a high opinion of the man who's behind this business, haven't you?"

Murphy nodded. "He's a cunning devil, and so are his blasted accomplices. It took brains to think out that trick of employing Langbridge to bid up high for the Shakespeare Lot. Besides, there have been three breakings, with not a smell of a clue, if you count the knife which nearly killed Mr. Terhune out of reckoning."

"Why should I do that?"

"Because, if it was bought somewhere in Europe that won't help much in tracing its owner."

"I didn't know you were a natural pessimist, Murphy?"

"Get away with you, inspector! I'm too Irish to be a pessimist. But I don't mind admitting that this case has had me beat from the first. There's been nothing to get me teeth into."

Sampson nodded sympathetically. "I know the feeling. Anyway, even if you are Irish, Murphy, I'm not taking any chances on your psychic powers. You may be right about thinking the man we're after was too smart to make himself conspicuous at the auction sale, but all the same I'll have our people check up on the three foreigners you mentioned just now, Mr. Terhune. Would you let me have all the particulars you can about them?"

Terhune related all that he knew of the three foreigners whose names or faces he had recognized at the sale, while the inspector jotted down some notes in his book. Afterwards Murphy passed on certain other information concerning his previous investigations and inquiries.

"Anything more?" Sampson asked presently, looking at his companions in turn. When there was no reply his thin lips tightened.

"There seems damn-all to go on with at the moment."

"Didn't I tell you there were brains behind this business?" Murphy complained.

"You did. Well, he'll need them if the man intends to smuggle the Little Bible out of the country. I only hope he hasn't already done so."

"Now who's a pessimist?" the sergeant asked not uncheerfully.

Chapter Seventeen

Following Murphy's quip the three men pushed their way to the temporary snack bar which the two Houlden brothers, opportunists both, had erected in a small club-room adjoining the bar. For the next fifteen minutes they ate plates of ham and tongue, and mustard pickles, followed by biscuits and cheese, and discussed every aspect of the crime in the hope of bringing to light some fresh fact which might help Sampson in his investigations. Nothing of any consequence resulted. Afterwards each went his separate way; Sampson to London, Murphy to Ashford, and Terhune to *Twelve Chimneys*.

When the sale was resumed in the afternoon Terhune had a busy half-hour, during which he bid successfully for several Lots which were quite unsensational but entirely resaleable. But when the higher-priced books came up for offer he found himself outbid by the better-known book-dealers and had, metaphorically, to take a back seat in the proceedings.

As soon as the sale finished for the day he obtained his ticket for his purchases, and passed it on to Wilson for collection. Then he cycled home for tea. Afterwards he relaxed in his chair in the study and began work on the new catalogue, of which his purchases from *Twelve Chimneys* were to form the bulk of the entries. For a time he worked with a will, but feeling a trifle weary he presently relaxed. Naturally, he began to think of *Eltzbacher's Bible*.

His first reactions were bitter. It was bad enough to reflect that he had handled the world's fourth most famous book without being aware of the fact. It was worse to realize that it was his carelessness which was partially, if not wholly, responsible for the thief's having finally obtained possession of it. If only he had taken the trouble of thumbing over the pages—or rather, trying to do so—he would have learned the secret of the *German-English Dictionary*; he would have found out that the apparently innocent-looking book did not open out, he would have investigated, he would have exposed—*Eltzbacher's Bible!*

He writhed mentally with misery, self-reproach, regret. What a discovery that would have been! What joy to have handled the Little Bible; to have been in personal possession of it, however temporarily! What pleasure to have been directly responsible for the return of the treasure to the custody of the church which it had graced for centuries! Instead of which, through carelessness that was almost criminal, the Bible was now on its way to God knows where, perhaps not to be available for exhibit to the common people of the world for generations.

Why hadn't he opened the dictionary, if only to make a quick check that no pages were missing? Had Julia's presence distracted him to the point of making him careless in neglecting his duty? If so then it was surely time that he took stock of himself, and forswore social pleasures.

This chastening mood persisted longer than the occasion deserved, but slowly he began to see things in their right perspective. He was, after all, an expert on the purchase and sale of second-hand books. What other expert would have wasted valuable time by giving more than a cursory glance at a badly-rubbed, obviously out-of-date, *German-English Dictionary* that wasn't worth more than a few coppers? Possessing a deep-rooted sense of justice he presently absolved himself from the charge of carelessness, or a dereliction of duty. But regret remained, and the inevitable: "If only—"

At this point his thoughts turned upon the things he had heard that morning from Sampson. He had read brief, and usually vague, accounts of the work of the Inter-Allied Committee of course. He was aware of the fact that the Germans had pillaged Europe of a large proportion of its art treasures; he knew that the art experts of the world had been meeting in committee for many years past in order to hear evidence of identity, and to order the restoration of this or that treasure to this or that museum. What he had not suspected was, firstly, the extent of the looting which had taken place during the years of German occupation, and secondly, the long-term plans of the German Nazis to start a Third World War in order to achieve the centuries-old dream of the German Junkers: world-domination.

What lay behind this incurable lust of the Germans to make slaves of the rest of mankind? he wondered. What kind of mentality was it that, even after two shattering defeats, could still believe that they alone—or that any race, for that matter—were destined to be masters of the world? Why were a people, whose dogged perseverance, patience, and outstanding organizing ability made them capable of conquering the world by peaceable means, such as scientific discovery, commerce and the like; why were these people so determined to; use martial force instead?

It was easy to admire them by thinking superficially: here are a people who refuse to admit defeat: here are a people who are determined to attain their ambition at no matter what cost to themselves; national death, if needs be. Yes, indeed, it was easy, especially for another people who were equally slow to recognize defeat, to find something to admire in this quality.

But what was the truth? The truth was that the German people; were as dangerous in defeat as in victory, because it was not national death which they used as a stake in their reckless gamble for supremacy, but international death. Civilization itself, for who could doubt but that civilization, which came so near to being wrecked in the Second World War, would inevitably collapse if it were to be involved in a Third World War. A fantastic, long-range war of automatons, he reflected. A hideous war that would force entire communities underground like so many moles. A war of electric buttons. A war of unmanned, unseen, unheard, and probably unheralded death. A war that would be won by the nation which committed the greatest possible destruction in the least possible time, by new and improved atomic bombs, or other weapons as yet undreamed of.

Could any sane, normal people deliberately plan such a holocaust? In spite of prejudiced forecasts, and sensational headlines, he would, of his own accord, have hesitated to believe it possible. But Sampson was not given to exaggeration or sensationalism: having stated, calmly and unequivocally, that the Germans were hoping to promote and win a Third World War by financing continued scientific research on automatic, long-range weapons, there could be no doubt as to the truth of what was happening behind the façade of normal German life. Somewhere, German scientists were at work perfecting the means of causing the wholesale massacre of innocent lives. And the money that was enabling this to be done was, in part, coming from the surreptitious sale of art treasures, looted from the very countries whose eventual subjugation was to be achieved as a direct result of the secret research! A perfect paradox for the cynic!

More ironic still was the fate which had apparently overtaken the Little Bible. Originally dedicated to the glory of God it had now, it seemed, become an instrument of the devil. Stolen from Greece at the cost of human lives and unparalleled human misery, it had been sold by the German looters for the equivalent of thirty thousand pounds sterling. Yet that comparatively small sum, invested in gilt-edged stock of a neutral country, was enough to produce in interest an amount round about one thousand pounds per annum, a competence large enough to employ a patriotic scientist full time, or perhaps two assistants.

Had many such treasures disappeared? he wondered. Sampson had been guarded when touching upon that aspect of German criminality, yet it seemed pretty certain that he would not have been seconded from his usual duties without good reason. In fact, reading between the lines as it were, Terhune had the impression that quite a number of art treasures were still untraced.

Not all, of course, were as valuable as *Eltzbacher's Bible*. Besides, even were there more than a handful of treasures which, as stolen property, could raise as much as thirty thousand pounds, it was doubtful whether there were many men who were, at the same time, both wealthy enough to waste so much money, and yet devoid of scruples. No sooner had he reflected upon this than the cynical thought obtruded itself that many men achieved wealth only by casting out all scruples.

But granted that many of the looted treasures were likely to realize only a few thousand pounds each, it could well be that the total amount realized would help to maintain one or two fully equipped and fully manned laboratories dedicated to the discovery and perfection of weapons that would eventually establish the supremacy of the German race. He possessed imagination—without it he would not already have achieved some success as a writer—but having a practical commonsense his imagination usually restricted itself to the limits of normalcy. For once it did not do so. It indulged in prophecies. He saw vague images of flood-lit laboratories, and workrooms, underground in both its literal and metaphorical sense, with grim-faced, square-headed, square-jawed men concentrating upon their experiments; draughtsmen bending over design boards and blue prints; skilled workmen fashioning intricate mechanism.

He bridged time with the ease of an athlete jumping a three-foot hurdle. Now he saw underground hangars filled with vague, indefinite shapes resembling the V1's and V2's of the past war, together with even more vague, more indefinite weapons which his non-mechanical imagination was incapable of delineating more clearly. He saw a military control room, map-lined, desk-studded, with men sitting in front of control panels, waiting for a signal. He heard rather than saw that signal given, but most certainly saw gloating-faced men lean towards their control panels.

Next his imagination transported itself to an unprecedented height above the earth. All Europe was stretched below him in relief, from the Bering Sea to the Mediterranean; from Cape Finisterre to the Iron Gate. He saw, at first glance, a continent where cows chewed the cud beside slow-flowing rivers, where factory chimneys smoked fitfully, where workmen processed the amenities of civilization, where their wives bent over washtubs in sunlit backyards and gardens, where children raced about in school playgrounds. A continent blissfully unaware of the Angel of Death hovering above. And then, one second later, he saw strange things happen in the land called Germany. He saw hayricks, cottages, garages, deserted factories vanish, to expose a thousand sites from which a stream of projectiles was being fired, north, south, east, west. Breathless moments later flames flashed in half a dozen capital cities, and smoke slowly mushroomed into the still air. He saw huge blocks of buildings disintegrate into mounds of rubble; he saw defenceless London, Paris, Rome, Stockholm, Moscow crumble into ruin as shells, rockets, flying-bombs and other incredible weapons crashed down upon them with unimagined speed and regularity.

He smiled wryly. Such fantasies were unduly pessimistic; not all the scientists in the world lived in Germany; surely during the years since the end of the Second World War scientists of other nationalities had devised some means of defence against unheralded attack? He sincerely hoped so, for had not the world already had a foretaste of what would happen if man's ingenuity were to remain directed on the evil of destruction instead of the blessing of construction? Yet even if some method of defence had been devised to come into operation before whole cities were completely demolished, the undeniable fact remained that, if ever an unsuspected attack were to be made, in the first few minutes of it thousands of people would die, and thousands of buildings would be utterly destroyed.

There was only one way of preventing such a catastrophe, he reflected. Science would have to be kept in the limelight of publicity, and prevented, at all costs, from working in secret. And wealthy art patrons who were ready to finance them indirectly by the purchase of stolen art treasures would have to be told that any such secret transaction would incur a severe penalty. Perhaps even death! Why not? A man whose selfish motives might later cause the death of innocent people deserved death or worse.

The Little Bible, unfortunately, had already served the damnable purpose for which it had been looted from Holy Trinity Church. But Sampson had indicated that there were other treasures still hidden in Germany which were only waiting for buyers who would pay the highest prices for them. They, at any rate, would have to be stopped from changing hands—

An interruption disturbed his thoughts at this point. The ring of the private door bell warned him that Wilson, the local carrier, had arrived to deliver the day's purchases.

Wilson carried the books into the shop, and left them where, twenty-four hours previously, he had left the others. As soon as he had gone Terhune began a quick examination of them. He did not expect to find anything unusual for he felt sure that he was merely doing something that was in the nature of locking the stable door after the horse had bolted. For all that, he meant to take no risks.

All the books were as they should be, so he stacked them neatly on what he called his packing-table. Then he selected half a dozen titles which sounded attractive, and took them upstairs with him. He pushed the cataloguing work on one side, and relaxed into the armchair with a sigh of satisfaction. No other side of his work gave him greater pleasure than the first quick browsing among new purchases.

He lit a cigarette, then stretched out his arm for the topmost book. This chanced to be a copy of *Anthony Adverse* in fair condition, one of the few works of fiction which he had found at *Twelve Chimneys*, and then not in the library, but in one of the bedrooms, a guest room presumably. He had read *Anthony Adverse* many years previously, within a year of its publication, but there were many half-remembered passages which he wanted to reread.

He began to read. Halfway through the first chapter he closed the book with an air of decision. He wouldn't just browse; he would keep the book back until he had had the opportunity of rereading through the whole of it. He rose from his chair and approached one shelf specially for books which he intended to read before selling them in the shop below. Then he chuckled. The shelf was so full there was barely room for fat *Anthony Adverse*. Such was the disadvantage of being at one and the same time book-lover, book-collector and bookseller. So many books had to go below which, if he hadn't his livelihood to consider, he would have kept upstairs for himself.

The next book which he lifted from the six he had brought up was another novel: *Rogue's Lute* by Philip Rush. He had vague recollections of having been told to read it, while in France on active service, by somebody in the King's Royal Rifles, who regularly received a parcel of books from an adoring mama. From that day he had never come across the book, but now, by happy chance, a copy had come his way. He dipped into the book, its slim, war-time standard size being in startling contrast to the previous title. The first paragraph—the first line, in fact, captured his interest. So François Villon was the rogue, was he? That rascal of the Middle Ages was one of his favourite historical personages—in company with Henry of Navarre, the Red Cardinal, the Sun King, and others—so *Rogue's Lute*, with difficulty, joined *Anthony Adverse*—to be read one fine day!

The third book was older, published in 1910, so the title page told him, and came under the general classification of "Travel." *Argentine Past and Present*, by W. H. Koebel. He glanced quickly at the illustrations, and grinned. Funny how some illustrations could date a book more effectively than mere figures, he reflected. Nineteen hundred and ten, now, seemed not so terribly long ago. But one or two of the pictures could have come from a forgotten age. Old-fashioned though they were the illustrations led him to the chapter-headings. They, in their turn, set him off dipping here and there until, presently, be turned to one which dealt with the *gauchos*, the picturesque peasant cowboys of South America.

Koebel's account of their history interested him. From browsing he turned to reading. Then, with unexpected drama, Koebel's book bridged four decades in time, and thousands of miles in space. From Argentina of the second decade of the century he was brought back to England of the fifth. For there, in print, was Koebel's account of the *gauchos'* method, part traditional—part superstitious, of curing a fly-blown sheep: the upturning of sods on which the animal had rested, and the cutting thereon of crude crosses.

So that was the explanation of the upturned sods which Julia and he had come across in Farmer Chitty's fields! Somebody had endeavoured to cure fly-blown sheep—and ward off further trouble—by adopting the *gaucho* method of dealing with the nuisance.

He read the paragraph through for a second time to make sure that he had made no mistake. Of course he hadn't, and as this fact became obvious his interest grew, for he recollected Pyke's story of the branded foal. It was fairly evident that the man who had cut the sods was also the one who had branded the foal—the significance of the cross could not be overlooked. Was it possible, Terhune asked himself, that the branding of foals with crosses was also an Argentinian custom? He read on with avid curiosity, and was quickly rewarded: according to Koebel the branding was indeed a *gaucho* cure for meningitis!

His first reaction to this information was scorn for the credulity of the *gaucho*—or was it faith, and not credulity? But Koebel explained that the branding often did effect a cure, and went on to give what he concluded to be the true reason underlying the custom. The use of the cross as a branding-mark was, true enough, evidence of a simple, peasant faith, but the effect of the heat was to act as a counter-irritant to the pressure which caused the illness; hence the reason for branding behind whichever ear was opposite to the direction of the circles turned by the foal: if the foal turned always to its right the brand was made behind the left ear; when the beast turned to its left, then the right ear became the venue for the brand.

Strange that somebody in Wickford should have been willing to try out a cure imported from one of the South American republics! Stranger, too, that that person was not Pyke himself, nor, so far as was known, one of his employees. Did that fact point towards one of Pyke's neighbours as the culprit? To someone who had read of the *gaucho* cure, and had experimented by trying it out surreptitiously on some other person's beast? That, he thought drily, was a possible explanation: most people are willing to profit at the possible expense of somebody else! But who was the experimenter? Whence had come his knowledge of the Argentinian custom? A traveller, perhaps.

He began making a mental list of people, living within a reasonable distance of Pyke's farm, who had travelled to any extent. He thought of three in as many seconds, but from the little he knew of them none was a likely choice. Then what of non-travellers? Had some local resident, who might be the sort of man to try out such an experiment, heard of the cure from a friend who had travelled to Argentina? Or had all this come about as a result of reading about *gaucho* customs—perhaps from the very book which was resting on his lap at that moment?

He nodded thoughtfully; telling himself that the last explanation was the most likely, for the copy of Koebel's book which had come from *Twelve Chimneys* had been published in the U.S.A. There might have been a subsequent English edition of it, but if not, then it was certain that the number of copies extant in the British Isles would be extremely small. It might well be argued, therefore, that Harrison possibly lent his copy of the book to somebody living in the neighbourhood.

Whatever the right explanation mattered little. What pleased him mostly was the knowledge that he had solved the mystery surrounding the upturned sods and the branded foal. It would probably repay him to read on: he might come across an account of some other *gaucho* custom which the unknown might be experimenting with at some future date. So he turned back to the Koebel book, but as he did so he remembered that the last owner of the book had been killed by a foreign dagger, and that the men who had broken into *Twelve Chimneys* the second time had spoken in a foreign language.

Could it be that the man who had branded the foal was one of those foreigners? It damned well could be, by jingo!

He reached for the extension telephone, to call Murphy, but at the last moment withdrew his arm. If the possibility of an Argentinian *gaucho* being involved in Harrison's murder had any foundation in fact, then that was just one clue which he could follow up better than Murphy.

For the second time he reached for the telephone, but this time to call the *Almond Tree*.

Chapter Eighteen

Julia waved as she turned into market square and saw Terhune waiting for her on the pavement. He felt comforted; she was evidently in one of her good moods. As long as she remained good-tempered he asked for no better companion.

She swirled round the corner, pulled over to the wrong side, and brought the car to a rocking halt alongside him. He ran round behind, and jumped into the offside front seat. She raced the engine, and pressed hard on the accelerator. The car shot forward, narrowly but skilfully missing Jessie, the Scotty bitch from the *Wheatsheaf*, who, with commendable tolerance, was ambling across the road to find a sunny patch in front of the *Almond Tree*.

"Well, my sweet, I'm dying to hear the reason," she said gaily.

"The reason for what?"

"As if you don't know as well as I! The reason for your being on the way to London instead of to the auction sale."

"The pleasure of a morning's jaunt in your company, old girl."

"Liar!" she exclaimed without malice.

"All right. If you have such a poor opinion of your own charms that you can't believe what I say, then I suppose I must tell you the truth. I'm on my way, thanks to you, to see a man about a sheep."

"Is that remark funny-vulgar, or funny-ha-ha?"

He grinned. "Neither, Julie. To begin with—am I usually vulgar-minded?"

"You're not, darling. That's why I like you."

"Well, there you are. That disposes of the charge of being vulgar. As for being funny-ha-ha, I wasn't trying to be that either. I really am going up to see a man about a sheep."

"I still don't believe you, Theo."

"Why not?"

"In the first case, I can't imagine what in the world could be more attractive to you than a book sale; in the second case, you're not interested in sheep, and in the third, even if you were, you wouldn't go up to London about a sheep. You would come down here."

"That's what I think the man did who cut those crosses in Farmer Chitty's fields."

"Theodore Terhune, I believe you are trying to make me bad-tempered." Her voice became snappy. "What man did what?"

"I think that the man who messed up Farmer Chitty's fields came down from London. Now I am going up to London in the hope of tracing him."

"Oh!" After a slight pause she went on: "Are you referring to that evening you and I went across the fields on our way to *Twelve Chimneys*?"

"Yes."

"I remember now. But why are you so interested in what happened to Farmer Chitty's fields?"

"Because I have a strong suspicion that the man who cut out the turf was the murderer of poor old Harrison."

"Theo!" Her voice became excited, commanding. "Tell!"

So he told her of the book he had read the previous night, and of his subsequent deductions.

"But how do you hope to find out anything fresh in town?" she asked him.

"Look, Julie, there isn't much doubt but that the murder and the subsequent theft of the dictionary was organized by a man who has both plenty of money and accomplices. Supposing I am right in thinking that Harrison's murderer was a *gaucho* from the Argentine, don't you think that the probability is that his employer, the man behind this affair, is also an Argentinian?"

"It is possible," she agreed cautiously.

"Very well, the next point to consider is this: is the head-boy of these murderers out to get hold of the book for himself, or only to make money out of it by selling it to someone else?"

She gave the question long consideration before replying. "It's difficult to answer that, isn't it, Theo? One is naturally tempted to think that the head-boy, as you call him, wants the book for himself, especially if one stops to wonder how an ordinary thief would have got all the information about the Little Bible and its whereabouts? On the other hand, I suppose there is nothing to have stopped an ardent book-collector from having hired the services of the head-boy to get hold of the book by fair means or foul."

"Whichever solution is the right one, Julie, it comes down to this: either the head-boy himself, or the man who hired the head-boy, is probably: *a*, wealthy, *b*, a book-collector, and *c*, an Argentinian, or at any rate a South American. There is one person in London who probably knows the name of every wealthy South American book-collector, and he is—"

"I know."

"You do, Julie?"

"I think I do. Is he the handsome, well-dressed man you pointed out to me the first day of the sale? Señor Francisco or somebody or other?"

"The very one. Francisco Perez is the London representative of Sánchez Hermanos, of the town which seamen the world over call B.A."

"Buenos Aires?"

"Yes. Sánchez Brothers is the biggest firm of antiquarian booksellers in South America. Perez told me some years back that the office in B.A. has for its clients ninety-five out of every hundred book-collectors in the Spanish-and Portuguese-speaking countries of the New World. If anybody is able to give me information about any South American book-collectors on visit over here he is the man."

"But suppose the collector didn't come himself, Theo, but only sent his hired man?"

"Then Perez won't be able to help except by negative means. For instance, if he says that he has no information of any well-known South American book-collector being on visit to this country then the betting is that the collector didn't come himself but sent somebody else, the head boy, to get possession of the Little Bible. Personally, I'm banking on the fact that a really ardent collector would not have entrusted the business to a third party. So if Perez tells me that Señor So-and-So has been over here for a few weeks I shall pass the name on to Murphy for further investigation."

"Why are you, and not Mr. Murphy, going to interview Perez?"

"For several reasons, Julie. I may be making a complete fool of myself, and if I am, then I'm not anxious to advertise the fact more than I have to."

"That's stupid of you. I'm quite sure Mr. Murphy thinks too much of you to believe you could be a fool, Theo."

He grinned his embarrassment, but there was a warm glow of genuine pleasure in his eyes as he glanced quickly at her to make certain that she was sincere. She was, so he said:

"Anyway, my principal reason is this: according to Sampson the Inter-Allied Committee doesn't want it to be generally known that the Little Bible has not been retraced. If an official police detective were to question Perez he might begin to smell a rat, and begin to circulate his own inquiries round the trade, possibly with results that would enable him to put two and two together."

"I thought Perez was staying at the *Almond Tree*. I saw him there quite late the night before last."

"He stayed there the first night of the sale. As a matter of fact I had hoped to see him last night, but when I 'phoned there Lomax told me that as he had accepted a previous booking for last night he had let the room to Perez only for Wednesday night."

"Doesn't Perez propose to be at the sale this afternoon?"

"As far as I know he does; he's after that copy of *Don Quixote*."

She turned a perplexed face towards him. "Then why are you rushing up to town, Theo? Couldn't you have talked to him this afternoon?"

He chuckled. "In the middle of a book sale!" His face quickly sobered. "It's the time element that matters, Julie. Every moment is precious. If once the Little Bible is smuggled out of the country it may never be seen again. I hope it isn't already too late."

"Wouldn't Mr. Sampson have made arrangements to try and prevent that happening?"

"Of course, but there was time, early yesterday morning before Sampson met us at Wickford, for someone to have caught one of the early morning 'planes to the Continent. Personally I don't think that that is what happened; the thief would have just as much to fear from the Continental police, who are co-operating with the Inter-Allied Committee, as he would from the English police. I think that he is more likely to try and catch the next ship outward bound for one of the South American ports."

"I hope you are right, Theo dear, and that something comes of your meeting with Perez," she said with a sincerity which she was usually slow to reveal. "I think that modern generations can ill afford not to be reminded of what miracles simple Christian faith can sometimes achieve. Many of us would be much better off for a little of Franz Eltzbacher's faith, patience and resolution."

By this time they had reached the centre of Ashford, where the traffic was temporarily piling up. By a kind of unspoken agreement nothing more passed between them until the northern outskirts of the town were behind them. Then Julia spoke of her mother, and the previous conversation was not resumed.

They reached Charing Cross Road, in good time, where they parted, she to drive off in the direction of Regent Street, to shop, he to proceed direct to Cecil Court, where a small plate-glass window announced:

FRANCISCO PEREZ
Antiquarian Bookseller and Exporter

London representative of Sánchez Hermanos,
Buenos Aires, Argentina.

He entered the shop, and in spite of the cellar-like gloom of the small, book-lined room, was immediately recognized by the stooping, grey-haired man who sat behind a table-desk, scratching out a letter.

"Good morning, Mr. Terhune." Precise formality gave way to surprise. "I didn't expect to see *you* here *to-day*, sir. I was sure you would be at that sale in Kent. Isn't it being held not far from your town?"

"Only a mile or so away. Don't worry; I shall be back there for the afternoon session. Is Mr. Perez in?"

"He is, sir, but——" The old fellow hesitated. "He's very busy, you understand. He has to leave soon to drive down to the sale."

"I won't keep him long for the same reason."

The remark reassured the clerk. He rose, somewhat shakily, from a chair which had a twanging spring-back, and entered the door behind him. Two or three minutes elapsed; Terhune began, for the first time, to experience an uneasy doubt about his impulsive journey to town. However, when the old chap returned his friendly smile offered hope which his words quickly confirmed.

"Mr. Perez will see you, Mr. Terhune."

With a "Thanks" to the clerk Terhune passed through a dingy door into a large room that was in surprising contrast to the dimly-lighted shop. In much the same fashion as the shop reflected the character of the old clerk who had to spend all his working hours in it, so the office supplied a natural background for the debonair Perez: powerful electric lights, chromium-plated fittings, two glass-topped desks—one for Perez, another for his blonde secretary—a thick pile carpet, ostentatious ash-trays, and a low, well-padded armchair for visitors.

Perez welcomed Terhune with a dazzling smile, and words which were almost a repetition of his clerk's.

"This is a surprise visit, Mr. Terhune. What has London more attractive to offer you than your own neighbourhood?"

"An urgent cabled request from a New York client who insists upon having a cabled reply within forty-eight hours. If he hasn't heard by then he cancels the order."

The South American smiled sympathetically. "These Yankees— They do not understand the restfulness of *mañana*. I trust you were successful."

"Not yet. The man who has a copy of the wanted book for sale is not expected in for another thirty minutes."

"I see." Perez paused politely for a studied moment. "You have something of an equally urgent nature which you wish to see me about, Mr. Terhune?"

Terhune nodded. Now that he was actually sitting in the office of the keen-eyed, astute South American he felt infinitely less confident of bamboozling the other man than he had twelve hours previously when thinking out his excuse for the inquiries he hoped to make.

"One of my best clients died quite recently, leaving a widow and a young granddaughter—the parents were killed during the war by one of the last German rockets to be sent from Holland. This client had been living on a comfortable annuity which, of course, ceased with his death. The widow now finds it necessary to sell most of the books and antiques which her husband had collected all his life."

He shifted restlessly beneath Perez's steady, slightly puzzled gaze. "I'm afraid I am not at liberty to tell all the facts, Mr. Perez," he hurried on. "But, shortly, she wants the largest possible sum in the quickest possible time. As far as the books are concerned I made her a fair, in fact a good, offer, which she accepted. She had the cheque a week ago."

The story, thus far, was true, but he had a nasty feeling that he was making it sound rather like a stupid fairy-tale.

"I see," Perez said smoothly—too smoothly. "And now, I take it, you have some titles which might interest the South American market. If you will let me have a list—"

"That is not why I am here."

"No?" The South American no longer concealed his surprise.

"Mr. Perez, your firm deals with almost every South American book-collector of note, I believe?"

"We have that fortunate distinction."

"If one of them were to visit England would he be likely to contact you?"

"It is likely. Several have, in the past, especially when they combined a book-buying expedition with pleasure. But, permit me to point out, Mr. Terhune—"

"Are any of them visiting Europe at the present moment?" Terhune blundered on.

A chilling silence followed. Terhune had not the courage to return Perez's angry glance. His cheeks burned with mortification, as he realized how completely he had bungled the interview. What a mad fool he was, he reproached himself bitterly. What a mad fool to think that he was better qualified than a trained police detective to handle such a delicate interrogation. Instead of allaying the suspicions of the South American, instead of persuading Perez to talk to him as one bookman to another, his crude diplomacy had resulted in creating precisely the opposite effect.

"May I ask your reason for wanting to know if any one of our clients is on a visit to this country?" the South American asked coldly.

Terhune nodded with the desperation of failure. "Of course. I—I wanted you to be good enough to put me in touch with him."

"Indeed!" Perez laughed, and a very unpleasant sound it made in Terhune's ears. "Perhaps you would like me to give you our mailing list at the same time. After all, by selling direct to them instead of to us, you would be sure of a better price."

Damn the man! Terhune thought. That was going too far. "What do you take me for, Mr. Perez? I wasn't suggesting selling any books direct to your client."

"Then why—"

"I mentioned antiques as well as books."

"Antiques!"

"You're not interested in antiques, are you?"

"Of course not. Are you, Mr. Terhune?"

"No, but I want to get the best possible price for those which the widow is selling."

Perez shook his head in bewilderment. "I am still at a loss to understand your meaning. Surely Christie's are the people to approach about antiques."

"England is not the rich country it was before the Second World War, Mr. Perez. Nowadays most of the wealthy people live in the New World. If the antiques are sold to British collectors they will not, generally speaking, get such good prices as if they were sold to one of your countrymen, Mr. Perez. I thought that if you were able to give me the name of any wealthy South American book-collectors at present in this country I would try to persuade them to buy some of the antiques which I am trying to sell on behalf of the widow. Naturally, I should give you my word not to sell any books."

"Naturally!" Perez repeated drily. His manner changed; he became more his old friendly self again. "Forgive me if I misunderstood your motives, Mr. Terhune. I should have remembered your reputation as an honest, straightforward business man. But do you think that a book-lover is necessarily interested in antiques?"

"It is my experience that he usually is."

"Is he?" Perez deliberated a few moments. "I have never given the matter thought, but it may be true: I know two book-lovers who are also collectors of antiques." He paused again, then slowly shook his head. "Unfortunately, I am unable to help you, Mr. Terhune. I know of no South American book-collector who is in England at the present time—"

"Or Europe?"

"Or Europe. We had one client who arrived here some months ago, but he returned to Montevideo—what was the date, Miss Wilkinson?"

"Do you mean Mr. Martinez?"

"Yes."

"He sailed on the fifteenth of June, Mr. Perez."

"Thank you." Perez shrugged. "Of course, others may have come—and gone again—without my knowledge. I can only say that if Señor Sánchez had known of their coming he would doubtless have advised me so that I could have communicated with them to offer my services, which has always been my custom." He showed his white teeth in a flashing smile. "That is all part of the success of Sánchez Brothers, Mr. Terhune." He glanced at his watch, and rose to his feet with outstretched hand. "And now, if you will excuse me—first I have to see a train off, and afterwards, well, I do not want to miss that first edition of *Don Quixote*, which I think you are offering far too soon after the luncheon interval." He laughed again. "As I am sure you know, we Latins like to spend a long time over our meals: we are not like our friends from the United States."

II

Julia arrived at the agreed meeting-place some minutes after Terhune, but as he stepped into the car her first words were not of apology, but of anxious inquiry.

"Were you successful, Theo?" Then she saw his expression. "Poor old Theo! You weren't?"

"I wasn't," he confirmed gloomily. "And what makes matters worse is that I can't decide whether it was my own fault that I was unsuccessful."

The car glided forward into the long line of moving vehicles streaming by. "Why not?"

"I thought I was being clever in talking to him as one member of the antique book trade to another, but all I did was to make him suspicious of me."

"Suspicious?"

He nodded. "He thought I was trying to worm the names of some of the firm's clients from him so that I could sell direct to them instead of to him. I gave him that story of trying to sell old Mrs. Rainsford's antiques to foreigners for the best possible price but I don't think that I convinced him. Anyway, he told me that the only book-collector from South America who, as far as he knew, has been in England this year returned home some time in the middle of the month."

"Do you believe him?"

"I don't know, Julie, but whether he was telling the truth or not doesn't matter now. I was mad enough to hope that I should be able to ring up Sampson, give him the name of Señor So-and-So, and say: 'If I were you, inspector, I should see to it that that gentleman doesn't sail for South America next week without having his luggage searched.' As it is—" He shrugged, and became glumly silent.

For a long time neither spoke. Presently, when the volume of traffic eased off, she turned to him, saying:

"There's nothing more that you can do, is there?"

"Not a cussed thing."

"That's too bad!" There was genuine disappointment in her voice. "Do you think Scotland Yard will be any more successful?"

"It's difficult to imagine how they can be, Julie. If there were any worth-while clue for them to work on they might have a chance, but there isn't. All they know is, that somebody broke into my shop the night before last, with the help of a duplicate key, and that he, or they, stole one single book. The assumption is that the thieves travelled to Bray by a car which they parked in some quiet spot, and that after the burglary they went back to town by the same method. Unless anyone was lucky enough to have seen and remembered the registration number—which isn't likely, and in any case, the plates might have been false—there's nothing about that trip to help the police. As far as the shop is concerned there were no fingerprints, tools, papers or any other blinking thing left behind which might help. Nor was there anything special about the method of entry which might help the Criminal Records Office—to report that it bore some of the hallmarks of Smith's, or Brown's or Robinson's handiwork."

"What about the man who got the impression of the key by calling at Mrs. Mann's?"

"That's the only possible bright spot, Julie, and the last I heard Murphy was working on it, but not very cheerfully. Unfortunately, Mrs. Mann wasn't very helpful. About the only points about the man which she noted were, that he had a hole in one sock, and that he had ginger hair."

"Oughtn't that to help—the ginger hair, I mean—if the man has ever been convicted?"

"Yes. That's the clue which Murphy was working on—and if he's a Kent man something may come of it. But Sampson is sure that Ginger also came from town—he thinks the man behind the burglary was too cunning to use local people. Naturally, Scotland Yard men are doing their share to find out what known ginger-haired crooks can't offer a good alibi for the time when the so-called inspector called at Mrs. Mann's, but that's not a five-minute business. Sampson fears that even if they do find him they won't do so until the head-boy has left the country, together with the Little Bible."

"Shouldn't you let Mr. Sampson know of your suspicions that the man who murdered Mr. Harrison might be a South American *gaucho*?"

"I'll 'phone him the moment I get back, Julie."

Terhune spoke too confidently. Some miles north of Maidstone Julia became aware that a fast, black car was overtaking her perilously near her offside wheels. She swung the steering-wheel round towards the near-side, but too late to avert a catastrophe. As the wings of the two cars clashed she lost control. Her car mounted the footpath, crashed through a paling-fence, cannoned against an apple tree, and overturned. One moment later both they and the car were enveloped in flames.

Chapter Nineteen

L ady Kylstone and Helena Armstrong arrived at "Twelve Chimneys"
just as Tuttell was beginning the final session of the three-day sale.
On this afternoon was to be sold Thorogood's *Kent Muniments*, which
Lady Kylstone had instructed Terhune to buy on her behalf. Her reason
for being present was, as she said in response to Helena's query:

"Why do I want to be there while Theodore is bidding for the book?
Because I do not trust him."

"Lady Kylstone!"

Lady Kylstone laughed as she noticed the expression of distress on
Helena's face. "My dear child, you don't have to look so shocked. It's
his conscientiousness I don't trust."

"I don't understand."

"If I were not here to prompt him his sense of values would probably
be too outraged to let him bid very much more than its real worth; he
would hesitate to involve me beyond a reasonable limit."

Helena smiled. "Dear Tommy!"

"Tut, tut! Don't ever speak of Theodore like that in Wesley's
presence."

"Why not?"

"Because, my dear, if I were a man I don't think I should like to hear
my fiancée use that tone when speaking of another man. You're not still
in love with Theodore, are you?"

Helena reddened. "Almost," she confessed. "If it were not for
Wesley—"

Lady Kylstone patted her companion's hand. "I know, my child.
I think quite a number of us are almost in love with that annoyingly

likeable young man. He is a positive menace to the female population of the neighbourhood."

Tuttell rapped his hammer. "Lot eight hundred and ten," he announced. "An interesting Lot, ladies and gentlemen. A complete set of a rare book, together with the still more rare plates. *Trials for Adultery, or The History of Divorce, being Select Trials and Doctors' Commons for Adultery, Fornication, Cruelty, Impotence, from the year seventeen hundred and sixty to the Present Time.* Seven volumes in half-calf, published in seventeen seventy-nine-eighty. Who will start me off at twenty guineas?"

Spirited bidding began, but Helena was not interested in Lot 810. She looked about, with puzzled eyes. "I can't see Tommy."

"Nonsense! He must be here." Lady Kylstone laughed her disbelief. "A local book sale without Theodore would be unthinkable."

"Thirteen guineas," Tuttell chanted. "Fourteen, fifteen, sixteen—"

Helena looked again. "He can't be here."

Lady Kylstone rose from the chair which Brereton had offered to her, and looked through her lorgnettes.

"You are right. I certainly cannot see him."

"Can't see who, m'dear?" questioned Brereton who overheard the remark.

"Theodore Terhune."

"Terhune!" Sir George's loud laughter boomed out. "He's probably hidden behind all the books he bought," he announced loudly.

"A little less talking, *if* you please, gentlemen," Tuttell called out.

"Then see whether you can see him, George," Lady Kylstone snapped in a low voice.

Brereton stared about him, and as he was tall there was no immediate part of the lawn that was not visible to him.

"B'Jove! You're right, Kathleen. He's not here."

She sat down again, frowning. "It's not like Theodore—besides, isn't the *Muniments* almost due, Helena?"

"It's the fifteenth Lot from now." Tuttell's hammer banged. "The fourteenth! Surely nothing could have happened to him."

"What an imagination you have, child! What could have happened to him?" But Lady Kylstone's voice was not entirely convincing.

"There were two Lots he wanted particularly just after the *Muniments*."

"Then he will turn up just in time."

The next few Lots sold quickly, but at flagging prices, because most of the smaller buyers had already bought up to their financial limits, while the larger buyers, having squeezed out or exhausted the lesser fry, were now prepared to let their rivals buy unchallenged Lots not specially wanted by themselves. Even to the uninitiated Helena it was obvious that, for the time being at any rate, prices were favouring the buyer; she was anguished at the thought of the number of bargains Terhune might have obtained. Meanwhile she watched and waited anxiously for his coming. With distress she heard Tuttell knock down Lot 826 to Francis Edwards for four guineas.

"Yours is the next Lot," she told Lady Kylstone. "What are you going to do?"

"Do! Why, bid for it myself, of course. Two guineas," she called out loudly as an opening bid.

Less than a minute later, Thorogood's *Kent Muniments* was hers—at a price. Thirty guineas she had to pay for it, thanks—or no thanks—to the mischievous bidding of a bookseller who was determined to make a mere amateur regret taking part in a professional contest.

For his part Tuttell did not miss the opportunity of making capital out of the Lot.

"Lady Kylstone," he announced. He stared primly at his audience. "It might interest you to know, ladies and gentlemen, that an ancestor of Lady Kylstone's family, the first Piers Kirtlyngton, is the subject of one of the early chapters of Thorogood's *Muniments*." He nodded his head. "Lot eight hundred and twenty-eight—"

"Come along, Helena, we will see whether we can find out what has happened to Theodore." She rose from her chair. "You can have your chair back. George. We are going."

"Thanks, m'dear."

"Take care of yourself if you want to make any bids. You won't be shown any mercy here."

He grinned amiably. "Don't worry about me, Kathleen. They won't try any of their forcing bids against me. I'm not a woman to be bluffed into exposing my hand."

"You're mixing your metaphors, aren't you, George?" she retorted as she swept away, followed by Helena.

As Gibbons, the chauffeur, sprang out of his seat to open the door of the Daimler a car drew up near by. A man alighted, and began to hurry up the drive towards the house.

"Isn't that Theodore's detective friend?" Lady Kylstone asked quickly.

Gibbons answered the question. "Yes, my lady. Sergeant Murphy."

"Quick! Call him back."

The chauffeur called. Murphy turned, and saw that he was being beckoned. As he walked back towards the Daimler he recognized its owner, and lifted his bowler.

"You want, me, Lady Kylstone?"

"To ask if you chance to know where Mr. Terhune is."

"Mr. Terhune!" He smiled. "At the sale."

"He is not. We have just come from the garden. Mr. Terhune was to have bid for a book on my behalf, but he hasn't turned up."

"Not turned up—to the sale!" Astonishment changed to a mood of anxiety that was part embarrassment, no doubt on account of Terhune's being a responsible person who was perfectly capable of looking after himself. "I've come here especially to ask him something."

"Well, he's not here," she retorted impatiently. "But if you don't know where he is, sergeant—"

Helena broke into the conversation. "I'm terribly worried, sergeant."

"But, miss——" he began reprovingly.

"Something must have happened to him, otherwise he would be at the sale."

Murphy's worry became increasingly apparent. "I must say it's not natural Mr. Terhune not being at the sale. I'll make inquiries, m'lady."

"Thank you, sergeant. Perhaps you would telephone me later."

"I will," Murphy promised. With a hurried snatch at his hat he jumped back into his car, reversed, and sped off in the direction of Bray. During the few minutes it took for him to reach Market Square his anxiety was in no way allayed. Only something really serious could have kept Mr. Terhune away from the book sale, he reflected, and in spite of everything commonsense did to contradict, he became increasingly worried. After all, the people who had organized the theft of the *German-English Dictionary* had already shown their lack of scruple by the cold-blooded murder of the unfortunate Harrison. Though why, if the Little Bible were in their possession, they should still be interested in Terhune was a question which assumed an increasing significance in his thoughts. If the gang had indeed engineered Terhune's disappearance surely it could only be for one reason: that in spite of all appearances to the contrary, the men had not yet obtained the thing—a book, or whatever else it might be—for which they had twice broken into *Twelve Chimneys*, and once into Terhune's shop.

He was still in this mood when he brought the car to a stop outside the shop. He ran across the pavement, and through the door. Save for Anne the shop was empty.

"Where's Mr. Terhune?"

"At the sale, Mr. Murphy."

"No, he's not."

Anne looked confused. "But he said he was going to be there."

"When did he say that? This morning, before lunch?"

She shook her head. "He didn't really say it; he wrote it."

"Bedad, girl! What the divil do ye mean, he wrote it?"

"I haven't seen him to-day, Mr. Murphy. When I arrived this morning I found a note for me to say that he was driving up to town, and that I was not to expect him back before I closed for the night as he intended to have lunch in Ashford and afterwards to go straight on to the sale."

"Did you say *drive* up to town?"

"Yes."

"But he has no car. Whose car was he going in?"

"I don't know, but sometimes he has gone with Lady Kylstone, and sometimes with Miss Julia."

"Miss Julia MacMunn?"

"Yes, sir,"

"I'm going along to the MacMunn's place. If there's no news there I'll be back. Meanwhile, be a good girl and see if you can find out from Mrs. Mann, or the neighbours, or somebody, whose car Mr. Terhune went in this morning."

She nodded her head, and said she would, but by that time the sergeant was already on his way back to the car. He drove back to Wickford, and beyond, to Willingham, at a fierce, dangerous speed, which was unusual for him, for he had very settled ideas about members of the police force setting a good example.

He found Alicia MacMunn in—but only just, as she was on her way out to tea at the Rectory.

"Dear me!" she murmured flutteringly, finding herself closeted with a detective-sergeant. "Don't tell me, inspector, that we've forgotten to take out the car-licence again. It was only the other day that I reminded Julia—my daughter, you know—"

Murphy interrupted, ignoring his promotion—he knew his Alicia, and was aware that he was just as likely to be officer or constable in the next breath.

"Is Miss MacMunn in?"

"Julia! What do you want with her? Has she been doing something naughty?"

"Is she in?" he demanded brusquely.

"No, she's at the auction sale—you know, at *Twelve Chimneys*—"

"Did she drive Mr. Terhune up to town this morning?"

She beamed. "How clever of you, constable! However did you guess that?"

The dear God give me patience! he breathed in silent prayer. Aloud he asked: "Can you be telling me when they fixed this trip up; ma'm?"

"Last night, about eight o'clock, I'd say. He 'phoned up. They planned to go to town early enough to get back to Ashford in time for lunch, and from there go on to the sale I was telling you about."

"Then the trip was fixed up out of the blue, was it?"

"I think so."

"Did Miss MacMunn tell you, Ma'm, why Mr. Terhune wanted to get to town so urgently?"

"Good Heavens! Sergeant, I'm only her mother." Her voice became querulous. "Julia never tells me more than she has to about herself. She doesn't treat her mother as I did mine. But there, you know what the modern generation is like if you have any children—"

No doubt Mrs. MacMunn would have rambled on—the modern daughter's lack of filial respect was a favourite discourse with her—but she was interrupted by a tap on the door, and the entry of the butler. For once Phillips's usual suavity was disturbed; his face bore an acute expression of surprise.

"If you please, Madam, there's another police officer outside wishing to speak to you."

Murphy's knowledge of police procedure warned him of the probable reason for the second visit; grimly—and perhaps deliberately—forgetful of his manners he snapped out: "Show him in."

Phillips glanced reproachfully at the sergeant, but he obeyed. Soon P.C. Simmonds entered. When he recognized Murphy his face registered astonishment.

"I didn't know you was here, sergeant. I suppose you've told Mrs. MacMunn about the accident—"

Murphy cut him short. "What's your news, Simmonds?"

"Mrs. MacMunn's daughter has been involved in an automobile accident, sergeant, on the Folkestone Road, north of Maidstone."

For once Alicia was natural. Her cheeks paled, and a deeply pained expression flashed across her eyes, but in a low, moderately steady voice she asked: "She is not—not dead?"

"No, ma'm. She's in Maidstone hospital, suffering from burns and shock, but her condition is not serious."

"Thank God! I shall go to her at once. Thank you for your kindness in bringing me the news. Phillips will see you out." She began walking towards the door. Murphy spoke.

"I'm just off to the hospital, Mrs. MacMunn, if you would care to come with me."

She turned, and nodded. "Thank you. I shall be ready within five minutes." With an upright, unhurried posture she continued her journey towards the door, and left.

Simmonds gazed after her with admiration. "She took that coolly, sergeant. I wasn't half expecting a scene, too."

"Never mind about her. Is there any news of Miss MacMunn's companion?"

"That there Mr. Terhune? He's not too good."

The sergeant felt a queasy spasm disturbing his inside. "Burns?"

"I suppose so. According to Piggott the Maidstone police said something about him having saved her life by dragging her out of the fire." Simmonds shook his head reprovingly. "I allus said that girl would pile up one day. Ruddy speed-mad she was, poor kid."

Alicia returned to the long drawing-room, not in the promised five minutes but not very long afterwards. She was still unnaturally calm, but her eyes, and her unsteady hands, betrayed her real feelings.

Little conversation passed between Alicia and Murphy on the journey to Maidstone. Upon arrival at the hospital Alicia was given permission to see Julia for a few minutes only, and hurried away. When Murphy asked to see Terhune the reply was an uncompromising shake of the house-surgeon's head.

"He's not recovered consciousness yet."

Murphy gulped. "He'll recover?"

"He should do, but it'll take time. Are you a relative, by the way?"

"No, a police officer."

"Have his next of kin been advised?"

"No. He hasn't any near relatives. I believe he has an aunt or a cousin somewhere in Scotland." Murphy saw from the doctor's face that something other than mere routine had prompted the question about relatives. "Is anything wrong, sir?"

"Not wrong, but he's in a delirium, and keeps calling out for a certain person. It might help a little if that person could be traced."

"Is he asking for Julia MacMunn? Or for Helena Armstrong?"

"No, for a man by the name of Murphy—"

"Bedad! That's me! For why should he be asking for me?"

The house-surgeon shrugged. "I can't say, but I should judge that he has something on his mind."

"Something on his mind!" Murphy's lips tightened. The news that Terhune was asking for him helped more than ever to convince him that the bookseller had discovered some fresh clue to the murder of Harrison, or perhaps the theft of the dictionary, or both. And meanwhile Terhune was unconscious. Bedad! What a time to have an accident. He had to hold himself in check to stop his exasperation changing to an explosive loss of temper.

"May I see Miss MacMunn when her mother comes out?"

"Not to-day. She's not really fit to see her mother."

"It's urgent, doctor. By the way, I am a detective-sergeant. Miss MacMunn may be able to give me some information concerning a homicide case I am investigating."

The doctor's eyebrows waggled, "In that case——" He hesitated. "I'll see her—perhaps if we let her rest for an hour—But mind, sergeant, I make no promises. My duty is to my patient, not to the police."

Murphy waited with what patience he could for the doctor's verdict. Presently he was joined by Alicia. She said little to him, but her trembling lips warned him that tears were not far off, and were only being kept in check by a self-control which he would never have suspected her capable of possessing. Once she burst out, impulsively:

"Her poor face——"

Then she lapsed into silence again, as though she had not consciously spoken aloud.

A little more than an hour later the house surgeon came along to the waiting-room.

"Miss MacMunn has agreed to see you, Mr. Murphy. But I cannot give you long; not more than five minutes."

He nodded, and after a word with Alicia, he followed the doctor to a private ward.

Julia was unrecognizable, for her face was swathed in bandages in which there was the merest slit for her eyes, and another for her mouth. A nurse sat by the side of the bed; she indicated a chair on the opposite side, so Murphy sat down with a feeling of shy embarrassment.

"Hullo, Mr. Murphy," Julia whispered.

"Hullo, Miss MacMunn," he replied gently. He glanced awkwardly at the nurse, who nodded. "Do you mind if I ask you a few questions, miss?"

"I want you—to—"

"You need only answer yes or no. Had Mr. Terhune's journey to town anything to do with the murder of Harrison?"

"Yes."

"Do you know what that something was?"

"Yes."

"Is it possible for you to tell me in a few words?"

"I will—try. Theo read in book about South—South American *gauchos* curing meningitis by branding foals behind ears, and cutting crosses—turfs—" She paused, giving him the impression, that she wanted to know whether he understood what she was saying.

"I remember, miss. Did Mr. Terhune have reason to believe that the crime was committed by a South American?"

"Yes. He went, to ask Perez—bookseller—if any South American book-collector was over here—perhaps he was a man after book—"

"Bedad! Well, what did Perez have to say?"

"He—said—no book-collector in—in—England since middle—middle—June—"

The nurse made a signal to Murphy, who understood that Julia was becoming exhausted.

"Bad luck, Miss MacMunn. Never mind, he did his best. And it offers another clue which I'll pass on to Inspector Sampson. One last question. How did the accident occur?"

"I lost—control—trying—avoid—black car—we were—both driving—fast."

"Then the smash was just an unfortunate accident?"

"Yes. I think—other car—skidded—"

"Thank you. Now I must go. I'll look after your mother until you return home."

"Thank—you—Mr. Mu—Mu—" The words tailed off.

"Good-bye, till to-morrow," he said softly, as he slipped quietly out of the ward.

Chapter Twenty

Having ascertained from Alicia that she wanted to remain near her daughter the sergeant kept his promise to Julia by driving her mother to the *Royal Star*, and making arrangements for her to stay there until further notice. Then he telephoned Phillips that his mistress would not be returning; at the same time he instructed the man to send Alicia's maid Rose to pack a bag and take it to the Maidstone hotel. Having completed these arrangements he felt that he was free to have a pot of tea.

While he waited for his order he considered the unfortunate turn of events which had resulted in Terhune's present state of unconsciousness. At first his thoughts dwelt upon the person; he had a sincere liking, an affection almost, for the bookseller, and hoped devoutly that the accident would have no lasting consequences. True, the house-surgeon had given an assurance that Terhune would live, but would the multiple burns leave permanent scars, or, even worse, was it possible that the shock might leave mental scars of the kind to which he dared not even give a name. The prospect gave him a queasy feeling somewhere below his waist line, but he realized that he was becoming morbid, so he comforted himself with the reminder that Terhune was no neurotic but a healthy-minded, healthy-bodied young man who should be perfectly able to recover from injuries which the doctor candidly admitted were "serious, though not critical."

As was only natural Murphy's thoughts presently reverted to the reason for the other man's mysterious journey to London. He considered Julia's halting story to be, on the surface, fantastic. Terhune, it seemed, had read in some book an item to the effect that South American *gauchos* were in the habit—a damn' silly, superstitious habit—of curing fly-blown sheep by carving crosses in the grass, and similarly, of curing meningitis in foals by branding a cross behind an ear. From this knowledge Terhune, apparently, had deduced the theory that Harrison had been murdered by a South American *gaucho*.

A long shot, and one to make the methodical but unimaginative sergeant writhe at the lengths to which amateur detection could carry an enthusiast. In fact, had the theory been suggested by anyone other than Terhune he was sure he would not have given the matter a second thought. But he had a deep respect for Terhune's opinions, so he conned the matter over, and tried to see the matter through Terhune's eyes, as it were.

To begin with, everything pointed to the fact that a close watch had been kept on *Twelve Chimneys* and the movements of its occupants, not only before the murder of its owner, but also afterwards. The field in which Terhune had found the mutilated sods was near enough to *Twelve Chimneys*—and far enough from the farmhouse—for a man to have been posted there to spy on Harrison and his small staff. The same applied to some of Fred Pyke's fields.

Then there was the un-British method of murder, stabbing; the foreign type of weapon; the few words spoken in a foreign language on the night of the second attempted burglary. All these facts pointed to the possibility of Harrison's murderer having been a foreigner. The reckless use of money to achieve a desired end suggested a background of wealth; a large proportion of the world's cash resources was now centred in the New World.

Murphy played absent-mindedly with the tea knife which was on the table before him; he made it spin round and round, and tried to tap the table-top in between each spin so that neither the blade nor the handle touched his flesh—a childish habit which he frequently indulged when he was in a thoughtful mood. On careful reflection it did seem as if Terhune's deductions were not quite so far-fetched as they had appeared

at first. Granted this fact, granted, also, that the man who ' had gone to
such lengths to obtain possession of the *German-English Dictionary* was
a book-collector, then there was every reason for believing that Perez,
the representative of the biggest firm of booksellers in South America,
might be aware of the presence in this country of such a man.

This train of thought increased his admiration for Terhune's reasoning. It might not have any genuine foundation, but on the other hand,
it might, especially as no alternative solution offered itself. It was all
the more disappointing, therefore, to know that the unfortunate visit to
London had produced such a negative result. Nevertheless, that line of
investigation was still worth following; the fact that Perez was unable
to name a book-collector offhand was not proof that one had not visited
the country unknown to Perez. Nor did Murphy's methodical reasoning
overlook the possibility that a South American book-lover might hire the
services of a criminal to steal the Little Bible, while himself remaining
in his own country.

He twirled the knife with added vigour—the more he considered
Terhune's theory the more it seemed well worth following up.

II

After tea he wandered along to the police station, where he recognized
Sam Warren behind the desk. Presently he said:

"A nasty smash that, this morning."

Warren was not complimentary to the victims. "Serve 'em right, the
ruddy road-hogs. P'raps they'll be more careful in the future. If they
lives," he added carelessly.

"You needn't be so blasted righteous about them, Warren. There's
not many a better driver on the road than Miss MacMunn."

The station sergeant looked surprised. "Friends of yours, Murphy,
me boy?"

"Mr. Terhune is and all. One of the best he is, begod! And you should know that as well as me."

"Terhune! Terhune! Am I supposed to know him?"

"You're no good as a ruddy policeman if you don't. Who helped to send Belcher to the gallows, and put Smallwood in the dock?"

"That Terhune!" Warren began to look interested. "It wasn't him!"

"That's what I'm telling you."

"I didn't know it was him. Poor devil! He's been pretty badly burned, Chester was telling me not an hour ago." Warren twitched a bald forehead. "Are you here 'cause of him?"

Murphy nodded. "He was helping on the Harrison affair at Wickford."

The station sergeant whistled. "Was he? Have you been to the hospital?"

"Yes."

"Will he pull through?"

"The house-surgeon thinks so."

"He's a good man, Jones. What's happening on the Harrison job?"

"All but damn-all! The Old Man's called in the C.I.D."

Warren grinned sourly. "Trust him, the old so-and-so."

"He doesn't give a man a chance. By the way, have you heard how the smash-up occurred?"

"Chester was telling me that a chap name of Taplin, who saw it happen, thought that the two cars were having a race. Suddenly the near-side car swung off the road, charged straight for the footpath, burst through the fence, hit a tree, overturned, and burst into flames. Taplin ran like mad for the scene of the accident—he was the best part of four hundred yards off, by the way—but long before he was near the car was blazing like a ruddy oil-bomb. Just as he reached the place he saw the man pull a woman out of the car, and carry her to a tree ten yards away. Then the man collapsed, so Taplin thought it time to call the police. He ran to the nearest telephone and asked for police. Exchange put him through to us."

Warren did not trouble to explain more; Murphy would know the routine probably better than himself.

"What happened to the other car?—Miss MacMunn said it was a black car, by-the-bye."

"That's right; that's how Taplin described it. What happened to it?" The station sergeant scowled. "The ruddy swine didn't even stop."

"Damn and blast him!" Murphy exclaimed angrily, thinking that if the driver had stopped to give a hand to the occupants of the other car Terhune's injuries might not now be so serious. "Have you got his number?"

"We have not!" the station sergeant replied in a disappointed voice. "Taplin was too busy staring at the burning car to worry about the one that got away."

"Have you got its description?"

Warren shrugged. "Taplin thinks there's only a difference of one between an Austin seven and a Ford V eight. Outside of noticing its colour the ruddy car might just as well be a Rolls-Royce, or a Morris for all the help he is."

"Nobody else see anything?"

"If so Chester hasn't nosed 'em out yet."

Murphy nodded, tight-lipped. "Think I'll take a look-see at the place."

"Good idea, chum, if you've got the time. I'd like to charge that bastard with not reporting an accident."

As soon as Warren had told him where to find Taplin, Murphy returned to his car, and drove there. He had no difficulty in finding Taplin's cottage, but his knock was answered by a pleasant-faced woman with apple-red cheeks who told him that her man was working in the fields farther along the road. He carried on another quarter of a mile, then he saw a man who answered Taplin's description. Taplin it was, a voluble Taplin who was obviously enjoying the tiny spotlight of notoriety which was playing on him. With many words, and in graphic detail, he retold the story of the accident, but he added nothing to what the sergeant already knew. Something, it seemed, had made him stop his work and look London-wards. Premonition was the meaning he tried to convey in his own phraseology, but Murphy had lived in the country too long not to recognize that the pause was one of those essential rests which the worker in the fields takes frequently. As he looked up, Taplin went on, he saw two cars racing along the road. Just as the middle 'un put on a spurt and drew ahead (Murphy understood him to mean the one in the middle of the road) t'other suddenly runned off the road, across footpath, crashed through fence, hit a tree—a fine Blenheim an' all—and bursted into flames. T'other didn't stop—t'other didn't knowed anything 'bout t'other crashing, guessed Taplin—so he runned as quick as he could to burning car to see if he could help, but just as he reached it he saw a man pull a black-'aired girl out of flaming car, carry her away from danger, and fall down.

There was more, of course, about the sequel: his run to the nearest telephone, his call to the police, the stopping of dozens of passing cars to see what was happening, the arrival of the ambulance, and so on, but stripped of all its trappings his story served merely as further evidence that Julia had unexpectedly lost control of the car, and crashed through the fence into the orchard. His own guess was, that the steering had developed a fault so, after some difficulty, he detached himself from Taplin and drove still farther along the road to the scene of the accident, where the remains of the burned-out car made an ugly scar against a peaceful background of a well-tended orchard.

He was no trained mechanic; he had merely a working knowledge of how a motor car functioned. Nevertheless that much was enough presently to make him discard his theory about the steering. As far as he could judge from the smoke-blackened skeleton, the steering still worked; it had not, for instance, become locked. Nor did there seem more play than there should have been.

He returned to the gap in the chestnut fencing, and with puzzled eyes stared at the road as he tried to imagine what had happened immediately previous to the crash. He had thought that a pot-hole might have wrenched the wheel out of Julia's hands, but there was no pot-hole visible, nor the crushed remains of a brick, a large rock, or anything else which might have been equally guilty.

He was still trying to find some theory to agree with the circumstances as he knew them when a voice at his side said:

"Hullo, mister."

He replied, absent-mindedly: "Hullo."

"What's the name of the film, mister?"

He was not aware of the question. What the divil could have made so experienced a driver as Julia lose control of her car? he wondered. Had she suddenly lost her nerve? Though, bedad! she wasn't one easily to lose her nerve.

He felt a tug at his sleeve.

"Mister!" Impatiently.

He looked round. A cheeky-faced, shock-headed boy stood by his side. About twelve or thirteen, he'd say.

"What do you want?" This also impatiently. As a general rule he liked kids; quickly made friends with them, but just at the moment—

"What's the name of the film?"

"What film?"

"The one they shot this morning."

"I don't know what the divil you're talking about, sonny. Clear off now, like a good lad. I'm busy."

The boy made no attempt to obey. "'Course you know," he stated with almost insolent confidence. "I saw you mucking about with that car just now."

"That car crashed this morning," Murphy explained irritably. "Now clear off before I help you with a kick up the backside."

The boy grinned; probably his intuition assured him that he was safe.

"Gee, mister! What a crash!" he continued rapturously. "Best I ever seen."

"Did you see what happened?" Murphy asked sharply.

"Cor! You betcha life I did. Right from the start."

"Why didn't you tell the police what you saw when they were here?"

"Not me." He shook his head so vigorously that curls fell across his eyes, and had to be brushed back again with none too clean fingers. "I did that once before when a film were being shot, and that time the man really did gimme a kick on me behind."

The sergeant realized abruptly that the boy believed that the accident had not been a genuine one but part and parcel of a scene for a film. "Where were you when it happened?"

The boy pointed across the road. "Just behind the hedge, putting up a rabbit snare."

Murphy thought it better not to inquire why he was there instead of in the class-room. "What made you—" He paused as he was about to add the words: "think you were watching a film being shot?" A more diplomatic method of obtaining information might produce a better result, he reflected.

"What made me what, mister?"

"What made you so quick in spotting that we were shooting a film scene, sonny?"

The lad looked pleased. "Cor! It was easy."

"Go on, then, tell me why it was so easy?"

"Cor lumme, mister! Anyone who'd seen so many gangster films as I 'ave wouldn't want telling twice that them two cars was acting for a film."

Murphy began to feel irritable. "But why? In the divil's name, why?"

"By the way the black car forced t'other car off the road, mister."

Murphy gripped the boy by the shoulder. "What's that you say?"

"You 'eard me!" the boy exclaimed, in the accepted slang of the gangster film, "Haven't I seen too many gangsters steer their cars so as to force other cars off the road not to rekernize what's happening when I sees it."

The sergeant's grip tightened. "You saw that happen?"

"Ain't I got eyes! I'll bet the black 'un were the gangsters' car, and t'other the 'ero's. Ain't that right, mister?"

"You're not making all this up, sonny?"

The boy grinned cheekily, and nodded at the burned-out wreckage. "If I'm making it up, what's that? Red Riding Hood's home?"

III

Murphy's journey back to Ashford was a slow, thoughtful one. In spite of everything he could do to shake his story the boy had never wavered in his conviction that he had witnessed a particularly thrilling scene from a gangster film. Except for the frequent use of gangster-film slang and American clichés his description of what he had seen had been simple and direct. At a certain moment he had looked through a gap in the hedge, and had seen two cars travelling in his direction at high speed. At first they had been one behind the other but suddenly the rear car, "the black'un" as he had called it, had swerved out almost to the far side of the road, and, with an extra spurt of speed, had deliberately steered across the bonnet of the foremost car, with its horn blaring loudly as it did so. Just as a collision had, to the boy, seemed inevitable, the front car had swung off the road at right angles and crashed.

The sergeant had children of his own; he knew how boundless is the childish imagination. For this reason he hesitated to accept the boy's story too readily; it was so very possible that it was his own invention from beginning to end. This possibility was to some extent substantiated by Taplin's account of the accident, and Julia's own version. On the other hand, to support the boy's story was the fact that the black car had driven on without stopping. Surely any driver innocent of guilty intent would have stopped to render what help he could. That he had not done so did suggest that, once he had made Julia crash, his one aim was to get away as speedily as possible.

But, granted that Julia had been deliberately manœuvred into crashing, what was the purpose behind such an outrageous design? To bring about Terhune's death? Or, if death did not enter into the proposition, delay? Of one thing he was sure. That, if the crash were no accident, the perpetrators of it were the ones who had murdered Harrison.

Assuming that the Little Bible had been inside the *German-English Dictionary*, why was Terhune's death so much desired? And why by so melodramatic and uncertain means? Surely it would have been easier, safer and surer for the would-be murderer or murderers to break into the shop and kill him, as they had killed Harrison, by stabbing.

The answer, decided Murphy, lay in one word. Time! The more he conned the matter over the more convinced he was that the element of time was playing its part. The murderers had tried to kill Terhune before he had had an opportunity of returning to his home district. Why? What did they fear from Terhune's return to Bray?

Enlightenment came with the asking of the question. Grim-faced, he drove to the nearest police station, and put a call through to Whitehall 1212.

Chapter Twenty-One

Unfortunately Sampson was not available, so Murphy left a message asking the inspector to telephone later in the evening. Then he started back for the County Police Headquarters at Maidstone, where he made out and handed in his report, after which he returned home. He had not been in ten minutes when Sampson 'phoned.

"Hullo, sergeant. Sampson speaking. I understand that you want to speak to me urgently."

"That's right, I do." Without wasting time in preliminaries Murphy gave the London man a clear account of Terhune's reason for the visit to London, the accident, and the boy's evidence. Then he waited for the other man's comments.

"It's a pity that Terhune didn't pass his ideas on to one of us."

Murphy believed that he detected a note of criticism in the inspector's voice. "He probably thought we should laugh at him unless he supplied evidence to substantiate his theory," he explained defensively.

Sampson laughed drily. "All right, Murphy, there's no need to get hot under the collar. I'm not criticizing him; all I'm thinking about is the waste of time. Look here, am I to take it that you believe the boy's story about Miss MacMunn's car being driven off the road?"

"Let me put it this way, inspector: I don't disbelieve it."

"Right! Then you think that the gang who killed Harrison, and stole the Little Bible from Terhune's shop, was also responsible for the crash?"

"That's the only answer which makes sense."

"All right! Then tell me their reason for trying to kill him. Wasn't the Little Bible in the *German-English Dictionary* after all? Did Harrison hide it in some other place, but does the man who's after the Little Bible believe that it was Terhune who's hidden it, and wants him out of the way while another search is made for it?"

"Personally I think the attack on Miss MacMunn's car is proof that the Little Bible *was* inside the dictionary."

"You do!" Sampson's voice was keen with interest. "Why?"

"In the first case, wouldn't the thief have taken the simple precaution of looking inside the dictionary just to make sure that the Little Bible was there? If it hadn't been wouldn't he have started ransacking the shop, then and there?"

"I don't say that I agree with you about that, sergeant. I think he's rather more subtle than that. If he had thought that it was Terhune who had taken the Little Bible out of the dictionary I'm sure he would have argued that Terhune, with his knowledge of books, would be bound to recognize the value of the Bible, and therefore would have taken thundering good care not to leave it about in the shop, or in any other place where it might easily be found. So what? He makes plans to try and kill Terhune, so as to leave him a more or less clear field for search."

"I don't think the thief could have planned the car crash ahead of time."

"Why not?"

"There's evidence that Mr. Terhune made up his mind quite unexpectedly to visit London, and that the only two people who knew were Miss MacMunn and himself. Neither Anne Quilter—the girl who helps him in the shop—nor Mrs. Mann, the woman who looks after him, knew until he had already left."

"What about that blathering mother of hers? Didn't she know?"

"All she knew was that Miss MacMunn was driving Terhune up to London, but not where or why. In fact, she complained to me that in these days daughters never told their mothers anything."

"Right! Let's assume that the gang did not have any previous information about Terhune's visit. How did they manage to organize the crash so quickly?"

"Because Francisco Perez gave them the information."

Sampson whistled into the mouthpiece; the sound travelled along the wires and echoed piercingly in Murphy's ear.

"If Perez did that it's because Terhune's theory about a South American being at the back of this business was right."

"I go farther than that, inspector."

"Go on."

"Suppose a South American Johnny had organized the robbery, and had already left the country with the Little Bible, then Mr. Terhune would have had his theory too late for anyone to do much about it. Miss MacMunn said that Mr. Terhune asked Perez if any South American book-collector was in this country at the moment. Perez might have put two and two together, and guessed that Mr. Terhune wanted to make certain of his facts before saying anything to us—"

"Assuming Perez to be an accessory?"

"Of course. Perez probably guessed that if Mr. Terhune hadn't already spoken to the police he would soon do so. To try and stop him Perez got moving, and sent that black car off after Mr. Terhune with orders to bring off a crash somehow or other, perhaps not necessarily to kill him, but at any rate to make certain of his being knocked out for a day or two."

"You mean, the Little Bible may not have left the country yet?" Sampson did not wait for a reply. "By God! sergeant, if you're right there's no time to be wasted. We'll get busy right away. I'll keep in touch with you by 'phone. S'long."

Murphy smiled wryly as he replaced the receiver. Sampson was a decent bloke; not one to claim all the credit for himself if he should be successful in recovering the Little Bible, and arresting Harrison's murderer. For all that, doubtless most of the credit would go to him; while the Assistant Commissioner in charge of the C.I.D. would, no doubt, conveniently forget about the poor devils of provincial coppers who had done the greater part of the work, and eulogize the excellence of the department for which he was responsible. That was the worst of being a provincial policeman; the C.I.D. got all the publicity,

"Coming, Tim dear? Supper's ready."

Ah well! The sergeant rose from the bed and went downstairs.

II

Early the next morning Terhune's consciousness struggled wearily out of the fog of oblivion into the light of returning memory. He stared up at an unfamiliar ceiling, and tried to focus his rambling, incoherent thoughts. The effort was too wearisome; he was vaguely aware that the fog was enveloping him again, but he didn't care. In a few moments he was unconscious again.

Some time later he became conscious for the second time. On this occasion the unfamiliarity of the ceiling worried him tremendously; it was nothing like the ceiling of his bedroom and he could not think why. A misted shadow passed by the bed. Mrs. Mann, of course. But why she should be dressed in white he could not understand. The idea of the big-bosomed, raw-handed, red-faced Mrs. Mann being dressed in white was too incongruous.

"Mrs. Mann—"

The white-clad figure moved swiftly to the bedside. A cool hand took hold of his wrist. A soothing voice murmured: "Do you want anything, Mr. Terhune?"

"Are you going to be married to-day, Mrs. Mann? No, I don't mean that, I mean—" What had he meant to say? He couldn't remember.

"Never mind," the soft voice murmured. "Just go to sleep."

"I've been asleep. All right," he protested weakly. "Asleep—and dreaming—" Why was the ceiling so strangely unfamiliar? And why was Mrs. Mann in white? The last remnant of fog vanished. "Where am I? Who are you?"

"You are in hospital, Mr. Terhune, but you have nothing to worry about. Go to sleep again. You will feel much better when you wake up."

"I know. I want to speak to Murphy. Where is Murphy? I must speak to him. I want him."

"Mr. Murphy is coming here later, when you have slept."

"You will wake me when he arrives?"

"I promise."

"Then I'll try—to—sleep—" Did he really want Murphy? What for? Murphy. Good old Murphy. But what for—

When next he awoke his brain was quite clear. He had no need to ask where he was, or why a nurse was tidying the room.

"Miss MacMunn—" he appealed.

Nurse Andrews smiled. "She is much better this morning."

"You—you mean that?"

She had learned from long service to understand the ways of men. She glanced at the round, boyish face, at the blue eyes so filled with anxiety, now, but with humorous lines at the corners.

"See this wet, see this dry; cut my throat if I tell a lie."

He grinned gratefully. "Thank you, nurse. Then she was not too—too badly burned?"

She was sure it would pay her to be honest with him. "She was badly scorched, Mr. Terhune, but not seriously. She will soon be about again."

"And me?"

"You too."

"But not so soon,"

"Not so soon," she agreed. "But you have nothing to worry about Are you in pain?"

"A little," he understated, wincing. "Nurse, can you do something for me?"

"Of course."

"Where am I, by the way?"

"At Maidstone."

"Would you telephone the police at Ashford and ask them to ask Sergeant Murphy—"

"Mr. Murphy has already telephoned to ask how you are, and to Say that he hopes to be here as early as possible in the afternoon."

"Afternoon! But it's that now—"

"You have been here twenty-four hours, Mr. Terhune." She saw the distress which the news caused him. "Are you worrying about Sergeant Murphy? You have no need to; Miss MacMunn gave him all the information about the South American gentleman."

He relaxed with relief. "Thank you, nurse." Then he added: "How do you know—"

"All yesterday afternoon you were talking in your sleep. But, in any case, Miss MacMunn sent a message that you were not to worry because she had told Mr. Murphy what you wanted him to know." She saw the door opening. "But here comes the doctor to see how you are getting on."

Terhune passed an agonizing morning, for the doctor, aware that when Murphy visited the hospital later he would wish the patient to be as alert as possible, prescribed less than the minimum dose of morphia. Consequently, when the sergeant arrived just before three o'clock he found Terhune with a drawn face but a clear brain.

Murphy's manner was embarrassed; although he had occasionally visited strangers in hospital in connection with police inquiries, he had not yet become accustomed to seeing people whom he liked in a hospital bed. He never knew whether to be very cheerful, at the risk of being thought unsympathetic, or to be grave and sombre, an attitude which, he was sure, might easily discourage a patient and make him feel dismal.

"Hullo, Mr. Terhune. Are you better?" he asked, feeling quite sure, when it was too late, that he had done wrong in asking a question which might suggest to Terhune that he was not as well as he might be.

"Not so bad," Terhune lied. "Did Julia tell you why I asked her to take me to Charing Cross Road yesterday?" he continued anxiously.

"Now you let me do most of the talking, Mr. Terhune. I'll repeat to you what Miss MacMunn told me yesterday. Then, if I've left anything out, you can tell me afterwards what it is."

As he added his own deductions the story took some time to tell, but as soon as he had finished with as much of it as Julia had told, Terhune nodded his head.

"That's everything, sergeant. You see, I had hoped to serve the murderer up to you on a silver platter, but there was nothing doing. I'm sorry. I suppose I was trying to run before I can even walk properly."

"Then Perez's evidence convinced you that there was nothing to your theory?"

"Not absolutely. There is still the possibility of someone's—some book-lover living in South America, of course—someone's having hired somebody else to get possession of the book, but I've been against that idea from the first."

"Because you do not believe that a one hundred per cent book-lover would risk hiring somebody else?"

"Not to be directly responsible for handling the book. For doing the dirty work is another matter."

"So now, in the light of what Perez told you, you think your theory about a South American being involved in the theft of the Little Bible is all cock?"

"It seems rather like that, doesn't it?"

"What makes you so certain that Perez was telling the truth?"

"I've dealt with him for a number of years, sergeant. To my knowledge he has never been involved in anything mean or tricky The trade trusts him—which speaks more in his favour than I can." Terhune essayed a smile, but the attempt was a poor one. It isn't easy to smile when the greater part of one's body seems to be on fire. "Don't you trust his word, sergeant?"

"Before we go into that, sir—by the way, do you still feel up to talking?"

"Yes. It helps me to—to forget myself—a little!"

"Well, I was going to ask you about the crash. What do you know about it? Did you see it coming?"

Terhune reflected for some time before replying. "Not really. I have a vague idea of turning my head just beforehand, and of seeing a big car slithering in the direction of our bonnet, but that's about all. A moment later everything seamed to happen at once."

"Would you be astonished if I were to tell you that there are good reasons for thinking that the crash wasn't an accident?"

Terhune's expression reflected his bewilderment. "I don't think I quite understand. How could it have been anything else?"

"If the other car deliberately drove towards your bonnet, for instance, in order to make Miss MacMunn crash through the fence into the orchard."

"But why would anyone want to do that?" Terhune chuckled drily. "Besides, that sort of thing only happens at the cinema."

"That remains to be proved. But as to why anyone should want to kill you—to stop you passing on your theory about Harrison having been killed by an Argentine *gaucho*, for instance?"

Terhune's cheeks flushed red with excitement—the sergeant began to feel nervous that he had put the question too abruptly.

"That would mean that somebody was afraid of inquiries being made along those lines."

"Exactly,"

"If so, it is because Harrison *was* killed by a *gaucho*."

"That's so."

Terhune frowned. "But that would mean that Perez lied. Of course, he might not have known that such a man was here in England, but if he didn't, what gave the man who arranged the crash the information that I should be passing on to the police a theory which might put them on the track of the murderer?"

"That's the question I started to ask myself the moment I knew that your crash was no accident. The answer was—Francisco Perez.

So I telephoned Sampson right away. Since seven last night he's been working along those lines. I heard from him an hour ago."

"Well?" Terhune asked eagerly.

The sergeant turned glum. "Bedad! if he hasn't all but exonerated the man," he replied, disgusted.

Terhune felt confused; perhaps he was incapable of thinking clearly, he reflected. Lord! It wasn't surprising if he couldn't. The burns seemed to be getting worse instead of better.

"If Perez is innocent, who fixed for the black car to chase us with the idea of causing a crash? Or was the crash an accident after all?"

"The divil knows!" Murphy exclaimed dismally. "All this morning men from the Special Branch have been checking up on the lists of passengers who have recently arrived from the Americas. The check has shown that the only known book-collectors who have visited England since last Christmas are two citizens of the United States of America—"

"Samuel Phillipson and Max Werner?"

"Yes."

"I sold Werner a couple of books last April. They are both back in the States."

"I know. Then there was that Johnny Perez told you about. He, too, left for home some weeks back. If one of the really well-known collectors is, or has been, in this country, then he must have slipped back incog.

"As for Perez himself, at least three independent people have proved an alibi for him for the afternoon Harrison was killed, and two for the evening when the second attempt was made, the night you and Miss MacMunn were there. Fifteen minutes before you crashed yesterday afternoon he was at Waterloo Station seeing somebody off on the French Line boat-train, so it is certain he wasn't in the black car. As for Wednesday night, he was only across Market Square from your shop, so he might have had a hand in stealing the Little Bible. By-the-bye, speaking of the black car, it's been traced."

"It has! Then—"

Murphy hurriedly shook his head. "No, Mr. Terhune. Nothing doing. It was stolen from Lincoln's Inn an hour before it pushed you into the orchard, and subsequently abandoned in Ashford, where it was found in the station car park this morning."

"Are there no clues to the identity of the thief?"

Murphy hesitated. "Nothing to speak about. One of the porters *thinks*—only thinks, mark you—that he saw it driven into the yard about an hour after you crashed. He also *thinks* that one of the two men who got out of it was a foreign-looking gent."

"Don't those facts add up correctly, sergeant?"

"I suppose so." Murphy did not seem very pleased with life at that moment. "The foreign-looking gent ties up with your theory, but if this Perez is innocent, who instructed the two men to steal a car with the idea of making you crash? And how did the news of your ideas leak out? Bedad, sir!" he burst out. "We're back at the point where we started."

"Not quite, sergeant. You have two clues you didn't have two days ago. The one, theoretical as it were—"

"The *gaucho* trick of branding foals?"

"Yes. And the second—the certainty, almost, judging by the hasty attack on me, that the Little Bible is still in the country."

"Is!" Murphy shrugged. "You mean, was, Nearly twenty-eight hours have passed by since then—more than time enough to have smuggled half-a-dozen bibles out of the country."

The two men fell into dismal silence. Murphy stared enviously at his boots; Terhune gazed enviously at the electric button close to his hand. He longed to press it so that he might ask the nurse for something to relieve the scorching pain which racked his body. Oh! for that oblivion, horrible in retrospect, which yesterday had spared his nerves such torture.

Presently, with the silence still unbroken, Nurse Andrews entered. Her skilled eyes saw *the* tiny beads of sweat which moistened the patient's forehead, and her quick glance at Murphy was reproachful. She said, with a note of implied asperity:

"There's *another* visitor asking to see you, Mr. Terhune. He says he's from London."

Murphy's head lifted sharply.

"Inspector Sampson?"

"No, sir." She looked back at Terhune. "Mr. Francisco Perez."

"Bedad!" gasped Murphy.

Chapter Twenty-Two

"Shall I tell him that he cannot see you for two or three days?" Nurse Andrews continued.

"Hey! Tell him nothing of the kind," Murphy exploded. "You tell him to come right up."

"I shall say nothing of the kind," the nurse retorted indignantly. "Mr. Terhune is not well enough to have any more visitors. Indeed, it's time you went, if you want my opinion."

The sergeant was contrite. "It's a poor specimen of a man I am, Mr. Terhune. Shouldn't I be realizing that you're a sick man, and not surprising after what you've been through. I'm sorry, nurse. It's the professional instinct running away with me commonsense."

"Go away with you. Don't you try your Irish blarney on me," She told him bluntly, but with a kindly twinkle in her eye. "Shall I ask Mr. Perez if he could come back here, say, Monday afternoon?"

Terhune looked towards the detective. "I ought to see him, oughtn't I, sergeant?"

"It's not for me to say."

"You would like me to?"

"What I'd like, and what the nurse here will allow you to do, are two different things."

Terhune swallowed painfully. "Ask him to come up."

She pursed her lips. "Don't you take any notice of that smooth-tongued policeman. If the doctor knew what was happening—"

"Please! It's very important."

She still hesitated. "Are you quite sure, Mr. Terhune? It doesn't matter how important Mr. Perez's visit is; it's even more important that you shouldn't take any stupid risks. You've had a severe shock, and should be having absolute rest and quiet."

"I'm quite sure."

"Very well. But I shall insist upon his stay being a short one."

As the nurse turned back towards the door Murphy rose to his feet. "I'll come with you—"

"Don't go, sergeant," Terhune gasped. "I'd rather you stayed. You could do the talking."

It was obvious that the invitation was one which the other man found it difficult to refuse. "Do you think that that would be advisable?" he asked with undisguised eagerness. "Won't my presence make him suspicious?"

A wisp of a smile revealed itself on the drawn face. "I thought he was exonerated."

"He is that." Murphy sat down again, so with one more indignant glance in his direction Nurse Andrews left. "But only in Sampson's opinion," he added significantly as the door closed.

"How does he know I'm here?"

The sergeant laughed. "You can't expect anything out of the ordinary to happen to a famous person like yourself without the whole story—and more than the whole story most of the time—being run in the newspapers. One paper even gave you a headline: Well-known Amateur Detective in Car Crash, or something like that."

"I wish they would leave my private life to me."

"Many people echo that wish," Murphy commented drily. "Not excluding some who would sue for divorce if it were not for the publicity."

Francisco Perez entered. His black, oiled hair reflected the afternoon sun; his even teeth flashed a welcoming smile.

"My dear Mr. Terhune! I cannot tell you how relieved I am that you are recovering so quickly from your unfortunate accident," he began cheerfully, and with such enthusiasm that one was forced to believe that he had received no more pleasing news in months. "Nurse tells me that you will be round and about again in no time." This with an eloquent wave of graceful fingers which disposed of pain, boredom, convalescence as mere nothings that would pass away with the night.

Murphy frowned; it didn't seem right that anyone else should be so much at ease in a situation which had caused him acute embarrassment. Especially a ruddy foreigner! Blasted hypocrite, that's what he was! trying to make Terhune believe that half the world was waiting anxiously for the patient's recovery.

It did not make the sergeant feel any less resentful when Terhune smiled with genuine gratitude and, apparently, with less pain.

"And that time can't come too soon for me, Mr. Perez."

"Of course it can't." Perez glanced at the glum-faced Murphy as though he were only at that moment conscious of the presence of a third party. "But I must not stay; I merely wanted to satisfy myself that you are not nearly so bad as some of the newspapers indicate."

"Please don't go on my account," Terhune pleaded. "This is Sergeant Murphy of the Kent police. He is making inquiries into the cause of the accident. Sergeant, Mr. Francisco Perez."

"But, of course." Perez nodded genially. "I recollect now that some of the papers hinted that your crash was not entirely accidental. Still, I cannot believe there can be any grounds for such a ridiculous story."

"Why not?" Murphy asked sharply.

"Why *not*! Surely, Sergeant Murphy, a more significant question would be: *Why?* Why should anyone want to involve Mr. Terhune in a car accident?"

"That is what the police want to know. By the way, Mr. Perez, perhaps you wouldn't mind telling me why you've come here to-day?"

"*Por Dios!* Do you suspect me of having brought about Mr. Terhune's accident?" The white teeth flashed in a smile which implied that his indignation was not really genuine, the question being too absurd to be anything but a poor sort of joke in which politeness and good manners dictated he should play his proper part.

"Well, Mr. Maggs hasn't come down from London to see how Mr. Terhune is. Nor has Mr. Edwards," Murphy commented heavily, mentioning the first two names to occur to him.

"Ah! I see what you mean. But then, maybe, neither of those gentlemen shares my liking for the patient. Perhaps I can ease your suspicions, Mr. Murphy, if I explain that I had a secondary reason for coming here to-day. True, a letter would have served as well, but it is a Saturday afternoon, the afternoon is an ideal one for a drive—except for all the other week-end motorists, of course!—so I decided to achieve both objects at the same time."

"Well?"

Perez turned to Terhune. "Yesterday morning you asked me if I could tell you of any South American book-collector whom you could approach about the antiques that poor old lady must sell. As you know I was, at first, suspicious of your motives—"

"I thought you had a high regard for Mr. Terhune?" Murphy interrupted with grim satisfaction.

The South American gave a disconsolate smile. "*Touché*, as the old novelists used to say, Mr. Murphy. You have pierced my guard, and wounded me in a vital spot. Your criticism is justified. I allowed my business training to override my liking for Mr. Terhune, a mistake which I regretted almost as quickly as it was made, and one which I promised myself to rectify at the earliest possible moment."

Murphy mistrusted this flow of eloquence. Just like a ruddy foreigner, he thought, trying to bluff me with a lot of high-sounding words.

"Go on," he ordered brusquely.

"Well, sir," Perez continued he bent his head to smell the carnation in his button-hole, "that opportunity came within a few minutes of Mr. Terhune's leaving my office. I mentioned the matter to my employer, Mr. Sánchez, who confirmed the fact that no collector from our country has visited England for several weeks. But what I had not previously known, and what I learned from him in the course of conversation, is that Senhor Nicolau Diniz will be arriving in London on Monday morning, en route for Rio de Janeiro via New York. As he is sailing on the Wednesday he will be in England for little more than forty-eight hours. You will realize, Mr. Terhune, that if you wish Senhor Diniz to see the antiques which you have to offer you have very little time to lose. As he is a keen amateur collector of antiques of European origin I urge you to write to him at the Ritz Hotel. If you tell him where they may be seen I am sure he will view the goods, and afterwards pay you a visit with the object of discussing terms. I suggest your mentioning Mr. Sánchez's name as an introduction, I'm sure he will have no objection. I would gladly have given a personal letter of introduction from myself, but alas! I have not the good fortune to have met Senhor Diniz." He coughed with embarrassment. "Naturally, I must leave it to your sense of honour not to sell any books to him, Mr. Terhune. That will be my business."

A feeling of shame made Terhune bitterly regret his invention of the antiques. It had seemed at the time an innocent enough story to tell, but circumstances had contrived to give it an unfortunate twist. Out of sheer goodness of heart Perez had given up precious hours of leisure to drive to Maidstone solely for the purpose of doing what he thought to be a good turn.

He found himself with neither the courage to confess his lie, nor the hypocrisy to express his thanks for a very real act of kindness. So he took the middle course by remaining silent.

Not so Murphy, who had few scruples about anything which concerned his work.

"Did you say this gentleman was en route *for* New York, and later, Rio de Janeiro?"

"I did."

"From where?"

Perez looked vaguely surprised at the question but he answered it with his usual impeccable manners.

"From Paris, Mr. Murphy,"

"How long has he been in Paris?"

The South American shrugged. "Mr. Sánchez did not specify the exact length of Senhor Diniz's stay in Paris. All he said was, just as the train was about to start: I nearly forgot to tell you, Francisco; my brother telephoned me last night to say that he has heard that Senhor Diniz will be in London next week from Monday morning to Wednesday, when he sails for New York and B.A. He's been in Europe for some time, with Paris as his headquarters, but I daresay he'll still have enough money left to buy anything which takes his fancy, so contact him at the Ritz and see what you can do.'"

"He's been in Europe for some time, eh?"

"They were Mr. Sánchez's words."

"And he buys books as well as antiques?"

"His chief interest is in books. His collection of antiques is a secondary interest."

"Is his collection well-known?"

"Ask Mr. Terhune."

Terhune nodded. "He is one of the best-known collectors in South America, sergeant."

"Then I suppose money isn't of much object?"

Perez assumed that this question was addressed to him—as indeed it was. He answered it, but not without a note of impatience in his voice.

"If you mean, is he rich? the answer is, yes. He is probably the fourth richest man in Brazil."

"Has he visited England before during his visit to Europe?"

"His present visit?"

"Yes."

"I really could not say, Mr. Murphy. If so, he has not visited me."

"Does he travel accompanied by his own servants?"

"I believe he does. Many wealthy people do, I believe. But really, Mr. Murphy, you must excuse me if I resent this interrogation."

"I am sorry, but I'm here to make official inquiries."

"Into the cause of Mr. Terhune's accident, I believe you said?"

"I did."

"Then I do not see what concern Senhor Diniz's affairs can possibly have with the accident."

"Perhaps not, but there's good reason for all that to think that they may have."

"Then please accept my apologies," Perez said instantly.

The stolid detective remained impervious to the other man's charm. "Who did you telephone to after Mr. Terhune left your office yesterday?"

"*I—telephone—*I do not understand—"

"Who to?"

"I telephoned nobody," Perez answered with signs of increasing anger.

"Then what about your staff?"

"How can I say if I was not there? I think you are going too far, Mr. Murphy—"

"Listen, sir, There is evidence to prove that somebody deliberately forced the car Mr. Terhune was travelling in off the road. We also have evidence that it was him and nobody else the men were after. Only three people outside of you and your staff knew that he had travelled up to London: himself, Miss MacMunn, and her mother. Does that fact mean anything to you?"

It obviously did; Perez became dismayed. "But that is a terrible accusation to make." He turned to Terhune. "I am a man of honour and integrity. You know that. You must know. Why, in God's name, should I desire to cause an accident to a man whom I like and admire?"

Terhune was just as unhappy. Less than ever now could he believe that Perez was involved in the sequence of events which had led up to the crash in the orchard. On the other hand there seemed little doubt that somebody had deliberately caused the accident, and though it appeared unlikely that Perez was the principal, undoubtedly nobody seemed a likelier accomplice.

Perez must have read from Terhune's face what was passing through his mind. He leaned nearer to the bed.

"I give you my word that I had nothing whatever to do with your accident, Mr. Terhune. You must believe me. As for the staff, I cannot speak for them, but why, why should they communicate news of your visit to would-be murderers—" He paused. His eyes filled with dismay, fear, horror. "Had your accident some connection with Harrison's death?"

"It had," Murphy interposed bluntly.

"Good God!" Perez exclaimed hoarsely. "Now I understand."

"Understand what?"

"Many things. The reasons for your interrogation, Mr. Murphy, and perhaps the reason for the accident. Had Mr. Terhune found a clue to the murderer?"

"Well?"

"The answer is obviously, yes. And the clue—did it point to a South American as the murderer?"

"What if it did?"

"A South American book-collector, perhaps? Ah!" Anger displaced all other emotion. "Perhaps all your inquiries, Mr. Terhune, were directed towards finding out if such a man was over here?"

"Yes," Terhune confessed unhappily.

Perez shrugged his contempt, but a moment later relented. "On second thoughts I understand your reasons, too. The murder was a brutal one. No man could have been more harmless than poor Harrison. The criminals deserve to be hanged. Yes, yes, indeed. I forgive your deception. Willingly. And now I repeat—aware as I am, of all the implications involved—that no book-collector has, to my knowledge, visited England since the Mr. Martinez you have heard about."

"Could any of your staff have been in communication with this Diniz man?" This from Murphy again.

"I should say—most unlikely." Then, with an expressive gesture: "But how can I speak for them?"

"Then you know nothing of Harrison's murder, and nothing of the accident to Mr. Terhune?"

"Nothing, I assure you, Mr. Murphy. Absolutely nothing."

I I

As soon as Perez had overcome his annoyance at the deception which had been played upon him his attitude towards Murphy became far more friendly. More than that he expressed his willingness to be as helpful as possible.

In the light of this offer the sergeant carried on a searching interrogation. Perez answered as best he could, but in the end it was apparent, even to him, that his eagerness to help exceeded his usefulness. So he soon left, after promising to make discreet inquiries about Diniz, also his small staff of two.

When his second visitor had gone Terhune wondered how soon it would be before the other visitor did likewise. For the first time in his memory he was anxious to be quit of Murphy; he felt so damnably tired, so weak, so incapable of standing much more. Unfortunately, Murphy was engrossed in his work.

"What do you make of that man, Mr. Terhune?"

"He seems very anxious to help, sergeant."

"He does that. I know you like him, and I don't blame you for that, but for my part I don't altogether trust him, and that's straight."

"Perhaps you are prejudiced because he's a foreigner."

"Maybe you're right," the sergeant admitted grudgingly. "It's this Diniz I'm anxious to know more about. From Paris he could have slipped over to Dover or Folkestone and organized the whole business from there without any of his friends being any the wiser." He became aware of Terhune's near-collapse. "Bedad! and it's more than time I was off meself," he muttered in contrition. "I'll be seeing ye as soon as there's any news, an' maybe sooner, say to-morrow afternoon, when it's your old self I shall be expecting to see." With that ingenuous attempt to copy Perez's easy manner with a sick man he hurried out.

Terhune closed his eyes with relief. Oh! blessed, blessed quietness! No more voices to keep one's nerves jumping; no more straining to concentrate on what was being said. Just peace, but unhappily, peace without contentment. The burns were scorching more than ever—and soon would come the added torture of the dressing.

He was not left alone for long. Nurse Andrews entered quickly. She had been warned by Murphy that her patient was not looking good.

"Drink this," she commanded.

He obeyed meekly, and later drifted off into sleep.

Later hours, for as long as he remained awake, were troubled. He experienced a feeling of restlessness and unease for which he was unable to account, for its root, he was convinced, was mental and not physical. An intuitive feeling almost, but though his thoughts rambled round and round in a vicious circle in an effort to trace its source at first he found himself unable to locate it. Later, he came to the conclusion that something to do with Perez's visit was responsible for his agitation. He could not think why, though he considered the visit from every aspect, past, present and future, At last he decided that he was on the wrong tack, but directly his thoughts drifted away from the South American intuition exerted a gravity-like pull, and brought them back to the point from which they had started.

At last, exasperated by a feeling of near-depression he retraced the three-sided conversation, as far as possible sentence by sentence, each of which he analysed to see whether it contained anything of significance. No easy matter this for his attention at the time had been frequently diverted by bouts of pain; sometimes he had almost lost the drift of the point at issue. But he persisted, as much to let the time pass quickly as in an obstinate determination to find out what was worrying him.

Was it something to do with Diniz? It wasn't? No. Something to do with Paris? No. The blonde-haired secretary—in striking contrast to Perez's blue-black hair. A stunning-looking pair they'd make. His thoughts began to ramble here, but at last he answered his own question. No. The old chap in the shop, then? No. The antiques? At this point he hesitated. Had his queer feeling some connection with the antiques? Was it nothing more than a feeling of guilt for having deceived Perez? It might be. It could be. It was just the kind of silly scruple which could stick in one's mental gullet, as it were. But was that the answer? Was it something to do with Perez's employer, Sánchez? With Perez's having mentioned Terhune's inquiry about the possible presence in England of a South American book-collector? Had Perez telephoned Sánchez, then? But no, he couldn't have done that, for hadn't Sánchez said something to Perez just before the train—the Cunard boat-train—had left—something about Diniz?

Then, the simple fact. Perez, in all innocence, had sworn that no *book-collector* had been in England. But what of a *bookseller?* Sánchez, himself—

Chapter Twenty-Three

He was too impatient to wait for Murphy's promised visit to him at some time later on in the day. As soon as the night nurse arrived to attend to him before going off duty he called out to her:

"Nurse, would you make a telephone call for me right away? Please. It's very urgent."

"Lands sakes! Mr. Terhune, what are you doing awake so early? And looking so feverish, too. Have you no slept the past few hours?"

"I'm not feverish, nurse. I'm much better—"

"That's gude, but stop blathering and open your mouth." She produced a thermometer.

He shook his head. "Afterwards, when you've telephoned."

"Whist!" she exclaimed irritably. "It's no time to be telephoning a Christian person on a Sabbath morn. Like as not the ring wouldn't be answered. Ask Nurse Andrews when she comes in."

"The call is to the police, and the matter really is urgent."

"The police!" Nurse Macdonald hesitated. "I suppose that's different now, though it's precious moments of sleep you'll be robbing me of. Who is the call to, and what is the message?"

He gave her Murphy's name and number, adding: "Ask Mr. Murphy if he would be kind enough to come here as soon as he can manage, and, if possible, would be bring Inspector Sampson along, too?"

She nodded her red head, and departed on his errand. When she returned her eyes were laughing.

"Why did you no warn me he had a wife, Mr. Terhune? Lands sakes! the trouble I had to persuade her to wake her man. You'd hae thought I was ringing up to propose an elopement with him."

"But you did speak to him in the end?" he asked with anxiety.

"Dinna fash yoursel'. I'm not that easily discouraged. I spoke to him, *and* I gave him your message, *and* he promised to ring up the Inspector Sampson person, *and* he said that, in any case, he would come as soon as might be."

"Thank you, nurse. One day, when I'm better, I'll kiss you for your kindness."

"Get away wi' ye! You men are all alike. You all think that the only thing a nurse wants is to be kissed an' cuddled."

"Well, don't you?"

She pushed the thermometer into his mouth. "You're too cheeky by two days or so; most other patients at least wait until they are convalescing before they start their blather."

Murphy proved himself to be a quick worker that morning. Soon after ten o'clock he and Sampson entered the sick room.

"I was sorry to read about your crash, Mr. Terhune," Sampson told the patient. "It wasn't until last night, when Sergeant Murphy rang me up, that I realized that your accident had any connection with the theft of the Little Bible. I take it from your message that you have news for us?"

"It remains to be seen whether you will regard as news what I have to tell you. Won't you sit down?"

The two men sat down. Terhune then told them, in as much detail as he could recollect, of his theory about the possibility of a South American's being guilty of Harrison's death, of his decision to pay a visit to London, of his interview with Perez on the Friday morning, of his disappointment with the result, of the little he knew of the subsequent crash, of Perez's visit to the hospital, and finally, of his own restless thoughts during the night, which culminated with his theory that the Sánchez who was on his way back to the Argentine via New York was responsible for the theft of the Little Bible.

"Is Sánchez a book-collector besides being a bookseller?" Sampson questioned eagerly as soon as it was apparent that Terhune had finished speaking.

"That I can't say; most of the booksellers I know like to keep for themselves some of the choicest volumes which pass through their hands. But if he didn't want to keep it, back in Buenos Aires, with the Little Bible in his possession he would be in an ideal position to sell it at a fancy price."

"Is Sánchez a rich man?"

"I believe so."

Sampson shook his head doubtfully. "That is where your theory seems a little thin, if you don't mind me saying so, Mr. Terhune. I can believe that a crazy-enough book-lover might have killed Harrison to obtain such a treasured possession; I can believe that a poor man would be willing to risk being hanged for the sake of the enormous return he would get from selling the Little Bible to an unscrupulous book-collector. But I shouldn't care to believe, without strong evidence, that a man already wealthy would risk death for the sake of adding another hundred thousand pounds to his bank account."

"One hundred thousand pounds is a lot of money," Murphy pointed out, tight-lipped with disapproval of the inspector's criticism. "I think I should take the chance of being strung up if I could be sure of getting even half that."

"But then you are not a rich man—"

"Bedad! and I'm not."

"So you wouldn't risk losing anything much except your life, To the man with a bird in hand, the two in the bush aren't so attractive, Still, I don't want to make too much of this point. Sánchez might be a collector as well as a seller of books. Before we go any further, can we be sure that nobody in Bray knew of your proposed visit to London, Mr. Terhune, other than yourself, Miss MacMunn, and her mother? Isn't

Mrs. MacMunn something of a chatterbox? Mightn't she have passed on the information to somebody else?"

Murphy grinned, and spoke for Terhune. "She certainly might, but I've questioned her very thoroughly, inspector, and she swears that she had seen nobody in between Miss MacMunn leaving the house, and my arrival with the news of the accident. Phillips confirms that fact."

"Then, barring the possibility of Mr. Terhune having been accidentally recognized while in town, the leakage must have come from Perez's office? You didn't visit anyone else, while you were there, Mr. Terhune?"

"No."

Murphy interrupted: "You can wash out the accidental recognition, inspector. If it had been that accidental the gang wouldn't have known that it was necessary to knock Mr. Terhune for six before he had a chance of passing his suspicions on to us."

"How do you account for Sánchez, or whoever ordered the crash, being so certain that Mr. Terhune hadn't already spoken to us?"

Again a broad, slightly mischievous grin spread across Murphy's unhandsome face. "If he had spoken to us beforehand should we have let *him* do the inquiries?"

The inspector smiled drily. "Perhaps you are right. So is this what you think happened, Mr. Terhune? Very soon after you had left, Perez goes off to Waterloo station—he had already said something about seeing a boat-train off—perhaps picking up his employer, Emilo Sánchez, en route, to whom he says casually, in the course of conversation, something like this: 'By the way, do you know if any South American book-collector has visited England during the past few weeks?' Upon which Sánchez, presumably having a guilty conscience, asks: 'Who wants to know?' Says Perez, innocent-like: 'That there Mr. Theodore Terhune from Bray; he has some antiques he wants to sell to a rich South American.' To a man of Sánchez's alleged intelligence the inference is easy; the story sounds phoney enough to make him realize that Terhune, whom he knows to be an amateur detective, has found a clue pointing to South America.

He further realizes, as you pointed out, Murphy, that as yet Mr. Terhune has kept his suspicions to himself in the hope of later announcing the *fait accompli*—"

He glanced sideways at the patient, who grinned back, shame-faced.

"Sánchez questions Perez. What answer did he give Mr. Terhune? Perez replies. Sánchez, being a bit of a character-reader, appreciates that Mr. Terhune, having failed to achieve success on his own account, will at last pass on his suspicions to the police—"

"Have a heart, inspector! He's still a sick man."

Sampson turned to Terhune. "Don't *you* think you deserve censure?" he asked drily.

"Not altogether. I thought that, as a bookseller asking questions about book-buyers, I should be less likely to cause suspicion than if the police made official inquiries."

The inspector nodded. "I see your point. But to get back to Sánchez. Presumably the first thing he did after hearing of your visit was to give orders to somebody or other to steal a car, chase after you like hell, and make you crash before you had a chance of seeing the police. Is that the suggestion?"

"Something on those lines."

"And who, do you suggest, were the men to whom he gave those orders?"

"His two or more South American servants."

"Are you really meaning bodyguards?"

"Not particularly. But he might have come to Europe prepared for trouble, and have brought one or two men along with him who would not only act as servants, but do any dirty work which had to be done."

"And where are those men now? Hiding in London somewhere until they can catch the next ship sailing for New York?"

"Why not? if they didn't charter a 'plane that same afternoon for whichever French port the liner went to after leaving Southampton."

Sampson shook his head, "The trouble about you, Mr. Terhune, is that you make all the pieces of your puzzles fit together too slickly. In real life that doesn't happen."

"Then—then you're not going to do anything about checking up on Sánchez?"

"Aren't I!" Sampson rose from his chair, his scarred face menacing with resolution. "Just you wait and see."

I I

Sampson was a sport. With unsuspected foresight he appreciated to what extent the boredom of an enforced stay in a hospital bed was likely to add to Terhune's natural impatience to hear what was happening. In consequence, after a word with the house surgeon, he contrived, from time to time, to send messages to the patient by telephone which were intended to keep him in touch with the progress of the investigation.

The first message to reach him from Sampson was to let him know that Sánchez had been staying in London, and had sailed for New York, en route for Buenos Aires, on the Friday, having booked his passage the day previously. This part of the message was not particularly exciting; Perez's conversation had already made this fact fairly obvious. What was more interesting was the second part of the message, which went on to say that Sánchez had first landed in England on the 26th of May, together with two male servants, by 'plane from Berlin, to which city he had returned, alone, on the 6th of June—the day following Harrison's murder. Three days later he was back in London again, two days before the second burglary at *Twelve Chimneys*.

It was possible, but not credible, that Sánchez's departures and arrivals were no more than a series of coincidences. The story, as Terhune deduced it from the scraps of knowledge which he now possessed, probably went something like this: During a visit to Europe Sánchez received information that the Little Bible was for sale. Possibly he went direct to the fountain head in Berlin, only to learn that it had already travelled to Paris. Perhaps he followed it there, to be told that, in the meantime, it had gone to Stockholm. So to Stockholm, and another disappointment. The Little Bible had been sold to a man named Harrison, living in an odd corner of England. Still the South American followed the treasure. On to England, via Berlin. He reached London on the 26th of May, engaged rooms at an hotel. The following day he probably bought a second-hand car. During the day he travelled down to Wickford, inspected *Twelve Chimneys* and its surroundings, left one of his servants to keep watch on the place, if possible to learn something about the movements of its occupants, and later on, returned to his hotel in London. Maybe, he did this every day, waiting for an opportunity to enter the house at a time most convenient to himself. His chance came early Monday afternoon. Accompanied by one of his men he entered Harrison's room by way of the French windows, and offered to buy the Little Bible. Harrison refused to sell, so he was callously murdered and his library was searched. This task was still uncompleted when the unexpected return of Miss Baggs and Mary forced the men to leave before they had planned. By that time, however, Sánchez had had a quick look at every likely spot in the library, and not having found the object of his visit, he began to suspect that he had been misled. He flew back to Berlin, and maybe on to Stockholm again, where his inquiries brought to light the fact that the Little Bible had travelled about Europe hidden inside a threadbare *German-English Dictionary*. Back in England he learned that the police guard had been relaxed so he withdrew his watcher and essayed to burgle the house again to look for the *German-English Dictionary*. Meanwhile, owing to his having taken away his spy, he did not realize that Julie and I were there in the library—Terhune reflected. He failed for the second time. Before he could make a third attempt the police guard was restored. He realized that he would have to substitute brute force with cunning. When he heard that all Harrison's books were to be auctioned he planned to buy the book, perhaps for a mere few shillings if, as might be hoped—though scarcely expected, Terhune thought with some bitterness—the secret of the *German-English Dictionary* is not discovered in the meantime. Then he got wind of the trap which was being laid for him—how? That was a separate mystery in its own right, to which no solution seemed to be forthcoming. The only reasonable explanation seemed to be that somebody among the Ashford police had been guilty of careless talk in a public place. When word reached Sánchez that the police intended to be present at the auction he evolved an expensive and complicated red-herring in the shape of Droopy Moustache. Meanwhile, he either sent someone to take a note of the number of the Lot containing the *German-English Dictionary*, or even himself visited *Twelve Chimneys*, during one of the days of showing. Who knows, perhaps in the company of his employee, Perez? Such a course would arouse nobody's curiosity or suspicion. Lastly, he made arrangements to steal the *German-English Dictionary* from whoever bought it at the auction. And that night he did, in fact, steal it. Having achieved success, the next day he booked a passage on the first ship sailing for New York, which happened to be the day following. All seemed satisfactory, but half an hour before he was due to leave for Southampton, Perez casually passed on an item of news which made Sánchez appreciate that he was not yet free from danger. At once he tried to protect himself by organizing a car smash—

The story was incomplete; possibly exaggerated at times, and possibly completely wrong in many particulars. But it held together, and gave the police something to grasp. That was the most important fact of all. As long as there was a clue of sorts, however vague, their superb detective organization would do the rest. They would fill in the gaps, and clothe the skeleton—dress it for the dock, as it were.

Some time later came the next message from Sampson. Late Friday afternoon two men had hired a taxi-plane at Croydon to take them to Cherbourg. They had arrived there in time to meet the ship on which Sánchez was travelling. The men had shown Argentinian passports; their names had been identified by the Ritz hotel as belonging to Sánchez's servants, one, a chauffeur, the other, a valet.

Still later, Sampson 'phoned up to say that Sánchez had hired an owner-driven Austin for two months, beginning 28th of May. It had been driven by Sánchez's foreign chauffeur, who spoke bad English with a very strong accent, and whom the employees of the hiring firm had nicknamed Ugly-Mug, for a good and sufficient reason.

Slowly but surely, it seemed, the trap was closing about the distant, and, no doubt, jubilant Argentinian. The thought made Terhune reflect upon his injuries. If, as an indirect result of them, Sánchez were brought to trial for the death of Harrison, and the Little Bible were to be restored to its historic home, then the accident was almost worth the cost to him of several days' suffering. Almost! But the mere idea made him feel better.

Then nothing more for more than sixty hours, the waking ones of which were spent by the patient fretting over the lack of news. Nurse Andrews scolded him severely, and brought books in the hope of distracting him. He tried to read, and to remain patient, but without success. Surely Sampson was doing something. If Sánchez were allowed to land with his prize, what hope would there be of recovering it? The hands of the Special Branch and the C.I.D. would be fettered; the F.B.I. would take over the case for as long as the thief or the property remained within the territory of the U.S.A. Not that the F.B.I. was less efficient, far from it, but in any country in the world, more particularly in a vast continent, was not a small book almost the easiest thing in the world to hide?

Then, early Wednesday morning, Murphy called at the hospital. A broad grin parted his lips; his eyes shone with unmistakable triumph.

Terhune did not wait for his visitor to speak. "You've good news, sergeant?"

"I have that, sir," the sergeant admitted, as he sat himself down on the bedside chair. "The New York detectives have recovered the Little

Bible, and arrested Sánchez and his servants. They went out in the pilot boat, accompanied by the inspector—"

"Inspector Sampson?"

"Yes. He flew to New York Monday night. He telephoned me an hour ago, and asked me to tell you that you were ninety per cent right in your deductions."

"Only ninety per cent?" To cover up his own bubbling satisfaction Terhune made a pretence of disappointment.

"That is what he said. It seems that you were wrong about—" Murphy paused.

"About?" Terhune prompted.

The sergeant grinned. "At umpteen pounds a minute for the cost of the call he said it would have taken a king's ransom to give me a complete list of your errors, so I told him—" The remainder of the sentence was inaudible, for he had just noticed that Terhune was inviting him to help himself to the dish of grapes which Alicia had left the previous night, and Murphy had a particular weakness for hot-house grapes—

III

Five minutes after Murphy left Nurse Andrews entered. Her manner was mysterious.

"There's another party asking to see you, Mr. Terhune. Shall I show the person in?"

"Who is it?"

"I don't know. The person won't give a name. Says you'll know the name soon enough. Shall I say that you're not well enough this morning?"

"I feel well enough to see anyone to-day, nurse."

"In that case—" Nurse Andrews shrugged her shoulders. "Only don't blame me if you have a relapse."

She disappeared, and Julia entered—a pale but radiant Julia, dressed in silk peignoir and satin slippers. A light glowed deep in her rich brown eyes.

"Theo!" she whispered. "Theo!"

And damfool Terhune, in all innocence, said casually: "How's tricks, Julia, old girl? Feeling better?"

THE END